Molly O'Hare (signature)

TENTS
& Tights

USA TODAY BESTSELLING AUTHOR
molly o'hare

Cover model: iStock photo
Cover art: Wildelake Creative
Editor: Klean Edits
Proofreader/ Continuity: Tracey Arcieri
Proofreader: Virgina Tesi Carey

Disclaimer: This title is intended for mature audiences due to adult situations and languages.

Molly O'Hare
First Print: April 2022
ISBN-13: 978-1-7328338-7-6
Be You Publishing, LLC

www.MollyOHareauthor.com

$\mathcal{D}$edication

To all my badass, takes no shit from anyone, unicorns out there. You are amazing. Never let anyone tell you differently, and if they do, throat punch those fuckers in the face.
I love you.
Can I have your autograph?

Also, to Katy, who helped spark this idea. You are freaking amazing!

Tents & Tights

MOLLY O'HARE

Chapter One

"I SWEAR TO EVERYTHING, Austin, you better stop laughing at me." Eve Morgan's eyes glared toward her best friend as she pursed her lips together. "If you keep it up, I'm gonna throw this pillow at your head."

At Eve's words, Austin Flynn cocked his head to the side for a split second before he burst into another round of laughter. "I can't help it."

Eve narrowed her eyes at him as an annoyed growl escaped her throat. When he continued to laugh, she couldn't help but glare harder at her muscled jerk of a best friend that she'd had for the better part of the last four years, trying to calculate if she could take him.

Sure, he'd win, but she might be able to knock him off his guard at first.

"I mean it, Austin. This isn't funny. He even tried to pick me up and *spin* me... Me." Eve pointed at herself, referring to her plentiful curves. "Like, does he even have eyes?"

"Stop! You're killing me here." Austin snorted as he fell back onto the sofa, gasping for air, his hand over his taut stomach.

Okay, so it was funny. Even Eve had to admit it. But that didn't mean she didn't want to maim Austin in the head. Because all in all, from an outsider's perspective, her horrible date last night was pretty hilarious. And if she couldn't laugh about it with her best friend, then what was she going to do?

Whine about it?

That wasn't Eve's style.

Nah, but she at least was going to give Austin a hard time for finding *too* much enjoyment in her joke of a life.

"How'd this even happen, Eve?" Austin's dark hazel eyes pierced through crinkled slits as he bit his lip and attempted to stop laughing at her mess of a situation.

At least she had to give it to him.

He *was* trying.

Failing, but trying.

Eve rolled her eyes. Tossing a pillow at him wasn't entirely off the table yet.

Leave it to her to somehow end up with a best friend like him. At least, it was always a good time when Austin was around.

Austin really was like a five-year-old boy sometimes.

Annoying, but he had his good moments.

Eve let out a heavy sigh as her shoulders slumped. "I don't even know." She glanced back at the ceiling, cursing the Universe, before turning her glare back to Austin. "It was horrible. And I mean horrible. After what I would consider the worst meal of my life, he actually made *me* pay for the bill. He then decided a walk on the beach would be a great idea. And because I just can't say no, and as you always remind me, I'm far too kind, I went along with it. What I should've said was fuck you and punched him in the face."

"Yeah, you should've." Austin sobered for a second, staring at her with hardened eyes. "*Anyone* that makes you pay on a date is a fuckface. You deserve better than that."

"Thanks, sweetie." Eve tapped Austin's knee. "I can't tell people no. You are well aware of this. It's not in my vocabulary."

Austin cocked his left brow. "You tell me no all the time."

"Yeah, 'cause you're a pig."

Both of Austin's brows shot up. "And he wasn't?"

"You're my best friend. I have to tell you no." Eve rolled her eyes with a slight shake of her head. "Can I continue?"

She loved Austin, but damn he was difficult ninety percent of the time. Especially when she was attempting to tell him a story.

"As your best friend, you should never tell me no." Austin sent her a pointed look, which Eve threw right back at him.

"As your best friend, it's never no. It's yes, sir. What else can I do for you, sir?"

If Eve didn't know he was joking, she would've kneed him in the balls, which he must have picked up on since she saw his hands migrate to cover his crotch.

Good.

As Eve quirked her left brow at him, Austin scooted back, holding up his hands in surrender. "Fine, I digress. For now..." He had the gall to glare at her. "Tell me what else pencil dick did?" Austin signaled for her to go on, all the while his eyes said they'd be talking about it later.

See, annoying.

But they *would* talk about it later because it'd be a cold day in hell before Eve let his *yes, sir, what else could I do for you sir,* comment go.

Did she say annoying already?

Because that's what Austin was.

Eve quickly looked him up and down, the corner of her mouth turned up. "How would *you* know what his dick looked like?"

Instantly, the playfulness of the room shifted as Austin

narrowed his eyes on her his face hardening. "Are you saying you do?"

Lord, her best friend was going to give her an ulcer.

Deciding to ignore his macho man behavior, she continued. "He tried hoisting me up in the air and then did a spin. Fuck me, Austin. A freakin' *spin.* Since you're all out there in the woods always hiking, doing God knows what else, and you've got all the muscles, maybe, just *maybe,* you could lift me, but this guy. Hell no, he was a scrawny, no good, weak piece of donkey crap." A small smile splayed across Eve's lips. "Hmm? Maybe you're right about the pencil dick."

Austin's brow cocked as his face held that 'I told you so look.' It took everything inside of Eve to stop herself from slapping it off him.

Again, annoying.

"The moment he tried lifting me off the ground, he realized his mistake. We ended up falling over in the sand. And to add insult to injury, the tumble ripped my favorite dress."

"Not the yellow one with the sunflowers?" Austin's face scrunched as his lower lip jutted out.

"Yes, that one."

"Damn, that's your favorite."

"I know! It was horrible!" she scoffed. "It's the first dress I ever made."

Stupid freakin' date.

Stupid freakin' Austin.

Stupid freakin' everything.

As Eve crossed her arms over her chest to continue sulking, out of nowhere, Austin dragged her off the couch into the air. And before Eve knew it, she was on his shoulder in a fireman's pose.

"Ahhh! What the fuck, Austin? Put me down!"

"You can't throw out a challenge and not have me follow

4

through. You know that," Austin stated matter-of-fact as he bounced her on his shoulder.

"For fuck's sake." Eve punched Austin's back, trying and failing to get him to put her down. "What the hell are you talking about? Put me down right now or I'm gonna bite you."

"I might like that." Instead of doing what she wanted, Austin did this weird move that once again had her flying. Although this time, she ended up in a full spin.

That bastard.

After her second spin, both of them fell onto the couch as Austin burst out into another round of laughter.

However, the moment Eve got her bearings, she punched him in the arm. "What the hell!" Quickly, she pushed her chestnut hair out of her face before she punched him again.

"Ouch." Austin rubbed the spot she'd just maimed. "That was uncalled for."

"Uncalled for? I should've kicked you in the balls."

Instantly, Austin's hands went to cover his junk as a flash of fear ran across his face.

Good. 'Cause I'll do it.

"Don't say stuff like that. You'll scare them."

"Eww, don't talk about your in-the-pants things." Eve shuddered while she fake gagged. Once she was done, she glared back at him. "And they should be scared. Why the hell did you do that?"

"You said I *maybe* could be able to pick you up. I had to test that theory 'cause *I* knew I could." Austin sent her a wink.

Oh God, she was going to murder him. Although she had to admit, it was partially her own fault. After all these years, Eve knew she should've worded it differently.

When it came to Austin, he never turned down a challenge. Even the most outlandish ones like picking her up just to prove it could be done.

Whatever. It'd be his back problems in the morning, not hers. "You're gonna regret that."

Austin sent her another wink as the corner of his lip turned up. "Nah. If anything, it just renewed my man card."

"Yeah, 'cause picking up the fat chick does that."

"Hey, I wouldn't let someone else talk about my best friend like that, and I sure as fuck ain't gonna let said best friend talk about *herself* like that."

"What? I'm just stating facts."

Austin narrowed his eyes as his lips formed into a thin line. "So am I."

"Put the caveman shit away." Eve glared back at him, her lips pursing together. "I'm gonna get you back for picking me up... And it'll be when you least expect it. Watch your back, Flynn."

"I'm looking forward to it."

When Eve saw the stupid smirk appear on his face, the one Austin always got when he thought he'd won, a growl escaped her. She might not be able to kill him, but she could at least punch him in the nose.

That'll teach him for finding far too much enjoyment in her misery.

"Whatever you're thinking about right now, it's not gonna happen."

"I'm not thinking anything." She glanced at him, her eyes doe-like as she sported a tiny innocent, 'I would never do that' smile.

Austin snorted, arching his brow. "After all this time, you think I don't know when you're thinking about punching me?"

Dang it.

Eve's mouth snapped shut.

"Now, if you wanna picture me in other ways other than punching, I'd be more than willing to—"

"Eww, Austin, shut up! Bleah." She shook her head. "Do you want me to continue or not? Because the falling over wasn't even the worst part."

Both of Austin's brows flew upward as his jaw dropped. "There's more? You're kidding me."

"Unfortunately, I'm not. It's like the date from hell that wouldn't stop. It took *foreverrrrr* to get the sand out of all my lumps, bumps, and places that shall never be named." Eve fell back onto the couch, defeated. "I think I might still have sand in my lady bits."

"Fuck me." Austin burst into a deep laugh as he fell onto Eve's sofa next to her. "Oh God, stop. I can't breathe."

Worst. Night. Ever.

Eve side-eyed Austin. Although, tonight wasn't shaping up to be the greatest either. But hey, at least they could laugh at her misery together. "I don't know why I agreed to the date in the first place..."

Austin pivoted his body to her, placing his leg underneath him, as he gave her a pointed look. "I'm wondering the same thing. You stood me up to go on some piss poor date, if you can even call it that, when you could have been watching movies and eating popcorn with me. But no, you had to abandon me for some fucking dweeb."

"He was cute."

Austin's left brow quirked. "Animals and babies are cute. You deserve smokin' hot, not *cute.*"

A playful grin spread across Eve's face as she looked at her best friend, cocking her head to the side. "*You're* cute."

Austin's jaw dropped the moment her words registered. "You bitch." In an instant, he flew into action as he quickly pinned Eve under him. "Take it back!"

"Ahhh. You fucking Neanderthal, stop it. For fuck's sake. What is with you tonight? Get off me." Eve thrashed under him, trying her best to toss him off, which was not working since Austin had somehow pinned her arms over her head with his legs on either side of her hips, keeping her trapped.

"Take it back," he growled.

"No."

Austin clenched his legs harder before he went deadweight on her body.

"You're gonna crush me, get off."

"Take it back."

Gasping for air while laughing, Eve squirmed under him. Realizing she was out of options, she gave up. "Fine. You're not cute. You're a huge hunk of sexy man meat. That better?"

"You think I'm sexy?"

That damn smirk was back.

"Kill me now." Eve groaned. "If I say yes, will you get off me?"

"Maybe. There's only one way to find out." Eve felt Austin's body go even more limp with his words.

"Fine, yes. You're a sexy hunk of man meat. Geez, you freakin' drama queen."

With zero effort, Austin pulled back before flipping over to his seat on the other side of the couch, with that ridiculously annoying smirk on his face.

"You're a piece of work." Eve righted herself as she pushed her hair back in place.

"And you love me for it."

"Sometimes."

The smirk on Austin's face grew into a full-blown, toothy grin. "All the time."

"Sure thing, *cutie*." At his instant growl, Eve held up her hands, letting out a laugh.

In all realness, though, Austin was anything but cute. He was one of those men that should be on the cover of magazines ... and damn it, he had.

Austin Flynn had been on the cover of multiple outdoor adventure magazines more times than Eve could count. You know when you're flipping through some magazine and you see those super-fit guys on the side of a mountain because they are outdoorsy and shit?

That was Austin.

He had muscles upon muscles, all from his outdoor adventures. Not just hanging around a gym for twelve hours a day.

Nope. That wasn't her best friend.

If it was any kind of activity you did outside, Austin was all over it. Hiking, rock climbing, backpacking.

You name it.

He did it.

That's probably why his business did so well.

Austin was the owner of one of the most successful and well-known outdoor shops in the area, if not the state. People traveled from all over just to shop there and *possibly* get a glimpse of the man himself.

Austin was, in a weird way, a celebrity in the outdoor world, and his business Anytime Adventure was well on the map.

And good for him.

Austin took his passion and not only made it a successful career, but he loved every moment of it. Plus, as he liked to say, the attention from the ladies didn't hurt.

Eve, on the other hand, was the complete opposite of him. She was plus-size, hated the outdoors, and more often than not, avoided anything that could be considered exercise.

Geez, they were such an odd pair.

How they became best friends, she still didn't quite understand it.

She was working one day in her plus-size boutique off the

corner of Mills and Brown when in walked Austin, asking a million questions.

She'd only had her shop a few months at the time and she was scrounging to make ends meet.

Eve had been so freaking tired of going to shop after shop and not one having her size. And if they carried her sizes, she was always thrown into the back of the store with the most god-awful clothes she'd ever seen. Or worse... they'd point her to the maternity section.

So one day five years ago, Eve said screw it and started making her own clothes. Sure, it was a learning curve, but she got the hang of it after a while. Thank everything for the internet and endless tutorials.

And before Eve knew it, she had her plus-size boutique Own Your Curves up and running.

Not to toot her own horn, but she was damn good at what she did. She could make or tailor anything now, from dresses, pants, shirts, skirts, really anything. You name it, she could do it. And if she couldn't, she figured out a way.

However, it had been a struggle at first.

Honestly, no matter how badly she'd hated to admit it, she owed her store's success to Austin.

Bleah.

The day he walked into her boutique asking more questions than she could answer, Eve nearly lost her mind. And she kind of did. She was after all, known for being a master of jumping to conclusions.

After calling him a chubby chaser and a creep, and tossing a few objects in his direction, which he perfectly dodged, they somehow ended up forging this fantastic business partnership.

Austin had only come into Own Your Curves to see if she could supply bigger activewear clothes for his customers.

Truth be told, that *shocked* her. Austin had gone on and

on about how pissed he was that his normal distributors had nothing above a large in anything. And even then he scoffed at their *large*. As he liked to put it, he wouldn't even get his head through their *large* size.

One of the many things Eve loved about Austin was his encouragement for everyone of all sizes to get out and enjoy nature. And he wanted to help provide that.

Fast forward another few months, and with Austin's contract and his guidance for making suitable clothes for all types of activities, he saved her business.

Now, four years later, and somewhere along his weekly stops by the shop, they became friends and not soon after that, best friends.

Maybe it was the fact she would give him shit all the time, or maybe he was just a glutton for punishment?

Who knew, but here they were. Just like most Friday nights.

They'd be at her apartment watching movies, laughing, joking, and eating popcorn.

And even if she hated to admit it and you would catch her dead before she admitted it to him, she loved it.

Because, all in all, Austin was her best friend.

He was always there for her. She'd never been more comfortable with a guy in her life. Everything was easy with him. And he was always there utilizing his business mind to help her along the way. Not only would he help with ideas for clothes, but he'd also give a man's perspective, and so much more.

He was like her rock in a lot of ways.

Austin was just an overall amazing guy.

Even if he was a pig-headed, know-it-all jerk half of the time.

As Eve looked at him, that tiny 'what-if' thought she had

shoved way deep down inside her crept up, begging to make itself known.

Oh, heck no. We do not go down that road again. We squashed that four years ago and that's how it's gonna stay. That's why you're trying to get out there and date you dumb-dumb.

"I'm gonna let that slide since you just had a traumatic experience." Austin's voice broke through her thoughts.

"Yeah, you picking me up was not fun."

Austin growled out a huff of annoyance as he picked up the popcorn bowl that was on the coffee table. After tossing a piece into his mouth, his eyes moved to her. "When are you gonna learn you need to find better men?"

"When are you gonna finally get off my couch and go find yourself a woman?"

"I found myself a woman already. I have you. And your couch is so nice and warm." Austin's lips thinned as his brows knitted together. "Besides, all the women I meet only pretend to like outdoor stuff. The first time I get them on a hike, they bolt. They just want me for my body."

"Yeah, 'cause the outdoors is hot and gross. I don't blame them."

Austin rolled his eyes. "At least you don't pretend that you like it. Although, it's been years and you keep saying *next weekend* when I ask you to go camping with me or go on a hike."

"Oh, would you look at that?" Eve grabbed her phone off the coffee table, pulling up her empty calendar. "Sorry, Austin. Turns out this weekend I'm booked, too."

"You're a lying little shit and you know it."

Eve shrugged, tossing her phone down.

Austin's brows wiggled. "It could be a business trip. We can do a more thorough test of the clothes you make."

"You know they work fine. We test them when I make them."

"Yeah, but you just put them on and make sure they feel okay. You don't actually get out there and put them to the test."

"Are you saying my work is shit?"

Austin cocked his brow. "You trying to prove me wrong?"

"I'm gonna throat punch you."

He barked out a laugh, shaking his head. "One of these days, you're camping with me."

"You keep telling yourself that, buddy."

"You say no to camping and hiking to me all the time. Then you go out on some bullshit date and leave me to my lonesome here. I get bored when we don't hang out. Some best friend you are."

"You've got other friends. Jake is a perfect example of one."

Austin's face scrunched. "Yeah, but you're more fun."

"Lies. Your friends do all the outdoor things you want me to do that I refuse."

"You admit you refuse?"

"Never denied it."

"You're a hell of a lot more fun than them. Your commentary alone makes everything better. Have you ever watched a movie with you? I swear the snide remarks under your breath make it ten times more entertaining."

"You tell me to shut up all the time."

"Just to rile you."

"Well, it works."

"I know, now can we get back to why you decided abandoning me, *your best friend*, was a better idea than watching movies with me?"

"What are you gonna do when one of these dates turns into more?"

Austin cocked his brow as he gave her the once-over. "Are you talking about sex?"

Eve's eyes widened as she threw a pillow at his head. "Ahhhh. No. We don't talk about sex. That's our rule. We've never talked about sex. I'm talking about a second or third date and I don't know, maybe a boyfriend."

"You don't talk about sex. *I* talk about sex." The right corner of Austin's mouth quirked. "Aren't you a little old to be using labels?"

"Aren't you a little old to be lounging on my couch on a Friday night, eating popcorn as you listen to your best friend tell you about her horrible date?"

Austin tossed a kernel into his mouth. "Nope. So tell me what happened next. Are we gonna get to the sex part soon?"

"God, you're infuriating."

"Not as bad as your cat." Marshmallow, Eve's Bengal cat, pounced into the room as if on cue. The cat took one look at Austin before leaping into his lap.

They both froze as Marshmallow sniffed him for a second. Then out of nowhere, her eyes narrowed and Eve knew it was coming.

Instantly, Marshmallow eyed her target and went for it.

"Ouch. Fuck. Why do you always do that!" Austin pushed the cat off his arm. The same arm that was now being attacked with a weird double hind-leg kick.

Marshmallow let go before plunging her face into the bowl of popcorn, grabbing a piece and hightailing it out of the room.

"Are you fucking kidding me? Does she have to do that every time? I would've given her one. Why the hell does she always have to fake me out?"

Eve shrugged before reaching over to grab some popcorn and tossed it into her mouth. "You're easy to mess with."

"One of these days I'm gonna have your cat fall in love with me."

"Doubtful. She barely tolerates me."

"At least the cat and I have something in common."

Eve's mouth fell open as Austin smirked.

"Ya jerk!" With that, the pillow was flying through the air again directly at Austin's head.

Chapter Two

AUSTIN PUSHED AWAY his unpaid invoices as he sat back at his desk the following Monday. Something felt off, and for the life of him, Austin couldn't figure out what it was.

The weekend had been like every other weekend he'd had for the past, who knows how long.

Friday night he'd spend at Eve's apartment, watching movies, talking, or doing whatever suited them. Saturday, he'd usually end up on a hike or anything that had him outdoors. And then Sunday, he'd stop by Own Your Curves and pick up a recent order or put in a new one.

Then he and Eve would go out to lunch and talk about new designs he wanted her to make for whatever upcoming season was upon them. That way, Anytime Adventure would be fully stocked and ready to go.

Or they'd just rag on each other.

It was usually the latter.

But to Austin, that's what made the weekends fun.

By the time he'd arrive at work Monday morning, he'd be refreshed and ready for whatever was headed his way for the week.

But today was different, and he couldn't figure out why.

And that annoyed him. Cool, level-headed Austin always had his head in the game. But right now, fuck, he couldn't look at another invoice.

What the hell is wrong with me?

Giving up, Austin groaned before taking a deep breath. Whatever it was he sure as hell needed to get over it, and soon.

He had shit to do.

However, as Austin sat there looking at the invoice, he couldn't help his mind from wandering to Sunday afternoon.

"Right on time, big man." Eve chuckled as he walked through the doors of Own Your Curves.

Austin winked, giving Eve his signature smirk. He loved their harmless banter, and he'd be a downright liar if he said he didn't look forward to it. "In more ways than one."

"Eww." Eve gagged as her entire face scrunched. "Remember, we don't talk about in-the-pants things."

"I could give you something to gag on."

"Austin! For fuck's sake, stop saying shit like that." Eve shoved her fingers in her ears to block him out.

Austin laughed, winking at her again. What could he say, he loved to rile her. "You're the one that keeps bringing it up, not me."

"No, I say something and then you do that weird, twisted words thing and make it about sex."

"Everything is about sex." His smirk turned into a thousand-watt smile as he teased Eve. This was their normal banter, so he assumed he was seconds from dodging whatever Eve was about to throw at him... but no.

Instead, Eve Morgan shocked the absolute shit out of him.

"Man, do I wish." Eve sighed as she turned on her heel, heading toward her backroom.

Austin stood there frozen for a few seconds as he processed what she'd said. It was almost as if Eve's words knocked the wind right out of him.

Yeah, they teased a lot, but it was mainly on his end. She'd always be the first to shut anything down when it came to bumping uglies.

Austin didn't know whether it was the guy in him or the best friend that needed to find out more, but he did. However, he was going to go with best friend since the whole 'guy' thing was a can of worms he didn't want to open at the moment. Lord knows he'd opened it too many times before, only to shove it down again.

Quickly, Austin followed behind her into the sewing room of her shop. He tried to be the attentive best friend and listen to her complain about some weird fabric she'd gotten in that she didn't think she could make anything out of, but his mind was in overdrive.

As Austin moved on autopilot, trying to jumpstart his brain while the 'Man, do I wish" played over in his mind, Eve plopped a box of breathable hiking tops she'd fashioned the week before in front of him.

Instead of looking through the box like he normally would, Austin couldn't keep his eyes off Eve.

He was stuck there, frozen, and no matter how hard he tried, he couldn't get himself together. The only thing that snapped him out of it was Eve clearing her throat while pointing at the box. "You good?"

Quickly, Austin cleared his throat. He'd deal with his brain short-circuiting later. "I'm sure the fabric is great. What are you planning on making with it?"

Damn, he was good. See, it was just a momentary lapse in his stupid head. Everything was back to normal.

"I already made a test dress." Eve pulled out a deep hunter green dress from a rack behind her. "Something is off. But I can't figure out what."

As Austin's eyes scanned the dress, he didn't see any issues. Then again, he hadn't worn a dress before, so he really didn't know what to be looking for. "It looks nice. What's the problem?"

Austin finally relaxed. Business things, dressmaking, stuff like that he could handle. Whatever the fuck happened just a few minutes ago, though, he was gonna file that away in a box never to be opened.

"Ugh." Eve held up the dress. "I don't know if I like the fabric. I prefer things with more stretch. You know, hug the curves versus trying to strangle them to death. This one is really tight and although I like the formfitting aspect, I don't know if anyone would be able to move in it. Wait, hold on, let me just show you."

Before Austin had time to respond, Eve walked behind a privacy curtain she had for her clients to try on their custom outfits.

And just like that, Austin's mind raced again.

He didn't know if he'd acquired some weird brain-eating amoeba on his hike yesterday or what. But as Eve stepped behind the curtain, just as she'd done a thousand times before, Austin stared in her direction like he was trying to burn away the fabric, so he could see her.

Instantly, he blanched as he staggered back a step.

Holy shit.

As soon as Austin realized what he was doing, he wanted to punch himself. What the hell had gotten into him?

He'd seen Eve go behind that drape more times than he could count and not since the early stages of their friendship had he wanted a peek.

No, absolutely not. That was long fucking gone. Eve was his best friend, and that was it.

Holy shit, maybe he did pick up some weird parasite on his hike.

At this point, he was going to have to get himself medically checked out. That's honestly the only logical explanation why his brain had lost its damn mind.

Austin took a deep breath, trying his best to center himself.

That's when Eve walked out from behind her hidden away fortress, and it was like someone had punched him right in the gut... or balls.

Okay, both.

It was definitely both.

A hard lump formed in his throat as he watched Eve's hands skim down her body, trying to smooth over the fabric against her plentiful curves. And fuck him. No matter how hard he tried to stop himself, his eyes followed right along with her hands.

Holy shit.

Wow!

Eve looked good. Not that she didn't look good all the time. But this time, as she walked out from behind the curtain, she didn't look like just his best friend.

And fuck him if he didn't know how to take that.

Yep.

Okay, that settled it. Something was eating away at his brain.

Clearing his throat, Austin pushed down whatever he was feeling and gave Eve the once-over.

Act normal, you idiot.

With a low whistle, Austin eyed her. "You look amazing, Eve. I don't know why you're worried. I think your clients would buy the shit out of that if they'd end up looking half as good as you do in it."

Austin wasn't lying. He always told her she looked good. And she did. He always thought Eve was extremely attractive.

But this was different.

What Austin really wanted to say about her in the dress was something more like, 'if your clients bought that, they'd be fighting the men away with a stick as they tried to rip it off. But you just don't say those things about your best friend.

Right?

Nope. Yeah, you don't say those things.

Not when that was exactly what his amoeba-infested brain was telling him to say.

Eve cocked her head to the side slightly before she let out a tiny laugh. "Aww, that's sweet in a weird kind of way. I didn't think I looked that good in this. I was afraid all my lumps and bumps would be too distracting."

Austin swallowed hard, giving Eve another once-over. Dear Lord, he hoped she couldn't see what he was thinking about in his eyes. Lumps and bumps his ass... And that's when his amoeba-eating brain took over. "Nothing sweet about it, Eve. You look fantastic. The only way it could look better is if it was on the floor."

Wait.

What the fuck? No.

Go back.

Wait, what?

Did he really just say that? Sure, he'd tease her all the time like that, but this time, fuck, this time, he meant it. He meant every single word of it.

"Really? You think it looks good?"

Eve did a little spin that almost sent Austin into a heart attack. Had she always looked this good in clothes? Sure, he'd always appreciated her body. Any man would.

But this, this felt different. No, this was different.

Yup.

He'd be making an appointment at the doctor first thing Monday morning.

Abort. Abort.

He needed to get the hell out of there, and go for a hike, or call one of his ex—

He stopped his train of thought.

Get your shit together, Austin. You're better than this.

He pushed his thoughts aside, taking another deep breath. "Yeah, you look great. Smokin' hot. I don't know why you thought that fabric wouldn't work." *The way it hugged her hips, dear God, it was like they called to him.*

Stop it.

Where the fuck were these thoughts coming from, anyway? Austin cleared his throat, as he forced his eyes to go back to the box Eve had handed him.

Do not have inappropriate thoughts about your best friend.

I repeat. Do. Not. Have. Inappropriate. Thoughts. About. Your. Best. Friend.

"Huh?"

Her voice forced Austin to glance back at her, rather than the box of tops. Eve had that little crease in between her brows as she studied him. The same one she got whenever she was thinking hard about something.

Oh no.

"Okay then. If you think it looks good, can you do me a favor?"

A favor? Yeah, Austin would do anything for Eve. Maybe she'd ask him to unzip the back and—

Oh, for fuck's sake, man. She's your best friend. Get your head out of your ass.

Besides, he'd do anything for her, no matter what Eve wanted.

Hide a dead body? Consider it done.

Make him try on a dress so she could see how it looked? Okay, he'd protest the shit out of it, but he'd do it.

Whatever Eve wanted, no questions asked, he'd do it. "Anything for you, babe. You know that."

"Can you take a full body picture of me?"

Austin's left brow shot up. That was a weird request, but who was he to say no? It was probably for some weird measurement or even to put up on the website. Besides, the sooner he got this done, the sooner he could put this all behind him.

Austin grabbed her phone, ready to snap a few pictures.

"Wait. Let me fix my boobs."

Then as Austin stood there like a deer caught in headlights, he watched his best friend bend and do a weird shimmy thing as she stuck her hand in her top and pulled her breast up.

Holy... fuck.

He repeated. Holy. Fuck.

Austin couldn't look away even if he tried. And he'd be a no-good dirty liar if he didn't admit another part of him took notice as well.

Holy shit.

Once Eve was upright, Austin cleared his throat again to ground himself. You know what, it was probably all the hiking he did yesterday. His blood oxygen levels were still off or something.

Or the amoeba was eating his brain.

He was definitely going with the amoeba at this point.

When Austin glanced back at Eve, he instantly choked, nearly swallowing his tongue. Those globes were now on full display and his eyes couldn't help but hone in on them.

"Eyes up here, butthead."

Fuck.

Quickly, Austin darted his eyes back to his best friend, who had a shit-eating grin on her face.

He'd been caught and she'd planned it that way.

"You little shit." Damn her. Austin chuckled as Eve shrugged, her smile growing wider.

"Sometimes you gotta use what you got." She pointed to the phone. "Take the picture, please."

Austin rolled his eyes as the two of them effortlessly fell into *their normal routine. It was like everything had gone back to normal in an instant.*

Thank fuck.

See, it probably was just the amoeba and now it was gone.

After he snapped a few pictures, he handed Eve back her phone. "Are these going up on the website?"

Eve shook her head as she scanned through the pictures he'd taken before glancing back at him with a massive smile on her face. "Nope. I'm trying to find another date."

"If you think any harder, your head's gonna explode."

Austin jerked out of his thoughts as his right-hand man and longtime friend, Jake, walked into his office. "What?"

Jake cocked his brow. "You tell me? I don't know if you were in pain or just needed to fart or who knows with that look on your face. You good? You need to take a shit?"

Austin barked out a laugh as he pushed the memory of Sunday away. Honestly, it was better that way, anyway.

At least better for him. It was probably just a one-off. He still hadn't fully ruled out the brain-eating amoeba, though.

Austin cracked his neck from side to side as he watched his friend. "What's up, Jake?"

The man dropped another load of papers onto Austin's desk. "Nothing much. Just Doug is down there fighting with some prick. Thought I'd let you know."

Austin groaned as he pushed himself away from his desk. "Isn't that nice of you?" He walked over to the window in his office which overlooked Anytime Adventure's sales floor.

"That's what I thought. Glad we agree on how nice it was of me to inform you."

Austin didn't need to turn back to his male best friend to know he had a shit-eating grin on his face. The bastard. "What's going on down there?"

"Who knows? I think the guy's mad he didn't get his girlfriend to put out in the tent he bought. When I walked by, he was complaining about the size."

A wicked smile formed on Austin's face as he turned toward Jake. "Sounds more like a him problem than an us problem."

"That's what I'm saying." Jake's face brightened as the corner of his mouth turned up.

"Do I need to go down there?"

"I don't think so, but just in case you get a phone call or an email, I'm giving you the heads-up."

"Thanks."

"Oh hey, before I forget, when I was chatting with Liz in women's apparel, she mentioned a lady was asking about bigger fleece shirts since it's about to get colder out. Something about her wanting to go with her husband on his next outing. I told Liz I'd let you know."

"I'll call Eve and put in an order. Was she looking at it for a certain time?"

"I don't think so. I think Liz told her about Own Your Curves."

"Good."

"Speaking of Eve, I have a list of things I need her to supply soon. We're actually running low on more items than I thought last week." Jake pulled out a folded paper he had in his pocket.

"Just put it on my desk and I'll give her a call."

"Thanks. That saves me from having to call her. She's feisty."

"Don't I know it." Austin laughed, the corner of his lip turning upwards, knowing just how feisty Eve could get.

"I'm sure you do." Jake's entire face brightened. "So, you gonna tell me what had your head about to spring a leak?"

Austin rolled his eyes. He should've known better than to think Jake would leave it alone. But what could he say? Austin didn't even know what he was thinking about. "Nah. I'll keep that to myself for now."

"Oooh..." Jake sat down in the seat in Austin's office. "This just got interesting. Can I guess?"

Austin's brows knitted together as he sent him a pointed look. "Can you not?"

"Whoa. Yeah, this one is gonna be good. Let me see, health..." He stared at Austin. "No reaction. Okay, food? Damn... okay, nothing. Hmmm... let me think. Okay, what about women?"

Austin flicked his eyes up.

"Ahh, so it has to do with the opposite sex. Let's see, how about—"

"Fuck man, do you ever stop talking?"

"Not usually." Jake smiled. "Is it someone I know?"

Just as Austin was about to tell Jake to fuck off right out of his office, the phone rang.

Thank the fucking Universe.

Austin walked over to his desk and grabbed the phone. "Austin," he answered.

"Bossman—"

As soon as Austin heard Doug on the other end, he let out a sigh, sending Jake an annoyed look. "I'll be right down, Doug."

"I guess I spoke too soon." Jake shrugged as an ear-to-ear grin appeared on his face.

Austin's only reply was a grunt and a glare directed at his friend as he walked out of his office.

Chapter Three

EVE LEANED against the counter at Own Your Curves as she swiped through the dating site, searching for anyone who piqued her interest.

So far, it wasn't looking promising.

She'd only gotten matched a few times, gone on two dates, and sadly, the best prospect was the horrendous one she'd told Austin about the week before.

Eve groaned as she shifted her weight to her other foot.

If that was the worst of it, she could deal, but sadly for her, it wasn't. If it wasn't a 'match and then un-match' right away, she'd end up receiving one of those dreaded dick pics.

She audibly gagged in the empty store.

The number of times she'd seen some random guy's eggplant over the last month was more than she ever wanted to count.

For real, in what world did these guys think 'as soon as she sees what I have in my pants she'll fall to her knees and worship me.' If they only knew how opposite the reaction truly was.

And as soon as another picture would end up in her

inbox, Eve would shut down the app immediately, and swear off going back on.

At least for a few hours.

Dating was hard.

And a person could only take so many dick pics.

It'd been a few days since Eve put the picture of herself in the new dress she'd made on the app. And truth be told, she was debating if she wanted to take it down or not since uploading it. The dreaded dick pics had gotten a little worse.

When Eve's phone pinged with an incoming dating app message, she swiped through, only to be accosted with another one. "Oh, for fuck's sake."

Okay, make that a hell of a lot worse.

"Whatcha doing, boss lady?" Mikayla's voice rang through the shop. "What's got your panties in a twist on this fine sunny day?"

Eve shuddered, closing the app after glancing at the image of what looked like a picture of a dick with a few extra bumps on it.

I guess ten in the morning seemed like a good time to vomit...

That image would be burned into her brain for at least the next hour.

Bleah, lucky her.

Trying to push it away, Eve looked up at the chipper Mikayla O'Neil, her employee and friend who'd just walked into Own Your Curves.

Not long after opening the shop, Mikayla bounced in one day going on and on about how she was thrilled there was finally going to be a store that carried her size and all the time. And before Eve knew it, she and Mikayla were well on their way to becoming friends and the rest was history.

Mikayla started work immediately. She picked up all the slack Eve couldn't do and was always there to lend a helping hand with orders. Hiring her was the best thing Eve could've ever done, and Mikayla made sure to remind her of that on a daily basis.

But hey, Eve didn't mind. Mikayla definitely made things interesting.

It was always a blast to have her in the shop. "Nothing much." Eve held up her phone. "I'm wasting my time looking for matches."

"You still on the dating site?" Mikayla put down her bag and headed over to Eve, peeking over her shoulder.

"Yeah, I have a few downloaded. So far, nothing interesting to talk about, other than that disaster." She flicked her eyes to the ceiling as she let out a sigh. "And you already know all about that." Eve closed out of one app and opened a second one. "I thought the new dress would get some good swipes since it made Austin drool."

"Let me see."

Eve pulled up the photo and shoved it into Mikayla's face. "So far, it's only caused me a bigger headache."

"Whoa." She took the phone. "*I'm* nearly drooling over your tatas. Damn, it's like they're following me." Mikayla moved her head. "See, look, *they* are following me." She circled her head again, her eyes widening. "I think they can see into my soul."

Eve barked out a laugh. "Shut up."

"What? It's true. Look, they follow me wherever I go." Mikayla moved her head from side to side.

Grabbing her phone from her friend, Eve shook her head with a quick eye roll. "I needed a picture like that to distract from my other parts."

"What are you talking about?"

"I needed a full-length picture so I wouldn't have a repeat of the disaster I had on the first date when the asshole took one look at me and walked out." Eve still wanted to punch the dude in the throat and it had been over a month. "I figured I'd have an out now. They see this picture, still meet with me and if they say anything about my size, I can kick them in the balls. Or something like that, I don't know. I just don't want to deal with a situation like that again."

Eve was confident in her body and size. She loved herself, but damn, it still hurt. It took everything inside of her not to tell Austin about it. On one hand, she was pissed. On the other, she'd be lying if she said she wasn't embarrassed.

How could she tell Austin how she'd been treated, when she hadn't even stood up for herself at the time?

It had been kind of a shock.

That's why putting a full-length picture on the app was the way to go... no more surprises.

"If someone doesn't want you the way you are, then fuck them." Mikayla's brows pulled together as her lips thinned.

"Down, killer. I know. Oh, trust me, I know my worth. It's just easier this way."

"Men are pigs."

"Preach it."

"It's one of the many reasons why I refuse to date."

Eve cocked her brow. "You've said you've sworn off men more times than I can count."

"You would too if you were left at the altar 'cause your fiancé decided at *that* moment to break up with you and confess he'd been cheating."

Eve winced.

That happened right before Mikayla came to work for Eve.

Eve knew it still hurt her. Mikayla now had this 'screw all men' attitude and you should love yourself for exactly who you are personality.

And Eve loved that.

She was all for loving yourself exactly how you are. It's one of the reasons she started Own Your Curves. But there was still a part of her that wished she could take away Mikayla's hurt.

No one deserved to be hurt like that. Eve could only imagine what it felt like to be left at the altar. And the worst part was, it'd been *years* and Mikayla still hadn't told her the whole story.

Changing the subject, Mikayla grabbed Eve's phone out of her hand. "Is this what you made with the new material we got in two weeks ago? The one you said you hated the feel of?"

"Yeah. It's not what I'm used to, but it's nice enough for a date or something that doesn't require a lot of breathing..." She winked. "And it showcases the girls nicely."

"That's an understatement." Mikayla swiveled her head again, watching the photo.

"For fuck's sake. You're just as bad as Austin." Eve plucked her phone from Mikayla's hand before swiping through the programs, closing all her apps. "You gotta do what you gotta do." After pocketing her phone, she frowned at her friend. "I wish dating wasn't so freakin' hard."

"Being single isn't that bad. Look at me. I'm as happy as could be."

Eve gave her the once-over as she watched Mikayla put on a fake front. She'd known her long enough now to see right through her lies. Eve swore if she ever just so happened to meet Mikayla's ex, she'd kick him in the balls just for good measure.

Before Eve could respond, Mikayla grabbed her bag and bounced off toward the backroom.

"I'm gonna run into the back and check our emails to see if we got any new orders."

That was her thing. When anyone brought up the opposite sex, Mikayla excused herself from the conversation.

That's how Eve knew Mikayla still wasn't over any of it. Again, if she ever saw her ex, she'd do more than just kick him in the balls. A good throat punch was justified.

Eve sighed as she watched her friend disappear. It wasn't her place to pry, and if Mikayla ever wanted to talk, she knew Eve would be there for her.

In the meantime, though, they could both at least have a good laugh at Eve's comical dating.

See, silver lining and all that bullshit.

Eve returned to her phone since the shop had been pretty dead most of the morning. Scanning through her pictures in the dress once again, she didn't get it. Eve thought she was drop-dead gorgeous, and anyone would be lucky enough to have her at their side, and yet, here she was on these dating apps, still invisible as ever.

That's kind of how it was Eve's whole life.

Invisible.

No matter how hard she fought it. She couldn't. Eve was invisible and she knew it. For the longest time, she tried to pretend that wasn't the case, but she saw it more and more as she got older.

Eve had always been picked last for sports in school when she was forced to 'sport'. She was *never* in the cool kids' club. Hell, Eve was lucky enough her shop got some good attention. At least enough to keep her afloat, and even then, that was mainly because of Austin's contract.

Besides, if it wasn't for Mikayla and Austin, Eve wouldn't have any friends.

Bleah, the world sucked sometimes.

Everyone always said things got better after high school, and in some ways they did. She was definitely more confident. But in other ways, it stayed the same.

There was always some cool kids' club. People changed themselves just to fit in. And God forbid you liked something or looked different from what society thought was acceptable.

Eve might be in her early thirties now, but not much had changed since her pimple-filled days.

Hell, there were still times she'd wake up with damn pimples.

Like, what the hell? Wasn't that supposed to stop? Stupid hormones. Stupid society standards. And stupid men on dating apps that send random strangers pictures of their junk.

"Ugh!" Eve pocketed her phone again, just as the door chimed, causing her to look at the door. However, as soon as she saw who it was, her whole face lit. "Holly Richman, how are you? Lord Waffles still keeping you busy?"

Holly walked into the shop, along with her best friend, Emma. "You'd think the kids would be the ones keeping me busy, but nope, it's always the Corgi. You're right on the money. Waffles always has me on my toes at all times."

"So does Twitch." Emma smiled at Eve.

Holly rolled her eyes. "Don't remind me. I still haven't forgiven him for the Christmas tree."

Eve laughed, walking over to the women who always brought joy to her day when they stopped by. "What can I do for you two lovely ladies today?"

"Ben and John are watching the kids, so we figured we'd go shopping." Holly bit her bottom lip, causing Eve to raise her brow.

Okay, that was a strange reaction, even for Holly. "Are you looking for anything in particular?"

"Umm, no." Holly's eyes danced around the boutique.

"Don't lie, Holly." Emma pushed her shoulder, causing the woman to lunge forward and lose her balance.

Holly flailed her arms around, trying to stop her fall. "Oh, for freak's sake."

Emma was quick to grab Holly, though. Kind of like she knew it was coming. Which in a way was true. With Holly around, they all knew what was bound to happen.

Eve bit her lip to keep from laughing. She didn't know if

there was ever a time Holly had come into her shop and *didn't* leave destruction in her wake somehow.

Once Holly was upright, she spun around and glared daggers at Emma. "I'm telling Ben you tried to kill me."

Emma rolled her eyes. "He won't believe you. Now, ask Eve."

"Ask me what?"

"Shut up, Emma."

"No. Your jerk-face forced me to babysit with *John*. I told you I was gonna get you back for that."

Eve heard a small growl come from Holly before the clumsy woman turned back to her. "Umm, okay, so I want to know if you'll start carrying underthings. Like... you know?" Holly waved her hands around her boobs and then her stomach.

Before Eve could answer, the door chimed and in waltzed Mildred, their local wildly inappropriate librarian.

"Did you ask her yet? Spit it out, young lady."

"Oh, for Pete's sake." Holly spun back to Emma. "I'll never forgive you for inviting her."

"Payback's a bitch." Emma shrugged, a wicked smile on her face.

Oh man, it'd been a while since these three had been in Own Your Curves, and Eve knew she was in for a wild ride.

Eve's whole smile grew from ear to ear.

At least Holly hadn't knocked anything over, and Mildred and Emma weren't in some weird fight like they normally were.

So far, so good.

Although Eve now contemplated what Holly had asked. Underthings as in —

Eve spoke too soon.

As Holly turned to Mildred, she lost her footing again and

toppled over, bringing a full rack of clothes with her to the floor.

"Ahhh!"

"Geez. Holly, can you go five seconds without causing a scene?" Mildred shook her head as she pulled the mound of clothes off the woman who was now thrashing around on the floor.

"Everything okay out here?" Mikayla came running from the back. "Oh, it's just Holly..."

"Hey!" Holly scrambled to get to her feet. Once she got there, she glared at the rack before flipping it off.

The whole room erupted into laughter as Holly glared even harder at the clothes.

"It's always a pleasure when you all come in." Eve laughed as she fixed the rack and began rehanging the clothes.

"Sorry about that." A sheepish look appeared on Holly's face as she picked up a bright pink top.

"It's all good. If this is all that happens while you're here, I'll consider this a huge win." Eve winked as Holly's mouth opened.

"Hey!"

Damn, it was always good to have this bunch in the shop, even if it caused me more work in the end.

Ignoring Holly's shocked face, Eve grabbed the top from her hands. "Now, what were you saying?"

That's when Mildred jumped in, pushing Holly out of the way and thankfully into Emma this time instead of on the floor again. "She wants to know if you ever thought about expanding and making lingerie? I guess our Benny boy keeps ripping them to shreds. I ask for details, but no go. She refuses to budge." Mildred sent Holly a pointed look.

"Can you blame her?" Emma chimed in, giving Mildred the side-eye. "You talk too much."

Mildred popped her hand on her waist and stared Emma

35

directly in the eyes. "And what about you, missy? How are you and John doing? Anything you want to get off your chest?"

Emma instantly spun back to Eve. Her eyes growing were as wide as flying saucers. "Holly wants you to make sexy clothes for us plus-size women!"

Eve erupted with a hearty laugh as Mildred stomped her foot, crossing her arms over her chest, staring the now nervous Emma down. Then, just to make matters worse, out of the corner of her eye, Eve caught Holly a few feet from them, somehow stuck in a dress, trying to untangle herself.

Yep.

She'd clearly spoken too soon.

"Actually, you know what, boss lady? That might be a good idea." Mikayla walked over to Holly to help free her.

"What?" Both of Eve's brows shot up as she watched her employee try to pull a bow back over Holly's head, which was impressive since Eve was positive that dress *didn't* have a tie.

"Expanding to an intimate section." Mikayla pulled Holly's arm out of some random hole. "Lord knows we need it."

"Huh." Eve hadn't thought of that. Actually, it had never crossed her mind. Eve mainly focused on seasonal wear, since she crafted everything by hand.

"I mean, there is a need for it." Holly ducked from the last bit of the dress Mikayla had finally detangled from her body and moved back to the group as if nothing had happened. "I'm so freaking tired of Ben destroying the ones I have. It's not cheap since I need to have every item shipped 'cause stores don't carry my size. Especially in *undergarments.*" Holly whispered the last word, making Eve laugh.

"That a girl! I knew you had it in you," Mildred hollered, throwing her fist in the air.

Holly let out another growl as Eve looked around her shop and then back at the woman standing in front of her. "I never really thought about it. I kinda just made clothes so I wouldn't be stuck wearing the shit that's out there. Most of it is degrading."

"And we thank you for that," Emma interjected. "Before you opened this place, it was lucky if any of us got something decent online. There is nothing worse than ordering something you fall in love with, only to find out it doesn't fit once you get it."

"Hear, hear!" Mikayla agreed, throwing her fist in the air.

Mildred placed her hand on her hip once more, focusing on Eve. "And look what you've accomplished so far, miss high fashion chica. You could add a whole new section to this place." Mildred winked.

"I'm not adding a sex shop, Mildred." Eve rolled her eyes only to hear Mildred sigh as she tsked.

"You're missing out then." The old woman shook her head. "Then at least you could do is add some sexy-time clothes. Although, I will say the idea of adding the sex shop—"

"Mildred!" Holly screamed, snapping her attention to the crazy old bat.

"What? She's this high fashion goddess, why not add a little extra spice to the mix?"

Eve barked out a laugh at the woman. Still the same horny old woman she always was. Damn, her husband was lucky. "I don't know about the high fashion part, Mildred, but I have come a long way since opening the shop. But even then, I don't think the jump from plus size fashion to sex shop blends well."

"I think it does."

"Of course you do."

"Mildred, if it was up to you, you'd turn the library into a sex dungeon," Holly chimed in.

"And I'd teach a few of you whippersnappers a thing or two."

As Holly and Mildred bickered, Eve bit her bottom lip as she thought about what they'd suggested.

About the intimate apparel, not the sex shop.

Dear Lord, Eve had thought Austin was bad, but nobody and she meant nobody in this world would ever come close to Mildred.

She was her own special brand of... well, Mildred. There was no other word for her other than her name.

Ignoring the women arguing, Eve thought about it harder. She *could* expand Own Your Curves. And in expanding, she could bring in more clients...

And more clients would always be a good thing.

Although there was that one pesky minor fact that could derail the whole thing. Eve had absolutely no clue about the first thing about making lingerie. Lord knows, she hadn't worn any in years.

"I'd buy up everything you make. Hell, I'll even pay for custom pieces," Holly interjected through Eve's thoughts as her cheeks heated.

"Me too." Everyone snapped their head around to Emma.

"Would you now?" Mildred looked her up and down.

Emma cleared her throat. "Yeah. I mean, pretty underwear isn't just for your partners. It's for ourselves. They can help us feel more confident."

"I'm going to have to agree with Emma there," Mikayla remarked, crossing her arms over her chest. "We all deserve to feel confident. And well, you know since all the stuff happened and well, uhh... well damn it, I deserve to feel pretty and sexy again even if I'm the only one that sees it." Mikayla snapped her hand to her hip.

Emma nodded in agreement as a flash of uncertainty rushed across her face.

"You both deserve to feel as beautiful as you are." Holly grabbed Emma's hand before looking at Mikayla.

"We certainly do." Emma nodded, pushing out a deep breath.

Realizing it was best to bring the focus off Emma and Mikayla, Eve spoke. "I like the idea, but I honestly don't even know where to start. I've never even attempted to make anything like that."

"Oh, my dear good woman, that is where I've got you covered." Mildred placed her hand on Eve's shoulder and somehow without Eve realizing it, began walking them toward the backroom. "How long do you have, 'cause I have more ideas than you can shake a dic—"

"Mildred!"

Chapter Four

As AUSTIN WALKED into Eve's apartment Friday evening, everything finally seemed like it was back to normal. Thankfully, somewhere along the week, he'd gotten his brain under control and life was good again.

And right now, all Austin looked forward to was spending the evening with his best friend, while attempting to dodge her menace of a cat that seemed to have it out for him.

Life *was* perfect.

"Honey, I'm home!" Austin joked, just as he'd done a thousand times before. As soon as he shut the door behind him, he placed his key to Eve's apartment back in his pocket.

"Did you bring the pizza?"

Austin instantly froze as he heard the tell-tale sign of the shower turning off.

Oh, shit.

Okay. So, he *thought* he had his brain back under control.

Against all his better judgment, Austin walked through the room and turned his head toward the bathroom.

As soon as he noticed the door was slightly ajar, his gut tightened.

That must've been how she heard me or, you know... she just took showers with the door open. I mean, I do that, but did she have to? Did that mean every time Eve got all naked and soapy, anyone could just walk right in there like they owned the place and see her? I guess you'd have to have a key first.... He swallowed hard. *I have a key.*

Austin cleared his throat as he forced himself to look away from the bathroom. No matter how hard he tried, though, Austin couldn't stop his heart from racing. Just the thought of Eve only a few feet from him, completely naked, was enough to have his body lose its damn mind all over again.

Get a grip, dumbass. What the hell is wrong with you? We already discussed this before we got here. We're playing it cool and calm with this shit. You hear me, body.

He pinched his eyes closed as he let out a strained breath. He'd already gone over this a million times. Eve was beautiful, probably more beautiful than any woman he'd ever laid eyes on, but this was weird.

And highly inappropriate.

Eve was his best friend and you just don't have those feelings toward your best friend.

Yeah, he knew Eve was attractive, but in all their time together, his body *never* reacted like this.

For fuck's sake, *again,* she was his *best friend.*

Your body shouldn't react the way it was.

That was not very best friend-like.

Austin was going to need to remind his body of that, because this - this right now, the stirring in his lower half was going to need to get on the same damn page.

But—

Eve stuck her head out, keeping her body hidden by the door. "Austin, did you hear me?"

It was a straight sucker punch to the gut.

Holy shit!

"Earth to Austin. Did you hit your head on some rock or fall off a cliff? I'm pretty sure you would've told me if you fell off a cliff." Eve's brows pulled together, making a small drop of water form and slowly drift down her skin.

Austin stopped breathing as his eyes followed the droplet as it ran down her face, stopping at her chin only for it to slide down her neck and then move to her —

He snapped his eyes away. Oh God, he had to stop.

This is your best friend. Dude, what are you fifteen?

Austin shook his head before clearing his throat, doing his best to restart his brain and slow his heart rate. He raised one brow as Eve stared him down, making sure to only look into her eyes. "If I'd hit my head, you'd know about it. Everyone would know about it."

Eve barked out a laugh as she threw her head back. "You're right. You'd probably be demanding I take care of you and you'd milk the crap out of it."

Although the second Eve tossed her head back, Austin honed in on her neck... there went his body again.

However, the Universe must have taken an ounce of pity on him since Eve shut the door. Once it was closed, Austin took what felt like his first breath since walking into her apartment.

Thank everything.

And then his unfiltered brain took over once more. "I'd only make you wear the nurse costume for a few days. A week tops." Okay, yeah, so he joked like this with her all the time, but it's not really joking if you mean it, right?

Maybe he *should* call the doctor.

"In your dreams, Neanderthal," Eve hollered through the door.

If only...

Ahh. He blanched. *No, not if only! What the fuck is wrong with you? No. Do not ruin the best thing you've ever had, just 'cause you've lost your damn mind. Get it to-fucking-gether Austin.*

Maybe he did hit his head and somehow forgot. That happens right? You fall, get a concussion and your brain fucking loses its mind? Maybe he hit his head at work and he was drawing a blank, or maybe he did fall off the side of a cliff.

It was plausible.

Pulling his shirt up and examining himself, he quickly checked over his body.

Nope.

No cuts or scrapes that he could see. Austin let his shirt fall back over his stomach. And, instead of doing what he should've done, which was leave it alone and sit on the couch and wait for Eve, his unfiltered brain decided to have a go at it again. "You'd love it, Eve. I'd even make sure it was one of those fluffy skirt ones. That way, you can twirl around for me."

Now he was just asking for it...

Eve swung open the bathroom door, revealing herself in a cloud of smoke.

Holy shit.

Abort, abort.

"Now, I'm positive you hit your head, 'cause there is no way in hell you'd ever catch me doing that." The look on Eve's face finally snapped his brain into working again. And this time, correctly.

This was safe. This was their normal banter. He could handle their normal banter.

Austin pushed out another deep breath.

Crisis averted.

For fuck's sake.

"A man can dream, right?"

"Absolutely not." Eve chuckled as she walked into the living room. Her hair was wrapped in a towel while she donned her famous Friday night cat-tus pajamas. The ones with cats dancing around cacti. Some were even pretending they were strippers.

And just like that, with the sight of Eve in her regular Friday night attire, everything was back to normal once again.

Thank fuck.

Because Austin was liable to end up in a crazy house. At this point, he really should make an appointment with his doctor. His own hot and cold behavior was enough to give him a migraine.

"Did you bring the pizza? You never answered me."

"Don't I always?" He held up their food.

"Sometimes." She laughed, taking the box from him. "What are we watching tonight?"

Austin snatched the box from her hands before grabbing a slice, sending her a smirk which only earned him another eye roll.

"Why are you so difficult?" She snatched the box back before grabbing a slice, sitting cross-legged on the couch.

Unfortunately for Austin, though, and his deranged, needed a doctor asap brain, the moment Eve moved he ended up getting a good whiff of her. How had he never noticed Eve smelled of flowers and honey before?

Why did that call to his need for the outdoors? And more importantly, why the fuck did he want to taste it?

His eyes scanned her uncovered arm. Would she taste like honey? *I bet she tasted sweet. Eve might be spicy and ready to throat punch at any moment, but I bet she'd be sweet, maybe even a little tangy, especially between —*

Bleah.

No.

Austin stopped himself again. What in the freaking world was going on with him? Now it was just getting ridiculous.

Okay, yeah, that settled it one hundred percent. First thing

Monday morning, he was going to the doctor and asking for a CT scan of his brain.

Maybe an MRI.

Or a frontal lobotomy.

Whatever worked.

All right. See, he had a plan now. Everything was fine. He just had to get through movie night, Sunday lunch and then he'd be in the clear. Or on the way to the ER. Either worked at this point.

Pushing aside his screwed-up brain, he grabbed another slice of pizza and sat back on the couch. "What do you have in mind?"

Eve quirked her brow at him. "You haven't even finished your first slice."

"I'm a growing boy." With a smirk, Austin placed the first slice over the other and took a massive bite.

"You got that right. A *boy* for sure." Eve reached over and grabbed a napkin from the coffee table and shoved it at his chest. "At least be civilized."

Austin chuckled as he took the napkin. Before he'd arrive on Friday nights, she'd have paper plates, napkins, and drinks set up for them.

A beer for him, and water or wine for her.

On the other hand, Austin was always in charge of the food.

"We watched some stupid action film last time, so let's do comedy tonight."

Austin snapped his hand to his chest over his heart. "It wasn't stupid. You're stupid."

"Says the *boy*..."

"If I wanted this type of abuse, I would've stayed at work," Austin grumbled, taking another bite of his double-decker pizza.

"I do love that Jake screws with you just as much as I do."

Giving her the side-eye, he grunted. "You're both evil."

"That we are." Eve smiled brightly as she took a bite of her slice. "Oh man, I love pizza. The more cheese, the better."

Before Austin could agree, out of nowhere, Marshmallow came running from the backroom and skid to a screeching stop the moment she spotted Austin on the couch.

Shit... wasn't it too early for her to attack me?

His eyes darted to the clock, but before Austin even had a chance to react, Marshmallow flew toward him.

"Damn it! What the fuck, cat? I haven't done anything. I just got here." Austin jumped back as she attached herself to his ankle and bit down.

As gently as he could, he pushed her away, narrowing his eyes at Eve. "Why does she always do that?" Austin growled as Eve hysterically laughed, holding her sides. "This isn't funny. Your cat is constantly trying to kill me."

"She likes you." Eve shrugged once she got her laughter under control. "Besides, you didn't bring her anything. What can I say?"

"Great." Austin rolled his eyes as he looked back to Marshmallow, who was glaring at him from the floor. "I guess I have to bring your mom *and* you food. Good to know. You're both pains in my ass. And if you think that she *likes* me, maybe I'm not the only one that hit their head."

"You've *always* known. It's the same thing every week." Eve sat her food down on the table before picking up the remote. "For some strange reason, I'm now in the mood for a shark movie." She winked, which caused Austin to toss a throw pillow at her head.

"Don't throw those around Marshie. She'll think they're toys and I'll never get them back on the couch."

"Good." Austin glared at Eve before throwing a second throw pillow at her. "I hope the cat causes you even just an ounce of annoyance like she does me." His lips thinned. "And you only said shark movie cause your devil cat was about to make me her dinner."

"Maybe..."

Austin glanced over to the cat again, crouching behind the table, studying him with only one eye visible. "Oh, for fuck's sake. You two are a piece of work."

"And you wouldn't have it any other way. Now, hush your face, the movie's about to start." Eve shifted, getting comfortable, and instead of arguing with her, Austin decided to do the same. But not before sending a death glare one last time in her direction.

"Don't forget, you choose to be here every Friday."

Austin's mouth fell open. "Are you saying you don't want me here?"

"Depends on the day." Her mischievous smile spread across her face. "I'm just reminding you, that's all."

That little shit.

And just like that, everything was back on track and normal again. It was just him, his best friend, his best friend's cat who had a chip on her shoulder and they were about to watch their Friday night movie.

He took another slice of pizza from the box and started eating it.

Things were perfect.

Finally, Austin relaxed into their night, kicking his feet up on the table and drinking his beer.

It was about thirty minutes into some unknown shark movie when Austin heard Eve's phone chime, signaling she'd gotten a message.

Not thinking much of it, Austin focused back on the movie until he heard her groan and toss her phone back onto the coffee table with an annoyed grunt.

That got Austin's attention.

"What's that about?" He stared at her with his brow cocked as he reached for his beer.

Eve shook her head. "Ugh, trust me. You don't want to know."

Instantly, both of his brows shot to the ceiling. "I'll be the judge of that and by your reaction just now, I'm pretty sure I *really* do."

"Fine." Eve rolled her eyes. "If you really want to know, I got matched again, and he sent me a *picture.*" Eve sent him a pointed look.

"Okay?" What was the big deal? It was just a picture. Although when she said the word *matched,* his heart did a weird clenching thing...

Eve moved her hand in a small circle in the air, encouraging him to think. "On a dating site, I got matched..."

Hearing the words *dating* site also made something twist inside of Austin. He was definitely realizing he didn't like the words *matched* or *dating site* when it involved Eve.

"And he sent me a *picture...* you know, the kind of pictures jerks send on dating apps... an eggplant?" Eve continued, looking at him like he was the problem here.

An eggplant, like in the food? Wait...

That's when he got it. "Oh, for fuck's sake. Guys really do that?"

Austin didn't know if he was more pissed at the fact some random asshole sent Eve a picture of their junk or that it was a real thing and guys actually sent unsolicited dick pics.

Are you kidding me right now?

Austin was going to push aside the fact Eve that being on a dating site still sent a weird wave of emotions through him and focused on the more important part.

The dick pic part.

Who the hell did that?

Jesus, the male species needed a time out.

Austin shuddered in disgust. It was one thing to send a dick pic to your partner, but it was something else to send to some random person you met online. Come the fuck on.

Eve groaned. "You should see how many I've gotten."

His brows shot up. "No shit."

"Yeah, shit. It's disgusting, but it is what it is. Normally, I just un-match and block them."

Eve said it so matter-of-fact, he gaped at her. "How many of them have you gotten?"

"Too many."

In an instant, Austin grabbed her phone from the table and entered her passcode, which he knew by heart.

"Give it back!"

"No." With zero effort Austin held Eve away with one arm as he scrolled through her apps. When he realized there was more than one for dating, he looked back at her, his brow cocked. "Damn girl. How many of these do you have?"

"Shut your face. I'm trying to get a date."

"It looks like you're trying to get a whole fucking team with this many. I hope you don't have to pay for these."

"Austin," she warned.

Deciding to pick one at random, he opened it up and boom, he was assaulted by some other guy's junk. "Holy shit."

On instinct, Austin threw her phone across the room.

"I know." Eve fell on the couch completely frustrated. "All I'm trying to do is get a decent guy to be interested in me and instead I just get dick pic after dick pic. It's exhausting." She narrowed her eyes at Austin. "And don't throw my phone, ya jerk."

It had to be exhausting. The fact Eve didn't get her phone or threaten to punch him was proof enough. "Do you ever reply?"

"God no. I don't want anything to do with someone who

sends me a picture of their dangly sausage. I mean dang, at least say hello first."

Austin's face scrunched as he cocked his head. "It wasn't very dangly."

"I know, right! If you're gonna send someone your man meat, please make it worth my time."

Austin had to agree with her there.

Although, he wasn't a fan of anyone sending Eve dick pics. Then again, he was just going to keep pushing that feeling into a box and not deal with it.

It'd worked so far... kind of.

Just then, an idea popped into Austin's head. He jumped from his seat and grabbed her phone that he'd tossed across the room. "I've got this."

"What? No. Austin, give me my phone." Eve lunged for him, but he easily avoided her collision. "What are you doing?!"

"Taking care of your problem for you." As he spun around in circles, avoiding Eve's attempts to grab her phone, he pulled back up the app and gagged when he saw the picture again. He then quickly got to work.

"Austin!"

"Done." He handed Eve her phone. And the moment she saw what he'd done, her eyes widened before she burst out into a hearty laugh. "You didn't."

"I did." Austin grabbed another slice of pizza in pure triumph before peering over Eve's shoulder at the phone to see his handiwork.

What am I supposed to be looking at here? 'Cause what I see is kinda small.

As he reread the text, he wanted to pat himself on the back. "Oh look, he's replying." A massive grin appeared on Austin's face.

"Great, here it comes." Eve groaned.

Within seconds, they got a reply from the sender, calling Eve a fat pig, and then he promptly unmatched her.

"Really, that was his comeback? Real original." Eve laughed completely unbothered. She took her phone from Austin before going back to the pizza box to get another slice.

As Austin watched Eve, completely unfazed by the guy's remarks, his lips thinned. This faceless asshole had just called his best friend a name. And that was sure as fuck not okay with him.

When Eve turned to Austin, she must've recognized the look on his face, because she thumped the seat next to her on the couch with her hand. "Down boy. When you reject people who are like that, they always have comments along those same lines. I'm surprised he didn't call me a bitch."

"*He's* the bitch."

"That's an insult to female dogs." Eve shrugged. "After a while, you just get used to it."

That made Austin see red all over again. "You shouldn't have to get *used* to it. That's bullshit and you know it." He stomped back to the couch, glaring at her phone.

No one talked shit about his best friend.

No one.

And she dealt with this all the time?

Fuck that, man.

Eve shouldn't let that shit slide, and he knew for sure he wasn't going to.

Effortlessly, Austin plucked Eve's phone out of her hand again. He was angry and what better way to take it out than on some assholes that thought it was okay to send pathetic dick pics to random women. "We're about to have ourselves a little fun, Eve Morgan."

With a mischievous smile on Eve's face, he knew she was down.

God, this was why he loved his best friend.

And the night was only just starting.

As they went one by one, Austin would rate each picture, critique it, and send his thoughts back to the sender. Most of the replies were met with choice words flung at Eve, but not all.

And as the night went on, they'd made a game out of it. By the time they'd reached their last dick pic, they were both dying of laughter, holding their stomachs trying to breathe.

"I can't. Oh God, Austin, we have to stop. I can't breathe." Eve choked out another laugh. "That last one. Oh my freakin' word, he really thought we were gonna tell his mom. I can't... Holy shit. My sides hurt."

Austin barked out a laugh along with her. "It wasn't hard to find her. Dude should've known better than to use his real name. One quick search and everything was there."

"Stop, please." Eve laughed harder. "My sides. They're gonna split and then I'm gonna die and that wasn't on my to-do list for today."

Austin snorted. "I honestly don't get why all the guys with such tiny dicks send those types of pictures. Do they really think they have anything worth showing?"

One last laugh escaped Eve as she took a calming breath, getting herself under control. "Yeah, yeah. So small." She waved him off. "Although the last one was the biggest I'd ever seen. He at least had something good to send."

Austin's eyes widened as he stared at his best friend. "You're shittin' me?" There was no way that the last picture was not much bigger than the first one that started the night. Fuck, he'd beat those guys by a lot.

She looked back at him dead serious with her brow arched. "What?"

"Oh geez, Eve, you really need to get with better men." That was an understatement at this point.

"I know. That's what I'm trying to do. Not my fault only creepers match with me."

Austin shook his head, tossing her phone down onto the table. Trying his best to erase the fact Eve said the last picture was the biggest she'd ever seen.

If she only knew...

"At least when you get a dick pic, we can rate them now."

Eve smiled, her eyes twinkling. "I'll save them just for you."

"I'm not sure if I like that." His face scrunched as he grabbed the second to last slice of pizza.

"Too bad. You started this, so now you've got to finish it."

Well, shit.

At least he'd be involved now.

As they relaxed on the couch to continue their movie, Austin watched as Marshmallow jumped onto the coffee table.

Crap.

The cat looked at the last slice of pizza in the box and then back at him. Back to the pizza and then to him once more.

"No, you don't."

Before Austin could do anything, Marshmallow was on his lap, grabbing his pizza crust right out of his hand. She then jumped onto the floor, staring him down as she devoured her treasure, making some weird hissing noise as she did.

"For fuck's sake, cat. You could've had the one in the box. You didn't need to go for mine."

"What's the challenge in that?" Eve laughed. "She wanted yours." Eve grabbed the last slice, taking off a chunk of the cheese and giving it to the cat, who happily dropped the crust and strutted over to Eve, glaring at Austin the whole time.

"Your cat is evil, and she has it out for me." Austin watched as the thing ate the cheese before moving back to the pizza crust.

"You love her."

"Sometimes," he huffed.

Once the commotion had died down, and the devil cat had disappeared as far as Austin could tell, they settled back into their shark movie. As per usual, Eve was doing her normal commentary as it played on. He knew it bothered most people, but he loved when Eve did it.

In a weird way, it was like getting to see the workings of her brain.

He liked that.

He liked that a lot.

And whenever Austin found himself watching a movie without Eve by his side, he realized he missed her adding in her two cents every few minutes.

Leave it to Eve to make everything more interesting.

Moving his attention back to the movie, Austin focused on the screen where the female lead was undressing, seducing her male counterpart.

Subconsciously, Austin swallowed hard, as he couldn't stop his mind from thinking about Eve doing the same for him.

"Do you think that's sexy?"

Eve's voice made him jump as he stared at her wide-eyed. *Did she hear my thoughts? Is she a mind reader now? She couldn't be a mind reader, if so, she'd have kicked my ass out hours ago. Especially after the water droplet cascading down her—*

Oh, fuck.

No. Not again.

Austin cleared his throat. "What?"

"That." Eve pointed at the woman on the screen in almost nothing. "Do you think that's sexy?"

Was this a trick? This had to be a trick. These were trick questions, right? Any second now, some camera crew was going to jump out from behind a fake wall and say he was on some reality TV show.

Austin swallowed again.

What happened to her rule they don't talk about sex?

Sexy equals sex, right? So sexy should be off-limits. Okay, this type of talk was never off-limits for him. He liked pushing those boundaries and to see Eve get flustered. But this was—

Wait, that's it.

Eve was just trying to fluster him... Now he got it. This was all payback.

Austin's eyes narrowed on her slightly. If she wanted to play, he'd play. Eve should know by now, though, he was always in it to win it.

Austin willed his dick to remember this newfound knowledge as he decided to tread very carefully here. "The actress?"

"No," Eve answered. "I'm talking about what she's wearing." She pointed at the screen and Austin saw the woman dressed in sexy, bright red lingerie that barely covered her tits.

If this was a game, it was by far the weirdest game he'd ever been a part of.

Austin shrugged, doing his best not to care. "I guess."

"Dang it." Eve crossed her arms over her chest as she bit her bottom lip.

Okay, that wasn't the reaction he was expecting. "Why'd you ask?"

Eve turned to him, her brows knitted together. "Some regular clients came in today and asked if I'd consider expanding my shop to more intimate things."

Austin jutted his chin toward the screen. "Like that?"

Okay, so this definitely isn't some game...

"Yeah. I don't know why I'm thinking about it." Eve sighed. "Actually, I know why. Clearly, there's a demand. But I don't know."

Austin cocked his head. "What don't you know?"

"Sure, I mean I know what *I* think is sexy, but what if

what I think is sexy isn't sexy? God, I don't even know what men would think is sexy anymore, since it's been so damn long. And I'm sure what looks freaking phenomenal on people like her." Eve motioned back to the screen. "Might not go over as well on a body like mine."

Austin immediately started coughing as images of Eve in the outfit the woman was wearing rushed through his head.

And no matter how hard he tried to stop it, he couldn't.

The sight of Eve standing in front of him in something lace, something almost see-through —

Fuck, Austin had to bite his tongue to stop from moaning. Quickly, he grabbed his beer and took a long swig, downing the rest of it.

Holy shit, he needed to get out of there.

"Wait!" Eve jumped in her seat, facing him. "Oh my God, Austin, I forgot you're a guy. You can help me. You can tell me what you think would work." She started bouncing as she spoke. "You'll know exactly what men want in their partners. Oh man, this is perfect. And you're my best friend, so you have to do it."

"Uhh..."

"I could really tap into this market. I mean, Holly already said she'd be my first client. So I already have at least one sale, but I want to do it right, you know?" She looked at him, excitement and worry in her eyes. "It's better than the sex shop Mildred wanted me to expand to."

"Uhh." He swallowed.

"This will be perfect."

"Wait." Austin's brows pulled together as his brain struggled to work. "A sex shop?"

Eve waved her hand in the air, dismissing him. "That was just Mildred. Ignore her."

Universe help him, he was trying... But now thoughts of Eve and a sex shop ran through his brain.

"But I know if you help me, this will work. I won't disappoint anyone."

"You'd never disappoint anyone, Eve," Austin's brain finally started working.

"I won't if you help me."

"Eve —"

"This will be perfect. You can give me the male perspective. You always say I should expand and bring more clients in. What if I started making custom lingerie? That's a perfect expansion."

Lingerie.

Damn it, she said the word. And fuck him, his dick took notice. If this was a game, she was winning by a long shot. This was a horrible, horrible idea, and he knew it.

Did he mention this would be a horrible idea?

Oh shit, what if it was more than just her showing him designs on paper? What if...

But as he watched Eve's entire face light up, how could he tell her no? And she was right, as a best friend, he had to do this.

He'd never be able to tell her no. It wasn't in Austin's vocabulary when it came to her. "Wait a minute, how did you forget I was a guy?"

The corner of Eve's mouth tugged up as her whole face brightened even further. "I just did."

That little shit. And as he saw her smirk morph into a full-blown grin that went from ear to ear, he wanted to growl.

She played him.

Like she always did.

Oh man, he knew this was going to be rough. But maybe he could use this to his advantage, too. Against his better judgment, the corner of his mouth quirked. "On one condition," he agreed, still trying his best to keep himself calm. "You have to go on an overnight hike with me."

"Gahh, are you serious?" Eve's face contorted into disgust, which made Austin chuckle.

This was one hundred percent going to be the death of him, but if he was going down, he was taking her with him. "That's the trade-off, babe."

"Ugh, you're such a pain in my ass. Fine. Deal." Eve huffed as she flung herself backward on the couch, crossing her arms over her chest, annoyed.

As Austin tried to relax on the couch, a small part of him was excited she was annoyed. And an even bigger part of him was over the fucking moon. She'd *finally* agreed to go out into nature with him, but... at what cost?

A lump in his throat formed as his eyes honed in on the actress wearing the near see-through garment.

Yep. This was an absolutely fucking horrible idea.

Chapter Five

EVE HAD such a new pep in her step the following Monday. The idea of venturing out to something new was exciting, and if she were being honest, a little bit scary at the same time. But she knew everything was going to work out, just as Mildred had assured her multiple times now.

No, like *multiple* times, for real, the woman was sending Eve email after email with her ideas and suggestions.

Eve rolled her eyes so hard it nearly gave her a migraine. Seriously, some of the pictures Mildred had sent were one hundred percent off a porn site.

Eve had zero doubt in her mind about that.

That woman really was a piece of work.

The corner of Eve's lip turned up as she pulled out her phone after hearing another ping.

Speak of the devil, as soon as Eve checked her phone, there was a new email from Mildred. A part of Eve wished it might have been a match, maybe even one she could share with Austin....

To her chagrin, though, this time it wasn't just a picture from Mildred.

Nope.

This was a full-on link to a porn site.

Look at how hot she looks! You can make something like this easy and watch how her hunk of burnin' love can rip it in two with zero effort.

Just think about how many times people will have to re-buy this piece just for that aspect alone. I can smell the money from here. I think this design would be a pleaser if you get my drift. And while you're at it, that man's meat isn't something to shy away from either... Whoo-wee, would I love to take a ride on that thing.

Oh, for freak's sake.

Eve rolled her eyes again, deciding *not* to click the porn link. And for the first time since this all started, Eve considered blocking Mildred's email address.

At least the crazy old bat wasn't sending them from her library work email like she was initially doing.

Eve probably had Holly to thank for that.

And even though Mildred was a different breed altogether, at least Eve got a good chuckle out of all her antics.

Well, maybe except for the blatant porn sites now... That was a little too much.

A laugh escaped Eve's lips as she pushed her phone to the side. She honestly couldn't blame Mildred for being excited because dang it, so was Eve.

With her excitement coursing through her, Eve pulled out the sketchbook she used when working out new designs for Own Your Curves. As she leaned against the counter, Eve mused over the few drawings she'd worked on the night before.

However, Eve kept going back to the first one she'd played with. She started out with the basic design, but then of course, added her own flair to it. She knew it still needed some work, but she liked where it was going.

It was still a little nerve-wracking expanding to an intimate section for her boutique. Sure, it made sense. Plus-size women already had a hard enough time finding any type of clothes, so why wouldn't they have a hard time finding suitable underwear?

Nevertheless, just because there was a need, was Eve going to be the right person to help fill it?

Like she'd told Austin, sure she knew what she liked, but thinking about what could be appealing to a client's partner... She didn't even know where to freaking start. In the past, Eve had never done the whole lingerie thing with the people she'd slept with.

It was more of a hurry, get undressed, keep the lights dim kind of thing.

And that was on her, she knew that. And she'd long since given up most of those fears about her body, but she'd be lying if she said they didn't creep up every once in a while.

See, she really was a mess when it came to this whole new expansion. Eve bit her bottom lip. Thank everything in the Universe, Austin agreed to help.

And for whatever reason, that somehow calmed her down, knowing he was on board. Austin really was a savvy businessman and if he thought it was a good idea, who was she to argue?

Austin had built Anytime Adventure from the ground up by himself. She was still in complete awe of everything he'd accomplished in his life.

So having him on board helping her expand was a huge deal.

And then, there was the fact that he was willing to help with the design aspect. Sure, he always helped with her active-wear designs, but this was different.

She'd be lying to herself if she wasn't excited about

possibly making Austin squirm again like he did when she was in the green dress.

Like she said, she used to have huge qualms about how she looked, but not anymore. Okay, not most of the time, anyway. And the thought of someone like Austin, even the tiniest bit remotely interested in what she had going on, was a tremendous ego boost.

Who said bigger girls couldn't turn every eye in the room? Eve might not be Austin's type, but it still felt good to at least know she still had it.

Curves and all.

And if you couldn't rile up your best friend, then what good is having an opposite-sex best friend, anyway?

The right corner of her lip turned up as she thought about it.

Damn, she kept getting more and more excited about this by the second. And why not start that excitement now?

After fiddling with the design for a few more minutes, she snapped a quick picture to get Austin's opinion.

"Boss lady! How's it crackalackin?" Mikayla walked into the shop with a massive grin on her face.

"Hey." Eve smiled back as she sent the text to Austin. "I'm working on some designs, wanna see?"

"You don't have to ask me twice." Mikayla tossed her bag behind the counter and walked over to Eve. "Whoa. That's hot. Mildred help you come up with that?"

"Nope." Eve chuckled as she cocked her head to the side, examining the design again. "You really think so?"

"Yeah." Mikayla waggled her brows before pointing at the drawing. "I think you should make the bow in the front... something that can be untied. You know, like they get to unwrap a present?" She winked. "Nothing better than unwrapping your gift before you get to play with it."

"Geez, you're as bad as Mildred." Eve let out a hearty

laugh before she looked back at what she'd come up with contemplating it. "I kinda like that idea." Eve grabbed her phone and quickly sent a follow-up text to Austin.

What about the bow in the middle being something that can be untied? Like her partner can unwrap her... Thoughts?

It wasn't even a second later before she got a reply from her best friend. However, her gut dropped a little as she saw it was only a thumbs-up emoji.

Not the reaction she was hoping for, but hey, at least it was something. And for the life of her, she didn't know why his reply kind of stung.

Maybe this is a bad idea all around.

"What's that face for?"

Eve shot her eyes to Mikayla from her phone, her nose still scrunched. "I sent the design and the idea to Austin to get his opinion and he didn't seem really thrilled."

Mikayla's brows shot toward the ceiling. "You're shitting me?"

"Nope." Eve's brows pinched together as she handed Mikayla her phone.

"Maybe he didn't really look at it, 'cause that's not the reaction I'd picture him to have. This is Austin after all, he's almost as bad as Mildred."

Exactly... Maybe that's why his thumbs-up reply stung a little more than she'd like to admit.

Sure, they had their 'no sex' talk rule that Austin always seemed to push, but she thought he would have had some sort of reaction, positive or negative. Not just a dang thumbs-up emoji. And this really wasn't about sex. This was business. And she was asking for his business opinion.

Maybe this was a bad idea.

Mikayla handed Eve back her phone. "You know what, it's Monday. He's probably busy."

Eve thought about it for a second. Dang it. Monday mornings were usually Austin's busy time since he took most week-ends off to do outdoor things. "You know, you're probably right. He's usually busy on Monday. Especially if Jake was in charge over the weekend. He thinks it's fun to get under Austin's skin once he gets back to work. Still, I kinda wanted some sort of better reaction, though. Even a heart would have been better than a damn thumbs-up."

"He's a stupid boy," Mikayla stated matter-of-fact.

And she kind of had her there. Most boys were stupid.

"I'm telling you it's hot and the idea of pulling the ribbon to unwrap the top is gonna drive anyone with half a brain cell wild. Even if Austin doesn't think so." Mikayla huffed, her annoyance with the opposite gender in full swing. "Why'd you send it to him, anyway?"

Eve shrugged with her reply. "He's my best friend, and he agreed to help."

"To help?" Both of Mikayla's brows nearly hit the ceiling.

"Not like that, you weirdo. Besides, Austin isn't like that. But he is a freaking business genius and a guy," Eve replied. "When I told him about the expansion, he agreed to help me along the way. Make sure I can market it correctly. And then somehow, I convinced him to give his opinion on the pieces I make. I need to get the opinion of someone other than you, me, and apparently Mildred, who is now sending me porn sites as references."

"She send anything good?"

"Mikayla!"

"What? It's Mildred. I'm sure she's got a stockpile of stuff I didn't even know was a thing."

Eve laughed. "You're probably right. But still, I thought it would be a good idea to get the viewpoint of someone that's attracted to people in lingerie."

Mikayla looked Eve up and down before nodding once. "Okay."

"What's that 'okay' supposed to mean?"

"Nothing." Mikayla gave her a strange look before shaking her head. "Actually, I think it'll be good. You're right, he is a genius when it comes to the business side of things. I mean, just look at Anytime Adventure. So I think you're smart to ask him for help."

"But not with the actual designs?" Eve cocked her brow, studying her employee, who was now acting far more interested in an invisible piece of lint on her shirt than she needed to be.

"He's a guy. Guys get stupid."

"Yeah, he's a guy. That's why I thought it'd be a great opportunity to seek him out for his business expertise with the expansion and use what he finds appealing in my designs. Seems like a win-win to me."

Mikayla looked her up and down once more as her brows knitted together. "I get why you did it. I just worry that's all."

"About what? There isn't anything to worry about here."

"You're right."

"I am. Austin is fantastic, and I don't think he'd steer me in the wrong direction. He'd rather cut off his arm before he did that."

"Austin would do anything for you."

"And I'd do anything for him. Okay, not anything. Although the jerk did finally get me to agree to go on an overnight hike with him," Eve scoffed. *That bastard.*

Mikayla's eyes widened. "You're kidding me?"

"Afraid not." Eve shuddered. "It was his condition for him to help me."

"Interesting."

"Ugh, it's gonna suck."

"True. Are you sure he's your best friend? He should know you and the outdoors don't mix."

"That's what I'm saying. But he's been begging to get me

out hiking for years. And he took this as a prime opportunity to make it happen."

Mikayla tapped her chin with her finger. "Huh, guess he is a smart man."

"Don't tell him. It'll go right to his head."

They both laughed for a moment until Mikayla's expression softened, worry flashing through her eyes. "Just be careful, okay?"

The pain in her eyes was almost too much for Eve to bear. She got it, though. Mikayla had been burnt so badly when it came to anyone of the opposite sex, she couldn't help but throw her guard up.

Eve just wished she could convey to Mikayla, not everyone was out there to hurt her. Besides, Mikayla had nothing to worry about. It would be nothing more than a friendship between Austin and her.

That's all it would ever be.

Eve wasn't his type, not just by looks, but with everything. Austin needed that outdoor, ready for an adventure woman.

And that wasn't Eve. She liked her calm and steady routine. She'd had enough adventure in her life. Add in her new mess of the dating sites and it was *way* more adventure than she'd bargained for. And she sure as shit didn't need anymore. Plus, she'd been there and done that when she first met him. It was only natural for her to develop a small crush, and just as soon as it arose, she squashed it.

She had to.

Eve wasn't Austin's type and never would be...

The outdoors... bleahhh. She shuddered.

"I promise, I'll be okay." She touched Mikayla on the hand, trying her best to convey what she already knew to be true.

Eve never needed to worry about Austin in a romantic sense. Even if he was the hottest man she'd ever laid eyes on in her life. She'd never be what he needed, and she'd resigned herself to knowing that a long time ago.

Once she realized Austin truly was a pipe dream, she was able to let that go. And in doing so, she got the best friend she'd ever had out of it.

That was good enough for her.

In an instant, just like any other time before when feelings got involved, Mikayla pulled her hand back and placed her walls around her. As a not so genuine smile appeared on her face, she looked at Eve. "You know what? You're right. This is a win-win situation."

And before Eve knew it, Mikayla was back to her usual self. "When are you gonna make some test pieces? Do you want me to put in an order for fabric?"

Shit, Eve really hadn't gotten that far to think about fabric yet. Doing a quick mental inventory of her stuff, she didn't really have anything that would work for the expansion. At least she didn't think so.

Stepping back from the counter leaving her sketch pad there, she went to the backroom to look.

Yep, she'd definitely need to get other fabrics, even just for test purposes.

Crap.

"I think I'm gonna have to see the fabric myself this time. Normally we can gauge if we wanna try something new from the online selection, but 'cause of what this is, I should probably feel them and stuff."

"That's probably smart. Nothing worse than scratchy fabric rubbing against your hoo-ha or your nipples. Bleahh." Mikayla shivered. "Hey, wait, boss lady, you can go today. I'm here, so the shop is covered." She narrowed her eyes at Eve. "Just get the right barcode numbers in case you do like the material after you've worked your magic with it, I can order more."

"This isn't my first rodeo, missy. Don't forget, I was doing this way before you came along."

A wicked smile spread across Mikayla's face. "I'm surprised it didn't crash and burn before I got here."

Honestly, same.

"Remind me why I keep you here?"

"'Cause you love me."

"Yeah, yeah."

Mikayla was about to walk out of the backroom to the front when she turned to Eve. "You should see if Austin can go with you. You know, since you're getting his perspective and all that jazz."

That wasn't a half-bad idea. And Eve liked that Mikayla was back on board with Austin helping.

Eve's face scrunched.

Although Austin did seem busy, at least if that text was any indication. But then again, he was usually better by the middle of the afternoon. Maybe he could slip away for an hour around lunch or something. That way, she could bring him with her to get some test swatches.

Then she could work on making some test pieces that night.

Yeah, that was a good idea.

"I'm gonna text him to see if he'll come with me." A mischievous smile appeared on Eve's face. "He's gonna hate it. He hates shopping to begin with."

Mikayla laughed. "And having to look at nothing but fabric would probably make him want to pull his hair out."

That was something Eve could one hundred percent get behind. Any day she could mess with her best friend would be considered a damn good day in her book.

"Today just got a hell of a lot better." This will serve as punishment for not being excited about the design she'd sent him. Eve pulled out her phone and quickly sent Austin a text.

Chapter Six

AUSTIN PUSHED his phone away as he willed his body to calm down. Too bad he was failing. So far, no amount of conjured-up pictures with sweaty old men or live operations on people shows, really anything gross and disgusting did the trick to still his body.

And that was saying something.

Usually, the sight of someone being operated on gave Austin the heebie-jeebies, but nope. Right now, he could probably be in the operating room and still be fighting a hard-on thinking of Eve.

Fuck.

Austin cupped the back of his neck with his palm, trying to massage away the tension in his muscles.

Eve nearly gave him an aneurysm when she'd sent him the design she'd been working on. It was a sketch, and yet, the image would be burned in his mind forever.

Damn.

And when he'd finally somewhat gotten his brain to function again, she sent him the part about *unwrapping*...

Austin was positive his heart stopped when he read the word.

Unwrapping... Fuck yeah, he liked unwrapping.

A low groan escaped his lips as his body's reaction took hold once again.

Fuck him.

Even if he tried, Austin couldn't stop himself from picturing Eve in the outfit and *him,* being the one to, oh so willingly unwrap her like she was his own personal Christmas gift. The one that he'd been begging Santa for all year long.

He'd be precise in his movements. Just like he would be as a kid as he unwrapped his high-ticket item.

He'd savor it.

He'd savor every single second as he'd gently pull on the bow, letting the ribbon untie.

Austin's eyes closed as he imagined the material slowly falling open, giving him the most perfect view of Eve's —

Fuck.

Austin's eyes shot open as he tugged at the crotch of his pants, desperately trying to make room. He was about to lose it.

No, scratch that, he was well past the point of losing it.

Austin groaned, pinching his eyes tightly together, his frustration ever-present. He was *well* past the point of losing it. Especially if you counted the mess he'd made of himself when he woke up that morning.

You can't blame a guy for what happened in his dreams, right? He was asleep and had zero control over the fact his *best friend* had made him come so hard he could swear it was real.

As images of dream Eve flooded his mind again, he banged his head on his desk.

Again... Fuck him.

This whole damn thing was wreaking havoc on his brain and body in more ways than one. And for the life of him,

Austin couldn't figure out where all this started. Something flipped in his brain the other day, and he couldn't flip it back.

He never once denied Eve was attractive. He'd always tell her what a bombshell she was. Men like to have something to hold on to and damn, he'd die to be able to hold on to her. Eve had curves for days, and even though she thought they weren't attractive, any man with half a brain could see how drop-dead gorgeous she was.

Where others were hard, Eve was soft.

Soft to cushion him as he —

Dude, fucking stop it. Come on, she is your fucking best friend. Stop right now. For fuck's sake, man, you really need to get laid.

Austin rubbed his forehead with his hand, hoping to ease away some of the tension he was feeling. This was the problem. No matter how attractive Eve was, he never wanted to go down that road. It wasn't safe.

Austin's fists clenched at his sides as he threw his head back with a growl. He wanted to punch himself right in the face.

And he knew he should do it too.

Eve was the best friend he'd ever had. She'd give him a hard time, and he'd give her one right back. He'd flirt with her, and she'd shoot him down. He loved that, since she was also fun to rile up. She'd threaten bodily harm on him, and he'd tell her she looked sexy when she was mad.

Which would only rile her up further.

They laughed, joked, watched movies... Everything just clicked with Eve. She was his best friend through and through.

Austin let out a heavy sigh as he pinched the bridge of his nose.

You're not supposed to have a hard-on for your best friend.

End of story.

Let alone sexy dreams.

Get your shit together, Flynn. You will not fuck up the best thing that's ever happened to you just because your dick lost its goddamn mind. Take ten hundred steps back and get your head in the game. You are better than this.

Now if Austin could only convince his body of that.

He took a deep calming breath, which only did the trick for about two seconds before his mind ran back to the image of Eve in the design she'd made.

His eyes slowly closed, this time as his head imagined images of Eve in the lingerie, but instead of *his* hand reaching out to undo the bow, it was someone else.

Austin's blood raced through his body as out of nowhere this faceless man that wasn't *him* appeared in front of the scantily clad Eve. And as that unknown man reached out to undo the bow that was rightfully Austin's to undo, something snapped inside of him.

Hot rage filled him as he clenched his fists, his knuckles turning white.

Fuck that.

Just the thought of Eve being around someone else dressed like that had Austin seeing a red he'd never seen before.

Austin's pulse raced as his mind kept going.

She'd be wearing lingerie for someone she'd no doubt met on one of her stupid dating apps. And fuck him if that didn't piss him off, too.

Austin's nostrils flared as he gritted his teeth.

How dare *anyone* think they'd be worthy enough to see Eve in all her glory? Sure as fuck, no dick pic sending piece of shit.

Austin slammed his fist onto his desk as his blood boiled.

Fuck, stop it. You're being possessive over someone you have no right to be possessive over. He pinched his eyes closed, letting out a strained exhale. *Okay, with Eve being your best friend, you have a little right to be possessive. But not like this.*

Everything was a mess inside of him. It was like someone had taken an eggbeater and gone to town on his brain.

And at this point, he didn't know if there was any way of fixing it.

"Fuck," he cursed under his breath.

Why in the hell he agreed on helping Eve with the expansion was beyond him.

Austin snorted, rolling his eyes at himself. He damn well knew why. He would do anything for her, but this... this *was* going to kill him.

And call it his stupid man-brain, but when he agreed to help her, he didn't realize Eve would more than likely end up wearing the pieces she created herself.

Austin's gut clenched.

And he knew beyond any doubt the lucky bastard that she'd wear them for would've come from one of those fucking dating apps.

Those damn fucking apps.

Austin's jaw tightened as his eyes narrowed even further.

It took everything inside of him not to go to Own Your Curves, grab Eve's phone, and delete every app she had.

Austin could picture it now. He'd march right into the store, grab her phone and lie directly to her face and himself and say something along the lines of, 'dating apps are dangerous and he was doing it only to protect her and there wasn't a damn thing she could do about it.' He'd stand tall, his shoulders back, as he'd try to convince both of them he was saving her life.

Austin snorted at himself. *Oh, for fuck's sake. Yeah, some dating apps were trash, but not all of them... Besides, she'd probably end up kicking me in the balls.*

Austin groaned as he shook his head.

Fuck me.

This was Eve. His *best* friend, and as a best friend, he could never interfere in something that might make her happy. And that's what he'd be doing.

You could make her happy.

His eyes shot open as the thought knocked the wind out of him.

Shit. No. Stop. Fuck.

Austin's heart raced as the palms of his hands began to sweat. He couldn't swallow over the lump that'd formed in his throat. *I could make her happy...*

No. Stop it. Right now.

He wasn't the answer here. If it hadn't happened between them when they first met, it would never happen.

Hell, Austin had never had a better friend than Eve. Let alone a friend of the opposite sex. The opposite sex was just that: sex to him.

But Eve was different.

Since day one, she'd kept him on his toes and he never wanted to screw that up, regardless of what his brain thought.

Eve was too important to him.

So, no matter what his asinine mind was coming up with, he was shoving it deep down into a box, labeled never open in fear of your face being melted off, just like in that movie when they opened the arc.

It was safer that way.

Safer for both of them.

Doing his best to push the intrusive thoughts into that box, Austin still couldn't stop the dating app shit rattling around in his head.

How many god-awful dick pics had she gotten?

That alone sent more rage coursing through his body. The thought of her having to endure looking at *other* men's man meat—

Wait. Not other men's man meat. Just man meat in general, he tried to convince himself.

Shit, Austin needed to get himself together.

It was just... damn it. Eve deserved more than some random assholes sending her their meat stick in his pants.

It really was a godsend he didn't delete the apps altogether when he first found out. And now that he thought back, he really should have.

Who the fuck does that?

Here, let me just take a random picture of my junk, and send it to a chick and maybe she'll what? Get all hot and bothered by it?

Give him a fucking break.

Yeah, right. Maybe if they were already dating or whatever, but just some random drive-by dick sighting isn't going to get any woman's motor running.

Dear Lord, he worried about the male species if they thought *this* was going to it.

The muscles in the back of his neck tightened even more. Fuck him, the weekend had been hard.

Literarily and figuratively.

And so far, the start of his week wasn't looking too promising, either.

Austin snorted again. While he was at it, you know what else pissed him off? The fact she'd *finally* agreed to go hiking with him.

He'd been begging her for *years,* and she'd always come up with some lame excuse. It took Eve needing his help and agreeing to pretty much torture himself for her to go.

That just added to his frustration with the whole situation.

Nonetheless, no matter how much it irritated him he had to bargain for Eve to go with him, he was excited to finally have the opportunity to take his best friend out to where he felt free.

It was the only place other than when he was with Eve where he felt at peace. He'd wanted her to experience that for years...

And if Austin were even remotely lucky, he'd be able to convince her to go out hiking with him again after this trip.

What's the use of having a best friend if you couldn't share in all the things you loved together? To him, there would be nothing better than hanging with his best friend out in nature. It'd be like combining the two things he loved the most.

Being outside and being with Eve.

A sharp exhale escaped his lips.

Finally, being able to get Eve out hiking with him: Good.

Holding up his end of the bargain and fighting these feelings he should not be having: Bad.

Eve was beyond excited to start her new adventure in lingerie, but damn him, he was only a man. And a man could only take so much...

"We gotta stop meeting like this."

Jake's voice shook Austin out of his thoughts. When he stared up at him, he could already feel it coming.

"I can't tell if you just ate bad food, wanna flip a table, take a shit, or somehow got news you're seconds away from your head exploding, and they called to warn you?" Jake walked into his office, his left brow cocked as he gave Austin the once-over.

Well, Damn. Austin sat back in his chair, his hand resting gently on the top of his desk. That was pretty much exactly how he felt. Other than taking the shit part. Austin didn't know whether he was coming or going. One second, he was on board with helping Eve and the next he was fighting the urge to strangle any man that even dared to look at her.

"What's up?" Austin exhaled, praying Jake had some catastrophe down on the floor that'd he had to fix.

At least then he'd be able to keep his mind occupied.

"Nothing much." Jake plopped onto the couch in Austin's office. "Just figured I'd come say hi. You know, the friendly thing to do and all that shit. You've been locked in here all morning."

"I'm working."

"You're always working."

"And you're always annoying me."

"Accurate."

Before Austin could throw something at Jake, his phone chimed. And without thinking, he picked it up, and as soon as he had, Austin wished he hadn't.

When he saw Eve's name flash across the screen, his stomach tightened. Being a full-on glutton for punishment at this point, he opened her message to see what other form of hell she was about to put him through.

Hey, you wanna go fabric shopping with me today? I'd like to get your opinion on textures and stuff for the expansion. Mikayla is here already and if you aren't busy, I'd really appreciate it if you came with me. I'll even buy food to bribe you.

Austin's eyes almost popped out of his skull. *Came with...*

"There's that look again. What? We got about thirty seconds before the big kaboom? Should I duck? Do I need to call someone for you? Does Eve know?"

Austin's eyes darted to his friend. He was still a little dazed, but after a few seconds of Jake's smile growing even wider, he decided he didn't have the strength to deal with him *and* Eve's request at the same time.

Ignoring Jake, Austin went back to his phone. He couldn't tell Eve no, but he was positive the idea of seeing Eve right now would be his undoing.

And to pick out the material she was going to use to make

lingerie... Yeah, maybe Jake was right. There was going to be a big kaboom soon.

"You sure you're okay? Your face is getting all red and weird... Are you havin' an allergic reaction?"

Austin's eyes shot back to his friend. "Yeah, to you," he grunted, still trying to work out his next move in his brain.

"That hurts."

Ignoring Jake again, Austin stared at his phone, swallowing around the lump in his throat. He couldn't say no. Even as his fingers hovered over the 'n' and the 'o'.

He couldn't do it.

If Eve asked him for help to hide a body, he'd be there. And this wasn't any different. He just needed to keep reminding himself of that.

And he could do that. He was a grown man, after all. He could keep his brain in check.

Austin looked back at Jake, eyeing him. "You good if I head out for a little while? You think you can keep the store from burning down while I take care of some stuff?"

Both of Jake's brows shot up. But instead of being met with Jake's playful side, Austin saw his concern. "You okay, Austin?"

"Yeah, yeah," Austin lied. Okay, it wasn't totally a lie. Part of him was okay. His brain and his dick were another story, though. "Eve needs my help with something."

Jake sat forward in his seat, ready to take action. "Is she okay? Is she hurt? Do we both need to go? Is Mikayla okay? I can run down to the front and get Doug to cover. I don't think I've ever seen you act like this before."

Austin let out a long exhale. *Shit.* Moving his neck from side to side, Austin did his best to get himself together. "Yeah, Eve's fine. No one is hurt. She's expanding Own Your Curves and asked for my opinion."

"Pfft." Jake scoffed, his face twisting. "That's what all of this is about? With the way you look, it's like she asked you to defuse a bomb." He waved his hand in the air. "I'm gonna have to text her. I'm a little hurt. She should've asked me. I'm really the brains behind this operation."

Austin cocked his brow. "Are you now?"

A wicked smile crossed Jake's face. "Yep. Now, go have fun. I've got this under control. Tell Eve and Mikayla I said hi."

"You seem all too eager to get me out of here." Austin studied him. "What are you planning?"

Jake shrugged, that stupid half-smile on his face. "I've always wanted to turn the back corner of the store into a play-place. You know, for kids and all that."

Austin's brow arched. "For kids, or do you mean you?"

"If you hadn't turned down the rock-climbing wall —"

"I said I'd think about it. And you and I both know if we added a play-place for *kids,* you'd never get any work done."

"Or would I work harder so I could use it?" He pointed at him.

Austin shook his head. "You're a piece of work."

"'Tis true, but I'm a glorious piece of work. I'd sell for millions in an art gallery."

Universe, help him. Between Eve and now Jake, Austin was bound to lose his mind, and then some.

As Jake went on and on about how much he'd be worth and how putting in a rock wall, or a play area, would be the next step for Anytime Adventure, Austin did his best to ignore him.

If he had to pick between Jake and Eve. Hands down, he'd always pick Eve. Pulling up her message, he sent her a text.

I'm on my way.

Chapter Seven

SINCE THE MOMENT Eve and Austin walked into the fabric shop, Austin had been acting strange. Wait, let Eve rephrase that. Austin was *always* strange. But this was different. This was, well, she didn't know how to describe it.

The entire ride to the fabric shop, not once did he crack a joke. Actually, the entire ride had been kind of intense.

Eve shuddered as she glanced over at her best friend. She knew something was clearly off.

As Eve felt uncertainty creep through her, she contemplated if she'd made the right choice. Maybe Austin really didn't want to help her in the new venture. And for some reason, that sent a weird pang of hurt through her.

Was it because it was intimate apparel and he just wasn't into that or was it...

Eve gulped, finding it hard to swallow.

Or was it the fact the items would be plus-size?

The thought had bile rising in her throat. He'd never seemed to bat an eye at her size or anyone that came into her shop before, but maybe —

"What exactly are we looking for here?" Austin asked, a

clear chip in his tone which had Eve instinctively wincing. She might've come a long way from her high school days and body acceptance, but right now she felt like she was thrown back a few hundred steps.

As Eve stared at him, that weird pang in her heart came back, and it hurt. She'd be a damn liar if she said it didn't. "Are you okay, Austin? You seem kinda..." She let the words hang in the air.

Austin darted his attention to her, his eyes hard.

Okay yeah, you know what, this was a horrible idea.

If Austin didn't want to help her with this, then she wasn't going to make him. He'd been weird about the whole thing since she'd decided to do it. And even if it hurt, she'd rather have someone on board that wanted to help, than someone who felt obligated. "Actually, Austin, I just realized I don't need your help with this after all. I think I've got it and what I don't, I can just ask Mildred. Lord knows she'll be pissed I didn't ask her here to begin with. As much as I'd hate to admit it, she'd be great at this." Eve laughed, trying to break the tension.

Austin closed his eyes for a second as he let out a heavy breath. When he opened them to look at her, Eve saw the pained expression on his face.

Yeah, we're done here.

As Eve moved to put back the shopping cart, Austin stopped her. "I'm sorry, babe. It's just been a long morning."

Eve could understand long mornings, but this was more than that. "You're kinda acting like a jerk and not the normal pain in my butt annoying jerk. What's the issue? Do you not want to do this?"

"Is that what you think?" Austin's face held a shock Eve had never seen before. "Dear God, Eve. No. Of course I want to do this. I always want to help you."

He could have fooled her. "I don't know. You've been acting all weird. I just figured —"

"You figured wrong." His voice was hard again. "And I'm kinda offended you'd think I wouldn't want to help you."

"Hey there, bud, you're not turning this around on me." She crossed her arms over her chest. "You're the one acting all weird, not me. I can't tell if you have a stick up your ass or you're just being a jerk to be one."

Austin swiped his hand over his face. "I'm sorry." His forehead wrinkled. "This is a me problem, not a you or a we problem. I promise. I think I'm just stressed."

Eve gave Austin the once-over. He did look stressed. Actually, he looked almost in pain. Maybe it wasn't the expansion and it was something else that was getting to him. Within seconds, Eve's best friend hat was on as a fresh wave of concern rushed through her. "Anything I can help with?"

Something flashed in Austin's eyes at her words, but Eve couldn't quite tell what it was.

"Do I need to throat punch someone? Maybe have Mildred call her *people*. I'm not entirely positive she has people, but it's also Mildred, so she probably does."

"Oh, hell no." Austin laughed. "Do not bring Mildred into anything. She scares me. Her people probably have people."

The corner of Eve's mouth tugged up as she chuckled. "And *they* probably have people, and they all somehow report to her."

"I wouldn't be surprised." When Eve saw a half-smile appear on Austin's face, she relaxed. "But I am sorry, babe. It's just work stuff. Jake made a mess of shit over the weekend."

"You want me to throat punch him?"

Austin's smirk turned into a full-blown ear-to-ear grin. "Maybe later."

Eve's eyes narrowed for a second, trying to pinpoint if Austin was telling the truth or not. But he did look more at ease, so she figured she'd let it go. If he wanted to talk about it, he knew she was always there. "He does that on purpose, just to get under your skin."

"Yeah, he's an ass like that."

"But a fun ass." Eve's face lit.

"If you say so."

"Kinda cute too."

Austin snapped his attention to her again, this time more aggressive than before as his face hardened. "What do you mean cute?"

"His ass," she reiterated as she pulled her brows together. "He's got this cute little tush that makes me wanna just pinch it." Eve pinched the air like she was a crab.

Austin stared at her for a split second before throwing his head back, laughing. "I'm telling him you said that."

"By all means. Hell, I'll tell him myself." She winked, causing Austin to laugh harder.

Thank the Universe.

Eve didn't know what was going on with him, but a grumpy, moody, not-fun Austin was blah. Eve didn't know if she'd be able to take another second of it. She preferred best friend Austin. Annoying pain in her ass Austin.

Not angry, grumpy face Austin.

That Austin wasn't any fun.

But now that he seemed to be back to his usual self, they might as well get to the fun part.

A wide smile ran across Eve's face as she reached to her right and grabbed a bolt of fabric. "What do you think of this?"

HOLY FUCK balls Austin needed to get his shit together and fast. Because right now he was acting like anything but a best friend and fuck him if Eve hadn't picked up on it.

In his defense, though, how could anyone be the doting best friend when their mind raced with nothing but inappropriate thoughts about said best friend?

And that was *not* being very best friend-like.

A prime example was right now as Eve picked up a black see-through fabric. Seeing it had his gut clench as he imagined the material on Eve's body cascading around her curves.

Was punching himself off the table? Because right now he was seconds from doing just that, right in the middle of the damn fabric aisle.

Now, it was just getting annoying. *Okay, body, I get it. You've lost your mind. We accept that fact. She's your best friend and you don't want to keep having these feelings... well then, do us both a favor and get it the fuck together.*

How much can one person keep fighting their own body? For fuck's sake, it was like going on a five-day backpacking trip that took everything out of him. Then again, those trips that seemed the hardest were always the most rewarding in the end. So maybe —

No. We aren't going down that path.

However, his pep talk to himself hadn't worked since his stupid man-brain took over once again. "What are you planning to do with it? How would you design a piece with that material, what are you thinking? Where would it fall along your —" He coughed. "A client's body?"

He knew.

Austin freaking knew what she'd do next. Call him a glutton for punishment because he stopped breathing as Eve held the material right across her ample chest, making his eyes snap directly there.

He swallowed hard.

Eve's *very* ample chest.

The chest he'd give his left nut to reach out and caress —

"I know this is kinda sheer, but I can use this as the base. I can either add a second layer so the boobies aren't as exposed or I can —"

"Keep it sheer," he barked out without thinking. Quickly, Austin coughed again, clearing his throat. "I mean, you should do both. Keep some of them sheer, that way there's just a hint of what's under the material. But then also make some where your... umm, well not *your* but the umm..."

She quirked her brow. "Tits? Boobies? Tatas?"

"Yeah." He cleared his throat again for the millionth time that morning, forcing himself to look only at her face. "Those aren't as visible, kinda like a surprise."

Eve cocked her head as she observed him.

Uhhhh... oh, shit.

Austin thanked every bit of the Universe when Eve spoke, since he clearly forgot what words were around her.

"I can see that," she remarked. "Maybe I can make a sheer robe that can double as a 'wear it alone' without a piece under it. But then it can also be worn on top, so there is an extra added layer of suspense and *unwrapping.*" Eve winked. "I think the unwrapping thing is going to be a huge seller. Who doesn't enjoy unwrapping their gifts?"

Oh, fuck him.

"Yeah, yeah, go with that. That's a good idea."

"I think so too. How about you go over there and pull anything fabric out that catches your eye? I want to buy some test swatches for a couple of pieces."

Austin looked behind him to where Eve pointed before turning back to her. "Okay," he choked out, feeling like a fool. And with the look Eve had on her face right now, Austin knew she was loving every single second of this.

That little shit.

Austin couldn't stop the growl that came from deep within his chest as he turned on his heel and headed in the direction Eve mentioned. She was going to be the death of him in more ways than one.

Pushing everything inside that box, which he was pretty sure was now ready to burst, he walked down the aisle.

Come on, Austin, get your fucking head in the game. This isn't that hard. Stop acting like a freaking tool and help your best friend.

End of story.

She'd help you in a heartbeat if the roles were reversed. So why in the hell are you making this so damn difficult?

And for both of you?

Austin was pissed at himself all over again. Maybe he was dehydrated? Didn't lack of water start fucking with your ability to function like a normal human being? He scratched his chin. He was going to make it a point to drink more water.

Maybe that was his whole damn problem to begin with.

And the more he thought about it, he was sure that was it.

See, he was good.

He was only a little bit of an idiot. A dehydrated idiot.

With his newfound knowledge, Austin scrambled through the endless avalanches of fabric and began pulling out the most ridiculous material. Some even had little foxes running after falling leaves on them.

Not very sexy, but —

Maybe it was his own preservation, maybe it was him just messing around and being childish.

He didn't know. Hell, he'd even pulled out some thicker fabric that had tents and campfires on it...

Hey, maybe we could use this for Anytime Adventure? Maybe pajama sets. Fun ones, like Eve's Friday night Cat-tus ones.

No, that would be dumb...

But Eve always did look adorable in her Cat-tus nightwear.

Instead of putting it back on the shelf, Austin added it to the pile in his cart.

And before Austin knew what was happening, something switched in his brain as he started going aisle by aisle, pulling out any fabric that he even remotely thought would complement Eve's skin tone.

Now that he used Eve as a guide, he was on a mission.

He'd grabbed satins, silks, lace, you name it, and in an assortment of different colors ranging from hunter green that would match Eve's eyes, to a deep fuck me red that he'd kill to see her in with matching red lipstick.

"Whoa, someone's been busy."

Austin jumped, his rapid movement causing a few bolts of fabric to fall off the shelf. "Shit. Don't come out of nowhere like that."

Especially when he was deep in thought about her wearing red lipstick that matched the red material he'd just tossed into the cart.

Eve cocked her brow. "I was calling your name for the past five minutes. Who knew you'd end up at the other end of the store?" She eyed his cart. "With a basket full of fabric."

Austin glanced down at his haul and grimaced. Okay, yeah, so he'd gone overboard, but he couldn't help it. As soon as his mind switched to material that would look good on Eve... damn it. How was he supposed to stop himself?

Eve picked up a few of the bolts of fabric that had ended up on the floor and started putting them back on the shelf as she laughed. "You are one funny man." She smirked, grabbing his cart. "Let's take this to the counter and get some yards of each."

After putting back the last bolt that had fallen, Austin

glanced at her, his brows knitted together. "Wait, you're not gonna see what I picked out first?"

Eve's whole face warmed as she beamed at him. "I trust you."

And for some reason those words went straight to Austin's soul.

Chapter Eight

"HONEY, I'M HOME!"

Eve chuckled at Austin's words as she wiped her hand on the dishrag by the sink.

Something about Austin being there relaxed her. It'd been a week, to say the least, but it felt like longer. At least now she'd be able to decompress, get some laughs out, and overall, have a damn good time with her best friend, and it was what she needed.

Believe her.

Eve could still feel the tightness in her shoulders from the past week. The number of times Mildred waltzed into Own Your Curves was more than Eve could count. She pretty much had to kick the old woman out when she came in carrying an old portable DVD player and a movie, which she, oh so desperately needed Eve to see.

Just thinking about it had Eve shaking her head.

Eve didn't even know they made portable DVD players anymore. Like for real, who doesn't just stream from a computer or phone these days? I guess leave it to Mildred to keep everyone on their toes.

Oh, and let's not forget about Mikayla encouraging the old bat ninety percent of the time. Eve was positive during at least one shift Mikayla and Mildred fancied their own research time and watched whatever the heck Mildred brought with her.

See, it'd *definitely* been a week.

Maybe the Universe was in some weird retrograde, as people like to say, and was throwing everyone off or whatnot. Either way, Eve was damn thankful it was Friday night.

"Hey, babe." Austin made his way into her tiny kitchen and promptly leaned against the doorframe. "Wanna explain why I wasn't supposed to bring the food?" He placed his hand over his heart. "I was gonna bring something yummy, like Thai food, but you had to go and crush my dreams."

"Pfft." Eve flicked her eyes up. "I do like the idea of crushing your dreams, though. Might have to do that more often." Her smile went from ear to ear as she looked him up and down.

"You wound me."

"Music to my ears." Before he could reply with no doubt some smartass comment, Eve winked at him and continued. "I wanted to make something *extra* special for us tonight. You know, set the mood."

Austin's eyes rounded as he coughed a few times. Eve could swear she saw a flash of panic fun across his face as he got control of himself.

"You good, big man?"

He cleared his throat, rolling his shoulders, trying to shake it off. "Yeah, yeah, I think I forgot how to breathe or something."

"I thought I was the only one that did that?" She laughed.

"Guess not. What do you mean mood?" His eyes darted around the room as his body stiffened.

Weird. I guess whatever the heck was wrong with the week

now extended to our Friday night as well. Damn you, Universe. You probably are in some weird retrograde thing and we're all suffering.

Figures. Determined to change the mood, she sent Austin a toothy grin. "You'll understand once it comes out of the oven."

Austin crossed his arms over his chest as he leaned on the frame again. "I'll give it to you. It smells amazing in here."

Eve's face brightened. "Good. I figured it was high time we had a home-cooked meal. Not that I don't love our Friday night takeout."

Austin shrugged, a warm smile on his face. "I'm not opposed to that." His brow quirked as he gave her the once-over. "But there is something you're not telling me."

Eve sheepishly looked at him, the corner of her mouth tugged upward. "Have I mentioned how grateful I am for you agreeing to help me with the expansion? I've been working every day with test pieces. I even brought some home to work on them."

Austin coughed, this time losing his balance as he stumbled backward.

"You sure you're good?" Eve's left brow cocked.

"Yeah. Breathing. It's a bitch sometimes."

Eve stared at him for a few seconds, contemplating what the hell was going on with him before shrugging it off.

It was definitely some sort of weird universal energy going on. She made a quick mental note to check it out later.

All in all, though, she couldn't help eyeing Austin.

Forget it. Let's not keep adding to the ridiculousness of the week. It was probably Jake annoying him anyway, or he went out hiking again and he fucked up his oxygen. She couldn't help looking him up and down again. *Well, he better un-fuck it, 'cause I got plans for tonight.*

Plans that involved a lot of humor and a damn good time.

Eve laughed to herself. Oh man, Austin had no idea what was coming and she loved every last bit of it.

Her eyes glanced at the oven. She had to stop from patting her own back. She was about to be a top-notch comedian in her book.

"Babe, you don't have to thank me." Something in the room shifted as Austin looked at her. "You know I'd do anything for you."

His eyes held something she wasn't quite sure of, but whatever it was, it made her stomach do a weird flip-flop thing.

Oh, heck no! Absolutely fucking not.

She'd been there and done that in the beginning of their friendship. She was not going down that road again. She'd cut off her own arm first.

Pushing whatever the heck that was down, Eve turned away from Austin and focused on the oven. It wasn't even a second later, the timer on her phone went off.

Thank freaking everything. It was like the Universe was finally on her side.

"Dinner's done."

Eve, still trying to forget her stupid body and its lapse of good judgment, quickly grabbed a potholder and opened the oven. "Just a little something I figured we could *enjoy.*" With that, Eve pulled out a heaping dish full of Eggplant Parmesan.

She was beside herself with her own joke.

Damn, I'm good! I should be a comedian.

She placed the dish on top of the stove and smiled at Austin. "You get it?" She bit her bottom lip to stop from laughing, but she knew her eyes twinkled with joy.

Austin glanced at the dish and then back to her. "I get it."

"Do you, though? *Eggplant...* I figured it would be the perfect accompaniment to the, I think..." Eve stopped for a second, her face scrunching as she thought. "About twenty-five dick pics we need to rate tonight."

Of all the years she'd known Austin, she'd never seen his jaw hit the floor that fast.

"Excuse me?"

Eve waved her phone in the air. "Our work is never done."

"I get that." Austin pushed himself off the frame and stood there, his mouth still hanging open. "Did you say twenty-five, as in two and five?"

"It's pretty close to that." Eve shrugged. "Maybe a few more or a few less. I stopped counting after twelve."

"You're shitting me." He crossed his arms over his chest, his whole body stiffening once more.

Crap.

Instantly, the energy in the room changed, and she cursed herself. *Ugh*, and here Eve thought they were back on track.

Dang it. Son of a monkey.

For some reason, when Eve planned out this whole 'rate the dick pic while eating eggplant' joke, she didn't think it would go over this poorly, or that Austin would look like he was seconds from snapping.

She figured they'd laugh about it, eat some yummy food. Destroy some men's lives and have a good night.

But right now, that did *not* seem to be happening. Instead, Austin looked like he wanted to strangle someone, and seeing as she was the only other person in the room... uhh.

Maybe I'm not as funny as I thought... I'm just gonna have to cross comedian off the list now. I really did think the eating eggplant thing was freakin' hilarious.

Eve glanced back at Austin... maybe not. "Why does your face look like that?"

"Like what?" His nostrils flared as his eyes remained hard.

Eve waved her hand around Austin's face. "Whatever you got going on there."

"That's just my face, Eve. If you haven't figured that out by now, I might need to take you to the eye doctor. Nothing I can do about changing it."

Eve burst out into a laugh for a few seconds before jutting her chin toward him. "You know what I mean. You're all grr and rawr in the face right now."

"Rawr?" Austin cocked his brow.

"You're a pain in my ass." Eve looked back at the food she'd made and then to him. "Do you not want to eat what I made? Is that what all of this is about?" And for some reason, the thought of Austin not appreciating her taking the time to make them food kind of stung.

Austin's whole body immediately softened as he grabbed Eve by the shoulders and pulled her into a hug. "Of course, I do. You're a fantastic cook. I love when you cook for us." He kissed the top of her head. "I'm sorry. It's been a long week and I'm somehow taking it out on you. Forgive me?"

Eve pulled out of his arms, a soft smile on her face. "Nothing to forgive. Trust me. It must be in the air since I've had a long week, too."

"Was it a full moon?"

"Sure seems that way. Lord knows the number of pictures I got somehow doubled."

Austin's body stiffened again for a split second before he seemed to relax. "So let me get this straight? You kept all the *pictures* so we can rate them and while we rate them, you thought eating eggplant was a superb choice for a meal?"

Eve nodded vigorously as her toothy smile reappeared. "Hell yeah, I did."

Austin barked out a laugh as he shook his head, his smile matching hers. "You're a piece of work, but I love you."

"As you should." Eve grabbed two plates from her cabinet. She then scooped some of the food onto one of them and handed it to Austin. "Now, let's pick out our movie. We've got some men to demoralize."

Austin took the outreached plate, his smile even wider than before. "That's my girl."

They headed to the living room to their respective spots and quickly decided on a comedy since it seemed the most fitting in their situation.

After all, they had work to do.

Well, by them, it was really Austin. She'd be lying if she didn't say she'd been looking forward to this all week.

It was the only thing that kept her going.

Like for fuck's sake. It's about time these *men* and she used that term lightly got a taste of their own medicine.

Bleah. She'd be happy if she never saw another dick pic in her whole life. She wasn't lying when she said this week, for some reason, the pictures had doubled.

It must have been the dress...

Eve sighed.

She was really beginning to love the way it looked on her, but no matter how much she loved the dress, she wouldn't keep it on the apps if this was the response.

Deciding it was time, Eve handed Austin her phone. If she was going to have to take down the picture of her in the dress, she at least was going to have some fun first.

And before Eve knew it, their massacre — and that's what she'd be calling it from now on — was in full swing.

Every single response they'd sent made the week just a little bit better.

Hell, at one point, Austin took a video of him stabbing his food and sending it to a guy with the words 'if you're looking to remove the warts, I have a knife and I think I can do the job. I've watched a lot of medical dramas.'

It was almost too much.

Actually, their food had been a perfect choice since it starred in most of Austin's replies. He even remarked how the eggplant they were eating was bigger than the one the guy had sent.

The weight of the week melted away with every reply Austin made.

It really did end up being a great evening.

And that included Marshmallow making an appearance. It only involved her biting Austin's ankle once before she snatched a piece of the melted cheese off his plate and high-tailed it out of the room.

"Your cat only likes me when I have food." Austin glared in the direction Marshmallow took off with the last bite of his meal.

"I only like you when you have food."

"Rude," Austin growled. "How can you say that when I just saved you from all of these horrible fuckfaces?"

Eve chuckled, putting her empty plate of food on the coffee table. "I'm sure not all of them are horrible. Just the ones that send an eggplant pic before a hello. Besides, on Wednesday, I matched with someone who seemed kinda nice."

Austin's brows nearly shot off his forehead as he stared at her. "You did? Why is this the first I'm hearing this? We've been texting all week." He looked at the time on his watch. "And we've been at this for over an hour."

"You say that as if we don't text all the time." Eve shrugged her shoulders. "I didn't think it was a big deal. I only replied to him a few times."

"As your best friend, I should be the first to know if you matched with someone that isn't a fuckface."

"Okay, Austin..." Eve cocked her head at him. "I matched with someone who isn't a fuckface."

Austin pushed the phone at her. "Who? Show me."

Quickly, she grabbed her phone, glaring at him. His swift

change in attitude annoying her. "What's your deal? It's not like I'm marrying him."

"You're getting married?"

Oh, for freak's sake! She rolled her eyes. "You really are a pain in my ass. It's not a big deal. We just exchanged a few messages. That's all."

"Not a big deal?" Austin stared at her like she had two heads. "Just show me. I want to make sure he's not a freak or something."

"Are you saying I'm a bad judge of character?"

"I mean, you did go out on that one date so —"

"Screw you, Austin." Fuck, that hurt. Okay, yeah, so that wasn't her best move, but he didn't have to throw it in her face.

Jerk.

It's not like everyone was like him and the opposite sex just fell to their knees, begging for a chance to be with him. "Maybe you're right. I am a bad judge of character. Maybe I've always been a bad judge of character. Including when it comes to you, so why don't you just go ahead and get the hell out of my apartment." She pointed toward the door, her anger still rising. Her week was bad enough. She didn't need his shit on top of it.

Austin held up his hands. "I didn't mean it like that."

"Then how did you mean it?" She crossed her arms over her chest, shooting daggers in his direction.

"Let's start over."

"How about not? Explain to me what you mean. Yeah, I know when it comes to guys I don't pick the greatest. That's why I'm in the position I am. I'm in my thirties and alone. All I've got is a damn cat," she huffed.

Yeah, tonight was definitely not going how she wanted it to.

Eve eyed the ceiling.

You happy now, Universe? You couldn't just give me one night after a work-week from hell... just one freaking night.

"And me!" Austin pointed to himself.

Ugh, and if that didn't annoy her more. Eve rolled her eyes. "Yes. How could I forget you? My soon-to-be-ex-best friend." She narrowed her eyes at him. She knew she was being dramatic, but damn. "Maybe I should call Marshmallow and give her the command to attack."

Okay, she might be overreacting a little, but Austin stepped on her last nerve.

"She doesn't know any command *other* than attack. So that won't do anything. And what do you mean you only have a cat and *me?* First, I'm amazing. Everyone knows that. Second, you own your own freaking store. Don't discount what you've already accomplished, Eve. You took what I said the wrong way." He softened while he looked at her, his eyes almost pleading. "I didn't mean it any other way than, you deserve better than some fuckface sending you dick pics or guys that make you pay for your own food. Or while I'm at it, dicks that are the size of a freaking crayon and yet you think they're huge." He growled out his last words, his jaw hard.

Eve's eyes dilated as she gawked at him, her mouth hanging open.

"I just wanted to see who you matched with to see if he was worthy of my best friend. Fuck. That's all I meant."

And for some strange reason, that kind of made Eve feel even worse for her reaction. She was stressed, and she really did just want to have a good evening with Austin.

There was definitely something off with the week. Even her fun eating eggplant while rating crappy men felt blah and was not going as planned.

Actually, this whole week wasn't going as planned. Eve was agitated, and when Austin questioned her on the match that she liked, she got even more frazzled.

Mildred had annoyed the crap out of her almost every day. Austin, although he did text as he mentioned, they weren't like their normal conversations. Most of his replies were short and snippy, and all the test pieces she'd made she wasn't happy with.

And now, to top it all off, she was in a stupid fight with Austin. And for the life of her, she couldn't figure out why.

And at this exact moment, as Austin stared at her she didn't know whether she wanted to take him and punch him in the face or burst out into tears.

Maybe both.

Because fuck her.

She wanted to scream.

The stress of everything started folding in on her. Do you know how hard it is to make designs for a clearly underserved market and have no freaking idea what you're doing? All while making them pieces so each person who wore them felt like the true Goddess they were?

That stress alone was enough to put her on edge.

Then the stupid dick pics. She *thought* adding the fun into their night would loosen her sour mood... Guess the freak not.

Eve huffed as she fell back onto the couch. Screw everything and the horse it rode in on.

"Eve, I'm sorry."

She side-eyed him. "You should be."

"I deserve that."

"You do. But I'm sorry too. I guess it really has been a week for both of us. I shouldn't have jumped on you. Can we just get back to our normal Friday night fun? Who knew rating dick pics would get you all growly and being a jerk?"

"I said I'm sorry."

The corner of Eve's mouth tugged upward. "I know. And I really am sorry too. I hate when we fight."

Austin sat back, exhausted. "Me too."

"Let's get past all this. Tomorrow is a new day and no matter how frustrating our weeks have been, the sun always comes back up giving us a fresh start."

Austin cocked his head at her. "That's very insightful. Who are you and what have you done with Eve?"

With a chuckle, Eve tossed a pillow at him.

"Do you want to tell me what pushed you over the edge this week?" He propped his leg under him as he faced her on the couch.

"Other than you?"

"Very funny. I'm being serious. Is there anything I can do to help?"

And this was one of the reasons why she loved Austin. They hadn't had many fights in their friendship, but even when they did, they never lasted long.

Austin was always there for her.

From bad days to good days to all the in between days.

To days when she didn't want to get out of bed.

To the days she was so productive she forgot normal everyday things like eating.

And she was there for him, too.

However, it was rare for them both to be having a shit week at the same time. "It was just everything."

"I'm all ears."

Maybe if she got everything off her chest and he did the same, they could get back to their regularly scheduled programming.

"Fine, but when I'm done, you have to get whatever's going on off your chest, too." She observed him, her face scrunching. "Putting aside the assault of dick pics, I had Mildred stopping by every day to *help* me. And I'm using the term help very loosely." Eve cocked her brow at him. "She showed up at the store with a portable DVD player and a porno..."

Austin's eyes widened for a split second before he burst into a deep laugh. "You're kidding me?"

"I wish I was. I had to kick her out."

"Did you get a look at the video?"

"Austin!"

"What? I'm asking for research purposes."

She looked him up and down. "And what research is that?"

"Manly research...."

When Eve just stared at him, he continued. "Okay fine, it's Mildred we're talking about. I'm dying to know what she's into. I mean, look at her. At her age and being the way she is, she's got to have a few tricks up her sleeve."

Eve sat up, laughing. "Believe me, I already know. I made the mistake of opening a few of the links she sent me."

"Do you have any of those links handy for research purposes?"

Eve grabbed another throw pillow from behind her and tossed it at Austin. And when he ducked out of the way with zero effort, she reached over and pinched his side.

"Ouch. What the hell was that for?"

"You're being a pig. Besides, I don't know how many times I need to remind you, *we* don't talk about sex. And we sure as shit don't talk about porn."

Austin cocked his brow. "I'm supposed to be helping you with your expansion. Newsflash, babe, we're gonna be talking about sex."

"Ahhhh." She jammed her fingers in her ears. "I'm not listening."

"Eve, stop being a child. It's human anatomy. It's how babies are made... Wait. Now I get it." Austin grabbed Eve's hand, tenderly holding it in his. "I'm sorry I didn't realize you had no idea how babies were made before now. See, there are these parts. One is a hole, and the other fits into that hole —"

Eve yanked her hand out of his as she glared daggers at him again. "I will murder you."

"Wouldn't be the first time you threatened me with that." He laughed, changing the tension in the room.

Jerk.

Thank the Universe. She didn't know how much longer she was going to last the way it was.

Finally feeling fully comfortable again, Eve rolled her shoulders. "And it won't be the last. Anyway, the expansion is the bane of my existence right now. All the test pieces I've made this week suck."

"I doubt it."

Eve quirked her brow. "Trust me. They do."

The room stilled for a few seconds before Austin cleared his throat. "What did you make?"

Eve turned on the couch so she was facing him. "I made three pieces, well technically two. A bodysuit, a bra and panty set with material attached to the bra so it flows around the body, and a robe, like we talked about."

It wasn't that she thought what she made was bad, it just... She didn't know. Something was off. Maybe she was too out of touch with what was considered sexy and what wasn't to venture into this new expansion.

Maybe she wasn't cut out for this?

Regular everyday clothes she could handle. She'd gotten that down pat by now, but intimate things... Ugh. She hated everything she'd created so far, and the amount of half-started projects at the shop was nauseating.

As Eve sat there, mulling over her disaster lingerie attempts, Austin jumped from his spot and headed over to Eve's work bag that was hanging by the front door.

"What are you doing?"

Austin grabbed the bag and brought it over to the couch before placing it on the coffee table. "What does it look like

I'm doing? You said you brought the projects home. I want to see them."

Instant panic raced through Eve as she lunged, trying to grab the bag from him, but Austin must have seen it coming, since he held his hand up, stopping her while his other hand rifled through her stuff.

"Didn't your mom ever tell you not to go through a lady's bags?"

"Yeah." He gave her a cocky smile. "But seeing as this is your sewing bag, it's fine."

"Austin..." she warned.

"I'm your consultant. So sit back and hush your face." He lightly pushed her, making Eve fall back into her spot.

Fine. Whatever. Why not add more to her shit-tastic week.

As Austin held up the black lace bodysuit she'd made, only then did it occur to her what he was actually doing.

She winced.

Eve made all of her test pieces in *her* size. It's not like there were many mannequins out there that served her body type. She *always* made her test pieces in her or Mikayla's size for that reason.

But as Austin examined the bodysuit, turning it in all different directions, testing it, Eve couldn't help her feel nerves getting the best of her.

Eve would bet her left arm Austin was used to looking at *this* type of clothing in far smaller amounts of material... As he put it down and grabbed the bra and panty set she wanted to vomit. The second Austin put his hand through the opening to check how see-through it was, she lost it.

That was enough of that.

Eve grabbed it from his hand in one fast movement and shoved it back into her work bag. "Stop fondling it like that. I know they aren't good, but you can stop staring at them like..."

I don't know." For some reason, adrenaline rushed through her body as she glared at her work bag.

As soon as Austin left, she was burning the whole damn thing.

Bag included.

"Not good?" Austin choked out. "What are you talking about? I like the black one the best."

Eve growled, snapping her eyes to him from her bag. "Stop trying to pacify me."

"Babe, I'm not." His brows were almost to the ceiling.

"Austin, now is not the time. Trust me. Can we just leave it alone? I only brought them home so I can tinker with them."

"Did or did you not ask me to help you with this? I'm pretty positive the agreement was for me to give you my opinion on what you make."

"Yeah, I know, but it needs to be at a certain standard before I ask what you think about it..." As the words left her mouth, she winced. "That didn't come out right?"

"Sure as fuck, it didn't. Do you want me to help you or not?"

"Of course I do. You're my best friend." She looked at him like he'd sprouted a second head. She wanted his opinion more than anything, but she knew they weren't good enough yet.

And as the room fell to complete silence, a new wave of something she had no idea what raced through her.

Great. Now, just freakin' great. At this point, she was burning down her whole shop.

"Try them on."

Eve froze.

Austin's words had been so low, she swore she misheard him. "What?"

He stared at her, refusing to break eye contact. "Put them on. Let me see."

It was like the whole room was sucked of all its available oxygen. "You're kidding."

She knew he wasn't. His face was stern, his eyes sharp.

This was not playful Austin ready to crack a joke at any second. No, this was not that Austin at all, this was...

Well, she had no idea.

"They aren't ready."

"Bullshit. You said you didn't think they were good and what am I here for? To help you. I can already tell they're good. You want my honest opinion. And if you want an honest opinion, I need to actually see them on a body. You asked me for help and here I am giving it to you. Put them on. As your best friend, I'll tell you if they're crappy."

"They *are* crappy."

"I won't know that for sure until I see them on a body."

"Not my body..."

"Who else's body am I gonna see them on?" He eyed her like she was the one making outlandish requests, not him.

Eve glanced around the room. She didn't know what to think. This had definitely taken a weird turn. Actually, a very weird turn. How did Eggplant Parmesan and movies turn into her trying on her designs for her best friend?

A fresh wave of panic rushed through her. What if he saw all her lumps and bumps? Wait, no, scratch that.

He *would* see all her lumps and bumps.

Like all of them.

Okay, she had pasties in her bag and thank the Universe the pieces she made covered more of the *downstairs* area so he wouldn't really be able to see that... but still.

Best friend or not, she didn't think she'd be okay with that.

"Eve, just do it."

"I don't know."

The corner of Austin's mouth quirked up. "Do you want me to put them on?"

"Oh God, no." Eve burst into a fit of laughter. "Please, dear Lord, no." That would be hilarious but he'd rip it... However, that gave her a wicked idea. Maybe she should get his measurements, you know, for research purposes.

"I don't know what you're thinking about over there, but I'm positive I don't like it."

"How would you know you don't like it if you don't know what I'm thinking about?" A mischievous smile formed on her lips.

"Eve..." he warned.

"Don't Eve me. You have no idea what I've got planned."

"So you admit you have something planned?"

Her smile went from ear to ear. "Maybe..."

Austin shook his head as he laughed. "Go try them on. Times a-wastin'."

Eve sat there for a minute before she jumped off the couch.

Ehh, fuck it.

This was Austin. He'd seen her stomach and legs before when she'd try on the active-wear she'd made for Anytime Adventure.

Plus, he *was* her best friend.

What was the worst that could happen?

He could take one look at me and vomit...

Eve blanched at her own thought.

Austin wouldn't do that.

Never in a million years would he do that.

And he was right. No matter how much she didn't want to agree with him, she wanted his help and his opinion did matter. It mattered more than she wanted to admit.

But still, being pretty much naked in front of him sent a weird wave of unease through her.

Crap on all the crackers...

If she really wanted his opinion, she needed to do this.

Eve had to do this.

Screw it.

You only live once, right? And if your best friend was disgusted with your body, then well, maybe he wasn't that good of a friend to begin with?

With her mind made up, Eve grabbed the pieces along with the pasties, out of her work bag and headed toward her bedroom.

Hopefully, she'd be able to cover herself the best she could and spare herself some dignity.

Thank everything in the world the bottle of tequila was still in her bedroom from the disaster of a date she had the other week.

Eve had no idea why she hadn't brought it to the kitchen, but maybe now, it was the Universe having her back, for what might be one of the worst decisions she'd ever made in her life.

Chapter Nine

AUSTIN DIDN'T KNOW if he should punch himself in the face or the dick.

Probably both.

Yeah, nope. The more Austin thought about it, both was definitely the correct answer.

What in the absolute fuck had he'd been thinking? Well, apparently, he wasn't. That was the problem.

The week had already been rough. He'd been on edge the whole damn time, with Eve clouding every part of his mind and then some. And at this point, Austin was positive he hadn't gotten a single thing done that needed to be taken care of at Anytime Adventure.

Sure, he'd make good progress on whatever task he was working on, and then boom, he'd get a text from Eve and his mind was right back where it shouldn't be.

How many times did he have to tell himself you weren't supposed to think of your best friend like that?

Apparently, more than a million since that was where he was sure he was at.

At this point, he was freaking annoyed at himself.

A strained huff left his lips as Austin looked around Eve's empty living room.

Fuck him.

They'd had some laughs, ate eggplant, which he had to give to Eve. That was fucking hilarious, to them freaking fighting and now... well now...

Austin groaned. Fuck him again.

It was like every sane part of his mind took a running leap off a cliff when he'd pulled out the lingerie Eve made.

As he examined the pieces, images of her wearing them raced through his mind. Seeing them on paper was one thing, but when it came to holding them in his hand...Again, fuck him.

The problem was, Austin didn't want to imagine it anymore.

He wanted to see.

No, he *needed* to see.

Austin needed to see what the material he'd picked out looked like against her skin. To be so close to her in them, he could reach out and touch her...

He was tired of the fantasies he'd had come up with in his mind.

He wanted the real deal.

No matter how bad of an idea that was. If Austin didn't see her soon, he might really explode.

A frustrated grunt left his mouth as he pinched his eyes shut. He really needed to upper-cut himself.

Austin knew without a doubt, he was being selfish when he encouraged Eve to try them on. His best friend, logical brain, had taken a hike and instead his screwed-up brain, the same one that had been giving him all this trouble, stepped up and took charge.

There was no thought involved, that was part of the problem. Eve turned his brain to mush.

Some freaking best friend he was.

Austin's fist clenched as he laid his head on the back of the couch. "What the fuck am I doing?"

The night wasn't going anything like he expected. Although, how good could it go, when all he'd thought about was her and those fucking dating apps.

I matched...

Austin's eyes shot open as Eve's words came rushing back to him in a flash. Everything inside of him tightened as his heart raced.

He glanced at her phone on the coffee table. Austin knew he shouldn't. Everything inside of him knew he should ignore it, but he couldn't stop his hand from reaching for the device.

However, the second Austin touched Eve's phone, out of nowhere Marshmallow came running into the living room and stared him down. She eyed him like this was going to be their ultimate battle and there was no doubt in her mind she was going to be the victor.

"Not now, furball. I've got something stupid to do."

The cat blinked at him slowly before narrowing her eyes. As she took a step toward him, he held up his hand.

"Okay, I'm sorry. That was rude. If I promise to *willingly* give you my ankle next time you want to attack, can you give me this one pass?" Marshmallow stopped, but looked him up and down.

"I need to check something for your *mom*. I want to make sure she's safe," he lied, not only to the cat, but to himself.

No, it wasn't a lie. Austin needed to make sure Eve hadn't matched with some creep. It had absolutely nothing to do with the fact the thought of her going out with anyone that wasn't him made him want to throat punch everyone and somehow vomit at the same time.

Absolutely not.

Yeah, no. That wasn't it at all.

It was clearly just a safety issue.

He was being a good friend.

That's what he was doing.

Austin nodded as he stared at the cat for a few seconds. Marshmallow looked at his ankle, then back at him, and then at his ankle again.

After a few more seconds, the cat stood, her tail high in the air with her nose doing the same, before Marshmallow strutted out of the room.

Why do I feel like I just signed a deal with the devil? Austin glanced in the direction the cat went. *Probably because I did.*

Deciding it was best to not think of whatever he just agreed to, Austin opened Eve's phone. Thankfully, since he'd been familiar with the app now, he went straight to her matches.

That's when he saw it.

Austin's eyes narrowed as he focused on the guy in front of him. He looked like a tool. Clearly, the dude was trying and failing to grow a beard, not to mention his fake smile.

He growled as he examined the guy further.

Okay, maybe he was being too harsh but Austin couldn't help it. Deciding to deal with his snap judgments later, he went to the guy's profile to investigate.

Hey! I'm 35, and I'm tired of playing the game. I'm looking to settle down with a woman who is ready for that, too.

Austin rolled his eyes. It sounded more like this guy was a fuck-boy, and now he wanted to be a reformed fuck-boy.

Strike one.

I love dogs. I can say for sure I'm one of those dog people.

Well, too damn bad. Eve was a cat person. Actually, as Austin thought about it, Eve was an animal person. She'd pet a crocodile if she knew it wouldn't eat her.

Either way...

Strike two.

I like entertainment. Going to concerts, going out to nice restaurants and the movies. I love the movies. There is nothing better than sitting down in a quiet place, just absorbing the film. It's like watching a real-life masterpiece.

Austin snorted out a laugh. Eve wouldn't stay quiet during a movie if you paid her.

And Eve would rather end up at some hole-in-the wall Mexican restaurant that would serve Eve her weight in queso rather than going to a fancy restaurant.

Or better yet, she'd want takeout.

Strike three.

Too bad, so sad. Austin snorted again. *You're out of here, bub.* Austin quickly unmatched them and blocked his profile. He contemplated deleting the whole app altogether, but that might be pushing it a little too far.

And when Eve asked him what happened? He'd shrug and say it was some weird technology glitch.

That shit happened all the time, right?

Austin wanted to pat himself on the back.

See, it would be fine.

Once he was done with what he was considering the Lord's work, Austin tossed Eve's phone onto the coffee table and sat back on the couch, mighty proud of himself. It was as if there were a weight he didn't know on his shoulders and it finally lifted.

Austin: One.

Pencil dicks on a dating app: Zero.

He let out a pleased sigh as he made himself comfortable.

Now, he'd be able to relax.

That's when he heard a noise come from the direction of Eve's bedroom. Instantly, everything came rushing back.

Austin's eyes shot open and stared at Eve's closed door. The same door which was the only thing separating him from his naked best friend.

Oh no. Oh, fuck. Oh fucking no. Somehow, in his freaking stupid brain-fog filled mind, he'd forgotten what was about to happen.

Austin wasn't ready.

No.

Not fucking ready at all.

It was like everything inside of Austin flipped. Holy fucking shit. Eve was about to walk out in front of him, modeling the lingerie she'd made.

He repeated, holy fucking shit.

And damn if his dick hadn't taken notice.

Fuck him.

What the hell had he been thinking?

Austin's heart raced as he stared wide-eyed at Eve's door. He tried to swallow, but his mouth had gone so damn dry.

"You sure you're ready for this disaster?" Her words sent an electric shock wave through him.

Austin should've said no. Even though he *knew* it wasn't a disaster. He should have said he had to go.

He should have left and come back another time, but instead, he was shocked to hear himself say his following words. "Get your ass out here or I'm coming in to get you."

Eve threw open the door, her hand propped on her hip. "I'd like to see you try."

His heart stopped.

Like full-on, he was dead now.

He one million percent forgot how to breathe.

"I know it's bad, but you don't have to keep staring at me like that." She crossed her arms over her chest.

Bad? Was she out of her fucking mind?

There were a lot of words he wanted to use to describe Eve right now and bad sure as fuck wasn't one of them.

Eve ended up putting on the lace bodysuit and added the

sheer-ish robe on top. And there was only one problem with what she'd put on as far as Austin could tell.

That fucking robe made it near impossible to see her.

He wanted to see more.

He wanted to see it all.

Austin's eyes slowly took her in. He scanned every inch of her from her feet, up her long, lush legs, all the way up to her chest.

Austin's heart pounded as his eyes honed in, as they refused to focus anywhere but the ribbon tied neatly in a bow right in the middle of her chest.

The one he would do anything to untie.

All the blood rushed from his head and straight down to his dick. The same dick that was now painfully pushing against the front of his jeans.

"Crap. It's so bad you can't even say anything. I knew this was a horrible idea."

Eve turned on her heel to leave, but Austin choked out a single word, causing her to freeze. "Stop."

"Hell no." Eve looked over her shoulder at him, and the second she did, Austin's brain short-circuited.

Not only did he get to see her ass through her sheer robe, but with the way she glanced at him, just peeking over her shoulder, he couldn't stop himself from picturing her doing the same thing as she laid under him while he took her from behind.

Her ripe ass pushed fully in the air.

She'd turn to look at him, begging for more. Begging for harder as he'd push inside her core, feeling her surround him.

Austin couldn't breathe.

He was about to die. And right now, Austin was positive he'd fucked up in a past life, and this was his punishment.

Thank every fucking thing he was sitting down.

Against his better judgment, he heard himself say, "Come

here. Let me get a better look at you. I can't decide if you're all the way over there."

Have you lost your fucking mind?

Yes, the answer was yes.

"Screw that. You look like you swallowed an orange."

"Eve Morgan, get your ass in front of me, or I'll grab you and do it myself."

Yeah, he'd lost his mind. Wasn't your brain supposed to have your back?

Guess not.

"Excuse you." Eve snapped her body toward Austin, crossing her arms over her chest as she glared at him. Too bad that was the wrong thing to do. Not only did it push her breasts up, but the movement also caused the robe to rise, giving Austin an even better view of her lush, thick, and would gladly suffocate between thighs.

"You heard me. Get your fine ass over here and let me take a good look at you. I need to see the full picture. You said you trusted me, right? So, trust me to help you make the best decision for Own Your Curves."

Eve grumbled, and he was sure he heard a fuckface somewhere, but he didn't give a shit right now. The only thing he cared about was getting a better view of the person who was going to star in every fucking fantasy he would have for the rest of his life.

No matter how wrong it was.

Austin might be headed straight to hell, but right now, he'd gladly accept his fate.

As Eve stomped over to him, he blindly grabbed one of the throw pillows and placed it over his lap.

Fuck him, he didn't know how much more he could take. With every step she took, her tits jiggled.

Breathe, Austin, breathe. Get your fucking head in the game and breathe. You don't want to pass out, and her come to help you only to find you with a hard-on. Idiot.

The moment Eve stood in front of him, Austin knew the sight of her like this was going to be burned into his head for all eternity.

It took everything in him to fight the urge to stand up, walk over to her, untie that fucking bow and let the robe fall open, finally giving him a better view of her curves. "Do a spin."

Oh, buddy, you really are a dumb motherfucker now, aren't you?

Eve cocked her brow at him. "Who died and made you king?"

"I'm sure someone did. Now spin for Daddy."

"Eww. Bleh." Eve gagged as her eyes narrowed on him. "I will murder you."

Really, Daddy? Austin was going to punch himself. There was nothing wrong with the daddy kink, whatever floated people's boats but fuck him for having zero filter.

He was blaming the lack of blood to his brain.

Fuck it. All rational thought had left and he was just going along for the ride... "You've been saying that as long as I've known you. Spin so I can see the full picture."

Eve growled, glaring hard at him. "Just know I hate you."

"You love me."

"The back is way worse than the front, trust me." Eve turned on her heel, and the moment Austin saw her backside, he was done.

A man could only take so much.

"I have no idea why I made a stupid butt-floss one. I hate butt-floss. Who the hell wants a string up their ass?" Eve grumbled as she turned back to him. "But it worked better for the design. I was able to add snap buttons that connected the front and back at my hoo-ha."

Austin stared at her, frozen in place, as his brain worked on processing what she'd said.

"Hey, at least I can walk around without them unbuttoning." The corner of her mouth turned up as her cheeks heated. "I was worried about that." Eve then rubbed her thighs together a few times to test her hypothesis.

Eve wanted him dead. Austin was sure of it now.

As she was off in her own world, spinning in circles, rubbing her thighs together, Austin closed his eyes, biting the inside of his cheek so hard he tasted blood.

Buttons... hoo-ha... I'm dead, absolutely dead, and this is my hell.

As Eve was turned away from him again, he quickly adjusted in his seat, trying to give himself more room, but failed miserably. This was more than a test of patience, this was fucking torture in every way possible.

When Eve finally stopped spinning and doing God knows what to see if the buttons would pop, she faced him with her brow cocked. "What do you think?"

Now or never. Head in the game. You've got this. Breathe in one-two, out one-two. In one-two, out one-two.

"I like it. The robe leaves an element of surprise, and the buttons are smart," Austin strained out the words. "You know, easy access."

See, that wasn't so hard. And you didn't lie. The idea of the buttons being the only thing in his way...

Just one quick flick of his fingers and —

"You think so?" Eve looked down at herself and then over her shoulder to look at her ass, making it so her chest was pushed forward.

He better get a goddamn medal for this.

"I know so. Trust me." Austin's teeth clenched.

He must have really been an asshole in his past life because the next thing Austin knew, Eve had grabbed her chest and pushed her tits up, and fuck him, he was done. Just go ahead and kill him now because another second of this and he was going to have a heart attack.

Or his dick was going to explode.

Eve's hand moved to the bow on the robe, and he couldn't hang on for another second. "Wait. No stop. I like the surprise element. Keep it like that. Always leave them wanting more?" he rushed out in self-preservation.

"Are you always wanting more?"

"Yes," Austin answered before he could think.

Eve's brows pulled together as she eyed him. "So you don't want to see what's underneath?"

Fuck yes, I do.

For the first time since this started, he was thankful his brain had some sort of filter because he didn't say it out loud. However, something worse happened other than him saying those words.

A weird wave of sadness ran across Eve's face.

Fuck him all the fucking way to the moon and back. Great, in his attempt to control himself, he'd somehow managed to hurt Eve's feelings. But how would you tell your best friend that same friend you should never have dirty thoughts about her design was so fucking good, he was liable to come in his pants at any second.

This is your best friend. And, right now, you are being anything other than a best friend. Eve doesn't look at you that way.

Austin took a deep breath. "Trust me, babe. You look like a bombshell. I don't need to see anymore to know this would sell like hotcakes at the shop. As a guy, I'd die if my partner wore this."

Eve cocked her head at him and he could tell she contemplated if he was telling the truth or not. "Really?"

"Yes, really."

She must've been pleased with that answer because an adorable smile formed on her face like she was proud of herself. "Huh? Alright, maybe this isn't so bad after all." Her eyes lit. "Wait, let me go try on the other one to see what you think."

Instead of waiting for his reply, Eve ran back to her bedroom and in doing so, Austin got another glimpse of her ass.

This time he couldn't hold back his groan.

Can you die from blue balls? Because if the answer was yes, he was about to.

As he sat there, he noticed his body shook. Like, actually shook.

Austin tossed the pillow next to him and grabbed the front of his jeans, trying to relieve some of the pressure. However, the moment his hand touched the bulge, he hissed.

Fuck.

He was seconds from coming in his pants.

Austin's eyes moved to the bathroom. Maybe —

No, fuck no. You have better control than to run to your best friend's bathroom and jerk off. You're fucking better than this. You aren't some high school pimple-faced kid.

For fuck's sake, man.

Sweat pricked his skin as he tugged at his pants, and he couldn't help but linger a little longer on his dick.

Austin grimaced toward the ceiling. *I hear you loud and clear, Universe. I fucked up big somewhere, and right now you are getting your payback. I fully accept that, but I beg you, please, fucking please have mercy on me. I don't think I can handle much more.*

Austin closed his eyes, trying to gain control, but that was a mistake. Instantly, images of Eve bombarded his mind.

Subconsciously, Austin's hand went to his dick and pressed down.

Forgive me.

He didn't know who he was asking for forgiveness from, but Austin knew he needed to ask for it. As his hand tightened around himself through his jeans, the bedroom door flung open.

Austin instantly snatched his hand back like he'd been burned before darting his eyes to Eve. And what he saw made his jaw drop.

There in front of him, Eve stood in a near see-through bra, which had material attached to the bottom that left an opening in front, kind of like a curtain.

It was just enough to see more of her delicious skin.

But no, that wasn't all.

The way the material flowed along her body, it was like it was made to draw attention lower. And boy, did his eyes do exactly that.

Eve had on a pair of black lace panties. And fuck him, he could tell even from how far away she was, he could see her skin poking out strategically through the lace.

Her skin.

Her soft, supple skin that was deliciously close to her core.

And even though at that exact moment he wished he had x-ray vision to see beyond the lace, his brain had the where-withal not to gawk at his best friend's pussy. As his eyes moved back up Eve's body on a mission to get to her face, they stopped at her chest again.

Her breasts were covered in an almost not big enough triangle with satin edges all around them that looked like it was hooked together by tiny little buckles before crisscrossing up her neck.

Austin swallowed hard, almost unable to do so.

"This one is pretty see-through. I needed to put on pasties," she announced like it was not a big deal.

Pastries? Like a cinnamon roll? Does she want me to lick icing off her nipples?

He'd do it. Fucking call him Chef Austin because he would sure as fuck do it.

"I'm glad I had some in my bag." She giggled.

"What?" he choked out. Did he miss the cinnamon rolls when he first grabbed her bag?

"The sticky things that cover your nipples." Eve eyed him like he had two heads.

Pasties. Not pastries... Oh, man, he was a goner.

Was he breathing? He didn't think he was breathing.

Eve did a spin unprompted this time. "These are cheeky underwear. I know butt-floss is a favorite. But, Lord help me. I wanted to make sure I'd like to wear it too. So I decided to make these, they only show half of the butt, but I think they are still sexy without giving me a wedgie."

Austin swallowed his tongue as he gawked at her, his mouth open.

"The material kinda cuts into me, though." Eve wrinkled her nose. "I'm not really sold on it. *But* I like this opening in the front design that's attached to the top. See?" She grabbed the two ends, tossing them through the air. "It makes me feel like I'm wearing a cape and capes are fun."

Austin nodded. "Capes are fun."

"That's what I thought when I came up with this." Eve's mouth scrunched to the left. "But would someone want this in the bedroom —"

"Yes."

Eve's brows nearly jumped off her face. "You didn't let me finish what I was gonna say."

"I didn't have to." Austin slowly scanned her body before reaching her eyes again. "Eve, holy fuck. You look damn—" He stopped, unable to form a coherent sentence.

"Cat got your tongue?"

"Yeah." Austin whistled low. "We'll go with that."

"I can live with that." Eve had a huge smile on her face, clearly once again proud of herself. "Score one for me."

And she should be proud because she did good.

Almost too good.

"Let's get down to business, then."

"What?" he squeaked out, his eyes widening.

Eve walked to her purse Austin's eyes following her every move. "What do you like and not like?"

Eve was confident in her skin and fuck him if that didn't turn him on even more. She quickly grabbed her sketchbook and trotted over to the couch and plopped down right next to him. Just sitting there in the lingerie she'd made like it was no big deal.

It sure as fuck was a big deal to him.

Okay, how do we play this? This is your best friend and no matter how inappropriate your thoughts are right now. You need to remember that. You cannot fuck up the best thing that's ever happened to you.

You cannot fuck your best friend.

Eve glanced at him, her pencil in her hand and her sketchbook open on her lap. "What should I change?"

"Nothing. I wouldn't change a damn thing."

"Oh, come on. There has to be something. Maybe I should make the bottoms higher in the back of this one. That way they show more cheek?" When she looked at him again, the line formed between her brows. "Is more better or worse?"

Austin swallowed, forcing himself to keep his eyes on her face. "Depends."

"On what?" Eve's nose scrunched as she looked down at the pad in her lap.

How fast he was going to rip it off her.

That's what.

Austin bit his tongue. "The situation."

Eve, not happy with his answer, sat back on the couch and pulled her legs up, and screw him if he didn't let his eyes scan down to her newly exposed skin.

How was she not affected right now like he was? It was like she had zero cares in the world, and he didn't get it.

He was about to come in his pants and yet, Eve was just sitting there, with her pencil in her hand and her sketch pad on her lap ready to get down to business stuff.

"What do you like, more or less skin? Butt-floss or no butt-floss?"

Fuck you, Universe. Fuck you and the horse you rode in on. "It's whatever she's more comfortable in."

"Hmm. Okay, not a bad answer." Eve tapped her pen on her chin. "If she's not comfortable, then what's the point, right?"

"Exactly. And you, Eve Morgan, look pretty comfortable right now."

She giggled again. "No butt-floss would do that to you."

Austin cocked his head to the side. Eve didn't giggle. No, that wasn't her thing unless she was —

Eve burped. "Shit, that hurt." Her hand flew to her chest.

"Eve, are you drunk?" That would explain a whole fucking lot.

When Eve pivoted her head to him, a smile spread across her entire face. "I think I'm between tipsy and drunk..." She wrinkled her nose again. "Maybe."

"What?" Austin's brows shot to the ceiling. "When did you drink? I've been with you all night." He looked around the room. He was the only one who had a beer. She was drinking water with their food.

Had he walked into an alternate Universe... or wait.

Did he actually die?

That's what happened, right? He died the moment she walked out in the first outfit and this was his purgatory.

"I still have the bottle of tequila in my bedroom from the night of the disaster date that ripped my favorite dress." Eve gave him a toothy grin. "I needed something to burn away the memory of me being practically naked in front of you, and a few shots seemed like a good way to do it."

Austin's head was about to explode.

Eve giggled again. "I know, I know. You're my best friend and it's not like you haven't seen me in shorts and a top before. Blah blah blah, this is business. Hell, you've seen me in just sports bras when I try on the pieces I make for Anytime Adventure. So, you've pretty much seen all I've got to offer, but I still needed some liquid courage."

"I've never seen your nipples or your pussy," he blurted out.

"Austin!"

"What?" He was kind of pissed. Okay, Austin was more than pissed. This sure as fuck explained a whole hell of a lot.

"We don't talk like that." She pouted, but let out a little burp at the same time. "Huh? Maybe I shouldn't have downed that last shot."

Okay, yeah, Austin was agitated. "Yes, we do."

"Yes, we do what?" She cocked her head at him, a lopsided grin on her face.

"Talk like that," he growled.

Eve narrowed her eyes at him, trying to intimidate him, but failed when she burped again. "No, we don't."

"Eve, look at the way you're dressed and what you're asking me to help you with. We're gonna be talking about nipples, pussies, dicks, and asses—"

"Stopppp."

"Eve," he warned.

Eve scrunched her nose at him. "Why are you so grumpy right now? Maybe *you* should take a shot. I'm not grumpy at all. In fact, I feel floaty."

"Floaty?" He cocked his brow. "I think you're past the tipsy part."

"Nahh." She nodded her head instead of shaking it.

Fuck.

Austin didn't think he could handle a drunk Eve right now, not while his lower half was still threatening bodily harm on him.

Don't get him wrong, he loved drunk Eve. Drunk Eve was fun and feisty, and he enjoyed the nights they'd end up letting loose while watching a movie. He'd always end up passing out on her couch and she'd make him hangover eggs in the morning.

Austin loved those nights even if they didn't happen a lot.

Although, he definitely needed to take some of the edge off. Austin grabbed his forgotten beer from dinner, realizing it was empty.

Shit.

He glanced back at Eve, a goofy smile on her face. At this point, Austin didn't know if Eve would remember half of this anyway. And he didn't know if that was a good or bad thing. He closed his eyes for what seemed like forever.

When he finally opened them again, he noticed Eve was now furiously sketching in her pad. That little line between her brows on full display.

Damn, he loved that line.

Austin took a deep breath.

He could do this.

He was her best friend.

And best friends did this stuff.

Huh, he didn't think the lounging around in almost no clothes stuff, but the being there for each other and well, helping her with her designs stuff.

And as Austin repeatedly told himself more times than he

could count. You do not have feelings like he was having right now toward your best friend.

Absolutely not.

But what if you did? What if —

"Oh my God, Austin. I've got it!" Eve's voice caused him to jump as his mind almost went to a place it shouldn't. "What about crotchless panties?"

The second before Austin's resolve broke, it happened.

Marshmallow must have decided the deal he'd made with her earlier was up, and it was time for him to hold up his end of the bargain.

As pain radiated through his ankle, he looked down at the devil-cat and had never been more thankful in his fucking life.

Chapter Ten

THE WEEKEND HAD damn near killed Austin and he knew it. He was a simple man and looked forward to his weekends. They are what really got him through the week.

The outdoors and Eve.

Just how he liked it.

Except for this last weekend.

This last weekend would go down in history and Austin would never be the same.

Holy shit, just thinking back to the whole thing had him contemplating changing his name and leaving town forever.

If you'd look up colossal screw-up in the dictionary, you'd see a picture of him, right next to the dates of the last weekend.

After Eve modeled for him, his brain had taken the next exit off the interstate and was never coming back.

And now, every single time Austin closed his eyes, Eve was there. Okay, well, she'd been there for a long time, but this was worse. If it wasn't her in the lingerie, it was replaying his oh-so-elegant exit.

Yeah, he was talking about the one that had him abruptly

running out of her apartment like a fucking idiot, shouting about needing to go to the Emergency Room.

Austin thought he'd never been more thankful for the devil cat to attack him, but when Eve jumped into action to help...

Fuck him.

The second Eve dropped to her knees in front of Austin with the wet paper towel to stop the bleeding...

You couldn't blame him for losing all control.

Oh man, and when she *looked* up at him.

Fuck him again.

Eve's hair was out of place, her eyes wide, and in that outfit... Austin moaned just thinking about it. It was enough to send any man over the brink, and that was exactly what happened.

In self-preservation to stop himself from further embarrassment, he knew he had to get out of there.

Like come on, Eve was on her knees in front of him in her outfit, inches from his dick.

His freaking *hard* dick.

The next thing he knew, Austin had pushed Eve out of the way as gently as he could and was bolting out of her apartment with an asinine, "I have to go to the ER to get this checked out. She probably gave me Cat Scratch Fever."

Just thinking about it sent a wave of ridiculousness through him as he banged his head on his desk.

Seriously, fuck him.

Did he mention the whole thing was a disaster because disaster was probably putting it mildly.

Austin was beyond thankful Eve hadn't followed him out of the apartment.

If the roles had been reversed, Austin knew he would have. But even in her drunken state, there was a sinking feeling inside of him, Eve knew exactly what she'd been doing.

Not entirely, and maybe not on a subconscious level, but there was something there that should've clued her in.

Austin knew he wasn't doing a very good job of hiding his arousal, so she had to have known. Eve was inches from his dick. His very hard, about to lose it any second, dick.

Shit, maybe she was too drunk to realize.

But then, even in her altered state, he'd catch her eyes honing in on him, watching him like he was a glass of water and she was dying of thirst.

Austin would never be able to get those looks out of his mind. They were burned there for good, her doe-like eyes staring at him through a set of naturally thick lashes.

Austin's fist clenched at his side as his body began to hum all over again.

And fuck him while he was at it. The same image, along with her little foray of dropping to her knees in front of him, Eve's mouth slightly open, were the reasons he'd damn near rubbed himself raw.

And fuck him again, if that alone didn't make him want to punch himself in the gut.

You shouldn't rub one out to your best friend and yet he'd lost count of how many times he'd done just that since Friday night.

Austin banged his head on his desk again.

How does one enter the witness protection program? Can I just apply? Maybe I should look into it.

As Austin's head throbbed, he contemplated checking it out. If Eve ever found out about the number of times he'd jerked off with her in mind, she'd kill him.

You'd think he would've gotten some sort of relief. No, that would mean the Universe was on his side.

And that was not the case.

Austin sat back in his chair as he pinched the bridge of his nose. If his own fucked up fantasies weren't bad enough, having to meet Eve Sunday and pretend nothing happened as he picked up the week's orders and had their weekly lunch was damn near torture.

Thank fucking everything after a quick apology and blaming it on the week, they left it alone and pretty much pretended it never happened.

Normally he'd push a situation like this and make sure they were actually good, but this time he was more than happy to leave it all alone and pretend it was all a fucked up dream.

But it wasn't a fucked up dream.

No matter how bad Austin wanted it to be, it wasn't.

You. Don't. Jerk. Off. To. Your. Best. Friend.

A painful throbbing behind his left eye formed.

How in the hell was he ever going to cross back over the line he'd crossed? How was he going to handle another weekend of her trying on what she'd made? Because he knew that's exactly what Friday night would end up being. He opened up that can of worms and now had to live with it. Okay, yeah, he was mostly to blame since he did encourage her to model... but still.

Austin opened his desk drawer and pulled out a bottle of pain reliever before popping two into his mouth and downing a bottle of water he had.

The events of the weekend had made him so freaking tense, every muscle in his body hurt. You'd think he'd gone on some two-day rock climbing adventure, but no. He saw his best friend in lingerie and probably gave himself an ulcer in the process.

Maybe Austin could skip this Friday. Get a date —

He blanched at the thought.

Austin didn't want a date.

Hell no.

He wanted to hang out with Eve.

He always wanted to hang out with Eve.

And that's your fucking problem, dumbass.

No matter how bad he wanted to continue Eve and his regular Friday night shenanigans, going back to her apartment seemed worse than torture. Going out to lunch was bad enough. But after a few laughs, it was fine.

Okay, it wasn't fine on his part, but he sure as fuck wasn't going to let her know that.

Austin knew for damn sure the moment he walked back into Eve's apartment he'd be done for. But at the same time, he didn't want to cancel.

Austin grabbed the bottle of pain reliever and looked at the label. *How long does it take for these to kick in?* His hand went to the back of his neck as he tried to massage away the tension.

"Dude, as much as I like to watch you annoyed, I'm not on the side of whatever the hell is causing you all this shit. Actually, come to think of it, a part of me thinks you enjoy it."

Austin grunted the moment Jake walked into his office.

"For real dude, it's like every Monday you've got this weird new stick up your ass. Do I need to call someone? You good? You're normally all woo-eee look at me, I'm all relaxed since I did some manly shit over the weekend. Not the last few weeks, though. I'm beginning to worry." Jake sobered, the permanent smile on his face slipping as he softened. "Man, are you okay? Like really okay?" Jake sat back on the couch, his full attention on Austin. "Is there anything you want to talk about? Any way I can help?"

Great. Freaking great. Fuck him.

Austin sighed, fighting the urge to bang his head on his desk once more. How the hell could he even begin to explain what he'd been going through? You don't just casually drop the fact he wanted to fuck his best friend and every second that went by the urge got stronger and stronger.

You don't.

You push that shit deep into a box and seal it away, never to be let out.

Austin straightened in his seat, doing his best to control his idiot mind and body. "Thanks, man. But there really isn't anything to talk about. I guess I'm just extra stressed since I'm helping Eve with her shop."

Jake studied him for a second before nodding. "Everything okay?"

"Yeah. Everything is fine."

It was not fine.

When Jake's brow shot up, Austin had to wonder if he'd said the words out loud.

"Ookaayy. Whatever you say." Jake eyed him suspiciously. "But if you need anything you know I'm here, right?"

"Yeah." Austin let out a heavy breath. "I appreciate it, man. Thanks."

"It's mostly selfish on my part. If something were to happen to you, I don't want to end up being the big boss here. There's no fun in that." A childish smile appeared on Jake's face. "Although I wouldn't mind having the weekends off." He scratched under his chin. "Now that I think about it, how about you go explode and I'll get to take the weekends off."

Austin rolled his eyes. Lord help him. "You already get most of the weekends off."

"Ahh, but not every weekend."

"I don't get every weekend off. I work Sunday," Austin reminded him.

"No, you go hang out with Eve and pick up inventory. That's not working. Buuuut, I mean, if you were to just disappear, I'd gladly assume that role as well. I like Mikayla. She has a fun sass to her."

"Jake," Austin warned.

"What, you can hang out with Eve and take her to lunch

every Sunday, but I can't do the same? Sounds a little sexist, if you ask me." Jake crossed his arms over his chest.

"I don't think you know what sexist means."

"Sure, I do. Now that we've got this girly talk out of the way—"

"See, you have no idea what sexist means."

Jake glared at him, giving him that duh look. "When you purposely discriminate against women."

Austin's fingers went to his head as he massaged his temples. "You give me a headache."

"Then I consider my work here done." Jake's hand darted to his chest as a smug smile appeared on his face.

"If you think your only job is to give me a headache, let me break it to you, buddy. If I were to disappear, you'd have a rude awakening."

"Yeah, yeah, whatever." Jake waved him off. "Fine. What's the plan for the week?"

Get through it as fast as possible so he could see Eve again — wait, no.

Ahh, screw him... Maybe Jake was right and he did like this new form of torture he was putting himself through. Although going back to Eve's apartment seemed a little too risky, even with his masochistic-filled brain.

Wait... Austin sat up straighter in his chair.

Oh, hell yes. Hell freakin' yes.

Austin rubbed his hands together as a new wave of excitement rushed through him. This weekend he was cashing in his end of their bargain.

The corners of Austin's mouth quirked into a colossal smile.

He was taking Eve on an overnight hike.

This was exactly what Austin needed. Now he not only got to spend the weekend with his best friend, which he wanted to do but there would be zero need to hang out in her apartment. The not-safe apartment. *And,* he'd get to be out in nature.

That's what he needed to clear his mind.

And all with his lovely best friend, who'd been avoiding getting out there with him for years.

His plan just became a win-win.

"That look on your face has me a little worried."

Austin's entire face lit as he eyed Jake. "How about we go shopping?" Austin stood from his desk.

"Hot damn. Where we going? Can I suggest burgers on the way? I'm starving." Jake thumped his stomach, standing up alongside Austin.

"Didn't you just have breakfast, it's only nine am?"

Jake shrugged unapologetically, a boyish grin on his face. "I can eat again."

"Same." Austin chuckled. "But no, you and I are going to raid the floor. Eve Morgan is going on a hike with me this weekend."

Jake's jaw dropped. "No shit. Really?"

"Yes, shit."

"Does she know this?"

The corner of Austin's mouth turned up as his eyes lit. "Not yet."

Jake did a weird jig at his words while he clapped his hands together. "Scheming against Eve. Hell yes, I'm all for it. What do we need? That'll show her for always making me the butt of her jokes." Jake was the first out of the office, Austin not far behind him as they made their way down the stairs to the main floor.

"You're never the butt of her jokes, *I* am."

Jake flipped around to him. "Huh? I guess you're right. *You're* always the butt of both of our jokes."

Austin narrowed his eyes at him. "Yeah. I know."

"Oh, but the stories this weekend is gonna bring..." Jake's

eyes twinkled with glee for a moment until a frown appeared on his lips. "I'm kinda disappointed I'm not going with you. I can only imagine the shit Eve's gonna say."

"I'll report back."

Jake glared at him. "You better. I want all the details. Make 'em good."

Austin laughed. He had no doubt it would be good. This was Eve, after all. And Eve hated anything that involved the outdoors... huh, maybe this was a little bit of payback after all.

As Jake walked through one of the aisles, he held up a bag. "What are her thoughts on dehydrated food?"

"She'd hate it." Austin's eyes danced. "Grab three." A wicked smile appeared on his face as he pulled out his phone to finally let Eve in on their upcoming adventure.

Chapter Eleven

"YOU'RE KIDDING. Please tell me you're kidding?" Mikayla held her sides as she worked to control her laughter.

If you asked Eve, though, she wasn't really doing a good job of controlling her laugh. "I wish I was."

It was Monday afternoon and Eve's mind still raced with the events of the weekend. And since this was the first time she'd seen Mikayla since then, she couldn't stop herself from telling her about the entire catastrophe when she asked how things were going.

"So you started downing shots in your room for the confidence to show Austin your designs. And when you did, he kinda just sat there but also didn't sit there. Then you ended up on the floor in front of him and he left shouting he needed to go to the Emergency Room? Do I have that right?"

"When you put it like that, it sounds ridiculous," Eve grumbled. "In hindsight, the shots were probably a bad idea, but being almost naked in front of you is way different than being almost naked in front of Austin. Trust me."

"Oh, I'm not arguing with you there." She nodded, but Eve could see the joy in her eyes.

"I want to punch myself in the face. 'Cause I knew after the second or fifth shot, I was way more confident than I should have been. Leave it to alcohol to just give you that extra push." Eve looked at the ceiling and groaned. "I can't believe I freaking sat on the couch in the test piece and worked on the design just, you know, sitting there with all my *things* hanging out and about like I had zero cares in the world."

"It sounds like you did have zero cares. How did Austin react to you sitting there?"

God, why couldn't Eve be one of those people that didn't remember stuff when they were drunk? She'd give her left boob to be one of those people right now. Because even though things were hazy, she remembered.

Eve remembered it all.

"It was weird." Eve sighed, still trying to process the events. "Austin kept saying what I'd made was good. He thought they were sexy and even in my uhh... tipsy haze, I can recall a lot of lingering looks at me. I mean, maybe Austin was just checking out the outfits. In his defense, that's what he was there for, right, to look at the outfits, not exactly look at *me* in them?"

"You don't sound really sure about that."

That's because Eve wasn't. Her mind raced back to Austin grabbing the pillow and putting it over his lap.

Maybe...

After all, there was the way he acted when she tried on the dress she'd made.

Huh? Perhaps she *could* turn on a guy like Austin.

"Why do you think he wouldn't look at *you* in the outfits, Eve? You're being silly. He'd be lucky to have *you*."

This poor, naïve soul.

Eve reached out and touched Mikayla's arm, giving it a slight pat. "We both know that isn't the case, but I love you for saying so."

Mikayla snatched her arm away from Eve. "You don't give yourself enough credit."

"Trust me here, Mikayla, the overly hot attractive guy and the whatever the hell I am, only end up together in the movies. That's not real life. Now, if I could only scrub the images of me making a fool out of myself from my brain, I can move on and pretend this never happened."

"I think you're wrong on many counts here. I know I wasn't there, but I don't think you made a fool out of yourself. Actually, I think there was a part of you that knew exactly what you were doing."

Eve gasped, her hand jerking to her chest. "Prancing around half-naked in front of my best friend as he looked me up and down unfiltered? Nahh."

"That's not what I'm saying. I'm talking about how it's always fun getting a member of the opposite sex hot under the collar. And this is Austin we are talking about—"

"And your point?" Eve cut her off.

Mikayla held up her hands. "I'm just sayin' I knew *exactly* where this was going to end up."

Eve snapped her arm to her hip. "What are you talking about?"

"Oh, nothing." Mikayla gave her a half-smile, which seemed to produce a new ounce of annoyance to run through Eve.

Forget it. She had bigger fish to deal with, like trying to come to grips with making an ass out of herself. She was still pretty mortified by the way she acted. Best friend or not... Ugh, and then Marshmallow....

Eve groaned, closing her eyes. *Universe, can we skip ahead a few years to where I can look back at this and laugh, instead of right now, when I want nothing more than the earth to open up and swallow me whole?*

"What?" Mikayla asked, forcing Eve to open her eyes.

Damn it. Eve looked down and saw no sign of a hole appearing, clearly letting her know the Universe was a jerk and didn't take her request seriously. Groaning again, she focused back on her friend. "At one point in my tipsy stupor, I mentioned crotchless panties and loud." *Crotchless panties. What the heck was wrong with me?* "Remember the whole part about leaving after Marshmallow bit him?"

Mikayla nodded.

"It was right after I mentioned the crotchless panties. As Marshmallow lunged, I jumped into action. Can I tell you how flattering it must've looked with me running around, chasing after my cat, while my tits and ass were pretty much hanging out, Austin screaming she'd actually pierced the skin and there was blood?"

The entire night was a disaster.

A huge fucking disaster. And Eve was more than happy to pretend it never happened. They'd done a damn good job of that when they met for lunch on Sunday. But as soon as Mikayla had asked how her weekend went, the words just sort of started pouring out of her.

It was like someone opened the faucet and there was no stopping the word vomit from coming.

"Oh, and yes, the 'I'm leaving to go to the ER moment.' We haven't gotten there yet."

"Stop sounding like you're enjoying this."

"That's like asking me to stop breathing." The merriment on Mikayla's face made Eve's eye twitch. "But I digress. Please carry on."

"I should fire you," Eve growled, her lips thinning.

"Pfft. I'd like to see you try. Now stop dilly-dallying and get to the good part."

"What good part? Nothing about Friday night was good."

"We can agree to disagree. Please, keep going."

I really should fire her...

Eve grunted. "I'm only finishing this story, so I can get it out of my system and move the hell on forever." She narrowed her eyes at Mikayla. "I know Austin can handle getting cut on his own, but my dumb ass must-always-fix-everything brain jumped into action and the next thing I remember is being on my knees in front of him holding a paper towel to his bleeding ankle and him pretty much pushing me away saying he had to go to the ER."

Mikayla stared at her, her eyes wide and her jaw open. "Wait, wait, wait a second. Back up. You were on your knees in front of him in your test piece, *taking care of him*, and then he left? This all happened when you were still in the lingerie?"

"Don't say taking care of him like that."

"I thought before your cat decided Austin was her next meal, you'd already changed?"

Eve glanced away. "Uhh, yeah, about that. No. That was right after I sat on the couch, all confident and shit like that."

It seemed like the entire shop froze as the room fell into an eerie silence.

Uhhh, maybe I should have forgone this part of the story...

"Let me see what you made." Abruptly, Mikayla walked past Eve and headed toward the backroom, leaving Eve's only option to follow her.

"I don't see what that has anything to do with the disaster of the night that will haunt me until I die."

Mikayla grabbed Eve's work bag and shoved it in Eve's hands. "Just show me."

"Austin said those same words."

"I'm sure he did."

Eve rolled her eyes. *Might as well get this over with.* She pulled the bodysuit and robe she'd made from her bag and handed them to Mikayla. As soon as she did, Eve plopped into her chair. "Ugh."

Ignoring her distress, Mikayla held up the bodysuit first,

her eyes wide before quickly putting it down and going to the robe to do the same.

"Why are you looking at them like that?" A weird feeling seeped into Eve's stomach. She didn't know whether it was bad or good, but she leaned toward bad.

Mikayla darted her eyes to Eve. "Was your goal to give Austin a heart attack? Because holy freakin' moly. I'll take five."

At Mikayla's reaction, Eve had to laugh. "Shut up."

"No, like for real. Holy shit. Let me see what else you made."

Eve flicked her eyes to the ceiling before reaching into her bag and giving Mikayla the two-piece design.

As Eve watched Mikayla inspect the pieces, her eyes focused on the *cape*. Why in the hell had she thought that would be a good idea?

Stupid cape. Who would want to wear a cape? It didn't even go around her neck. Just her boobs. *Universe, any day now. Just go ahead and put me out of my misery... No wonder Austin ran out of there like he did. A cape... freakin' really?*

"Holy shit balls."

That got Eve's attention, pulling her out of her annoyed thoughts. "What?"

Mikayla's eyes were larger than Eve had ever seen. "I think you knew exactly what you were doing when you modeled these for Austin."

"Why do you keep saying that?" Eve jumped from her seat and snatched the pieces from Mikayla's hand. "I wasn't doing anything but trying to get the opinion of an extremely intelligent business owner who also happens to be a guy."

"Okkayyy," Mikayla replied. "Are you sure you weren't trying to give him a hard-on? I think I have a girl boner and I haven't seen you wear it yet."

"You've been hanging around Mildred too long if you're using terms like girl boner."

Mikayla shrugged unapologetically with a laugh. "What can I say? I like her."

"Don't get any ideas from Mildred. She's bound to end up getting you arrested."

"The story she tells about the time she got arrested on a girls-only vacation before she met her husband... I think I'd be okay with that."

"Mikayla."

"What?"

Eve laughed, glad some of the weird feelings had finally left the room. "You both are a piece of work."

"And so are you, if you don't think the reason Austin ran out of there was 'cause he had a little problem he had to take care of..." She smirked. "Well, maybe not so little."

And just like that, the feeling was back.

"Eww. No. Austin ran out of my apartment 'cause I made a fool out of myself and my cat bit his ankle so hard it bled. We talked about this when he picked up the order yesterday."

Eve shuddered, thinking about how awkward it'd been. Thankfully, it all settled pretty quickly. You know, just shove all the things into the box labeled never to be opened.

"You keep telling yourself that."

"I will 'cause it's true."

"Okkaayy."

"Mikayla, stop saying okay like that. I'm serious. Trust me when I say this, Austin doesn't think of me that way and never will. Sure, he's a dude and I'm a dudette, but that's as far as it goes. I'll only ever just be his best friend."

"Dudette?" Mikayla cocked her brow.

"Yeah, opposite of a dude. Duhh."

"I know what it is." She laughed, flicking her eyes up.

"Okay, new subject, kinda. Were you happy with what Austin thought? Are you going to add these to the shop?"

Eve sat back in her chair, her face wrinkling. "He seemed to like them and even though I had a few shots in me, I liked the way I felt in them. They might sell well."

Although, the cape might have to go...

"They will sell. I'm for sure of that. I want the bodysuit in every color you can make it." Mikayla strutted over to the computer. "Actually, that's exactly what I'm going to do right now."

· "What's that?"

Mikayla turned to Eve like she was the one who'd lost her mind. "I'm gonna order every color they have in the material."

Eve barked out a laugh. "Let me make other prototypes before we go crazy. Simmer down there, missy."

"I'm not going crazy. I know the second Holly sees them, she's gonna want to buy more. I'm getting us prepared."

Eve laughed again. Ehh, at least someone was eager.

Mikayla ignored Eve, turning back to the computer to order other colors.

As Eve rolled her eyes, ready to go back to her sketchbook and forget all of this happened, she heard her phone ping.

There was a part of her that wondered if it was another match, since Friday night she'd sworn off the dating apps for a while.

A match might be a good distraction.

But Lord help her if it was another dick picture.

With how things had turned out Friday, Eve was going to go back to deleting and blocking them and never telling Austin about them again.

When she pressed the screen of her phone, she saw it was a text from Austin, causing her stomach to flutter for the briefest of seconds before she clamped that shit down.

Abso-fucking-lutely not.

Not today, Satan.

Ignoring her idiotic body, Eve opened Austin's text. "Oh, fuck me!"

Mikayla snapped her head around to Eve, the concern on her face. "What's wrong?"

"You have gotta be freakin' kidding me." As if the past weekend wasn't bad enough. *Son of a bitch.*

"What in the world are you talking about?" Mikayla's brow raised.

It's not even like I can say no... fuck me.

Eve groaned loudly as she painfully looked at Mikayla. "Guess who's going on an overnight hike this weekend?"

The room was silent only for a few seconds before Mikayla burst into a fit of hearty laughter. "Payback's a bitch."

"There is no payback needed."

"Mmmhhhmm." Mikayla nodded.

"Do you think I could break an ankle before the weekend, maybe get sick or something?" Eve pleaded, searching around the room to see if anything could help her avoid the inevitable.

Mikayla laughed even harder, throwing her head back. "No can do, boss lady. You, my friend, are going on an overnight hike, whether you want to or not."

Eve glared at her. "Aren't you supposed to be on my side?"

"You don't see it yet, but I am." With that, Mikayla jumped from her seat and bounced out of the room, as happy as could be, leaving a gawking Eve in her wake.

Fuck me. This is going to suck.

Chapter Twelve

"THIS IS IT. I'm gonna die. Right here. Boom. Death," Eve huffed as she leaned against a tree, her whole body feeling like it was moments from saying fuck this shit, I'm out. "No more Eve. Poof, I'm gone. Just like that. Who's gonna take care of Marshie?"

When Eve finally moved her eyes to Austin, he was staring down at her, his brow cocked like it wasn't a thing in the world, all while she was about to pop a lung.

"You aren't going to die, Eve."

"I am," she panted. "It's hot and gross and my body is tired and I'm just gonna die right here and now. And then some wolf or bear is gonna come eat me."

"That's not how—"

"Oh my God, what if it's some rabid animal? Like, I don't know, maybe a wild rabbit? It's minding its own business just hoppin' around the forest and then wham-o it comes across my dead body and goes, *ohhh, what a fun snack. There sure is a lot of her* and then starts going to town, munching down on my corpse. And then it realizes I'm the best meal it's ever had—"

"Rabbits aren't carnivores."

Eve snapped her eyes to Austin, who stood completely still, not even remotely out of breath.

That bastard.

"The rabbit would take one look at my plump ass and go, oh, she's not what we'd normally eat but it could work. Might as well broaden our food diversity. Plus, she looks fun to eat." Eve glared daggers at Austin as she put her hand on her side, pushing in, trying to ward away the sharp pain in her ribs.

Is this how death starts? Sharp pains? Oh my God, what if it's not my lungs about to pop and instead whatever the hell organ is on my right side.

"Hmm." Austin scratched his chin, grabbing Eve's attention from her impending doom. "I'd have to agree with them there. You look fun to eat."

"Austin! I'm being serious."

As he scanned her body up and down, he licked his lips. "So am I."

If she wasn't about to die, she'd kill him. "If I had any strength, I'd punch you in the face."

"Glad you don't have any strength, then."

Eve growled deep in her throat as she flipped him the bird. "If I didn't have to hold up this tree to keep it from falling, you'd be a dead man right now."

Austin's head slightly tilted to the side as he watched her.

Jerk. The enjoyment that radiated off him was nauseating. Or it might've been the hiking either way she felt like she was about to vomit.

"Is that what you're doing there? Holding up the tree?"

"Obviously," she grumbled, glaring at him like he was an idiot. "Who else is gonna do it if I don't? The tree looked like it was struggling, so I figured I'd be a hero and help save its life. And you're just brushing past the big issues here."

Austin raised his brow, not even attempting to hide his smirk. "And what issue is that?"

"I'm gonna disrupt the whole freakin' food chain with my apparently tasty, too good to pass up body. I'm gonna die and then some non-carnivore rabbit is gonna find me and eat me and then *I'll* be the one that ends up changing the entire ecosystem and we're gonna have meat-eating rabbits who have a taste for blood." She flung the hand not holding her side together in the air. "Who knows what'll happen next? What if one of those rabbits is the key to starting the zombie apocalypse?"

"But according to the logic you're using, you'll be dead. So why do you care what happens after you kick the bucket, which is apparently gonna happen any second." Austin glanced at his watch and then back to her, his eyes even brighter than before.

Oh, yeah, she was going to kill him as soon as she knew the tree was safe from falling over. "You think this is funny?"

Austin's sly smirk turned into a full-blown toothy grin. "I think *you're* funny."

"Well, you're funny lookin'."

"Ouch." His hand shot to his chest like he'd been shot. "And here I was ready to ward off the meat-eating rabbit that's bound to come our way any second."

"It could happen!"

"I know, that's why I'm waiting."

"Austin, I swear to everything, I'm gonna murder you in your sleep tonight."

He raised his left brow, as he failed to hold back his smile. "We'd have to get to the campsite first."

"Mark my words, jerkface. If I had any idea how to get back to the car, I'd have already disposed of your body and been on my way."

Austin looked down at Eve for a split second before

throwing his head back and bursting into a deep laugh. His hand moved to his taut stomach, trying to calm himself. "Eve, my Eve." He shook his head, his smile brighter than the damn sun that was beating down on them. "Good thing you can't read a map. I think if you look hard enough in that direction, you can still see the car. You just gotta squint through the bush."

Eve snapped her eyes in the direction Austin pointed. Coming up with nothing but trees upon trees, she did as he said and squinted, trying to find anything that even remotely resembled civilization.

Still nothing.

Eve moved her focus back to Austin. "You're lying."

"Nope." Austin's smile reached his eyes, the jerk thought this whole thing was a good ol' laugh. "We haven't really gone that far, Eve."

Son of a biscuit.

Eve pushed herself off the tree. Straightened her shirt, and then, as eloquently as she could, hitched her pack a little higher onto her back. "Then I guess I was a little premature in my almost dying. I should've waited until we were farther in."

Eve's eyes glanced back in the direction Austin pointed at.

Stupid car.

Stupid hike.

Stupid Austin.

The moment she took a step, her legs wobbled in protest as a groan escaped her lips. Eve might be a bigger person, but she was pretty healthy and in shape... at least she thought she was.

But hiking, dang, hiking was a different beast altogether. It used muscles Eve didn't even know she had.

If I make it out of here alive, I need to walk more. Eve's eyes narrowed on Austin as she gave him a dirty look. *Without you, though. You'll be lucky if you make it out of here alive.*

Austin nodded, but Eve could tell he was holding in his laugh. "If you say so. Should I set a reminder on my phone for you to almost die in what..." He gave her the once-over, his eyes even brighter than before, which Eve thought was impossible. "Let's say an hour?"

"Shut. Up."

With his hand Austin made the motion to zipper his mouth shut, locked it, and threw away the key behind him.

"Oh, real mature," Eve grunted. "Just so you're aware, not everyone is built so they can withstand the elements of the outdoors. I'm pretty sure I'm a mile away from a heart attack."

He shrugged.

"Don't you shrug at me."

Austin shrugged again, his smile growing even wider than before, which Eve didn't think was possible.

Oh, for the love of all freaking things.

This weekend was going to be the death of her, either by some zombie starting rabbit or her best friend. "What are you, eight? Ya jerk. Unzip your mouth or I'm going back to the car."

Austin's whole face lit, as his megawatt smile got even *bigger* while his chest bounced with a chuckle. "You'd have to find it first."

"I hate you."

"You love me. Let's get a move on. We have at least another five miles to the campsite I reserved."

Eve's jaw hit the ground. "Five miles? Five as in, one, two, three, four, and *then* five? Is that the five we are talking about? Because if it is, I don't think so."

Austin laughed harder. "It won't be that bad. Most of it is a straight shot, with only some uphill at the end."

"*Uphill?* Hold on there, mister. What in the hell have we been doing this whole time? We've been doing nothing but uphill."

"This has only been a slight incline, definitely not uphill, babe."

"I'm pretty sure your definition of uphill and mine are vastly different."

Damn. Who knew you needed to update your freaking will before you went out on a hike?

"I promise the view is worth it."

"Doubt it."

"Trust me." Austin turned on his heel and took off walking in the opposite direction than the car, leaving Eve with no other choice but to follow him.

"If I really wanted to see a nice view off the side of a mountain, I'd look it up online."

"It's not the same."

"Says you."

"I do." Austin glanced back at her and winked. "Come on before that rabbit finds you."

Eve's lips formed into a thin line as her eyes narrowed on the back of Austin's head.

I could just pick up a tiny rock and boom, toss it right in the middle of his head. He'd think a bird dropped a stone or something. I'd play the innocent bystander as he —

"Whatever you're thinking about, stop," he warned, without looking back at her.

"How do you know I'm thinking anything?"

Austin spun, the corner of his mouth turned upward. "Stick, rock, a nicely packed pile of dirt. What's your poison?"

Eve gasped, her hand shooting to her chest in shock. "I would *never.*"

Austin cocked his head to the side as he watched her. After a split second, he crossed his arms over his chest. "Eve…"

"Fine. A freaking rock," she blurted. "Why do you always know when I wanna maim you?"

"Call it best friend intuition." Austin shrugged, his smile

back on his face. "You done plotting my death, so we can get back on track? We're already running behind."

"Behind for what? You got a hair appointment on the side of a mountain?"

Austin shook his head, chuckling. "If I knew you'd be this entertaining, I would have forced you out here with me years ago."

"Over my dead body."

Austin scanned his surroundings, his enjoyment of the situation evident. "Are the rabbits coming?"

"You really do have a death wish, don't you?"

"We'll have to see now, won't we?" With that, Austin turned back toward the trail, leaving Eve no other choice but to follow him once again or be stranded. Even though he'd said they hadn't traveled far from the car, there was no way in hell she'd get back in one piece.

Might as well call me patient zero 'cause with the rate we're going, I'm bound to be the one that starts the zombie apocalypse from some dang rabbit after I die on this hike.

Screw her life.

The view better be worth it. If not, Eve was pushing him off the nearest cliff.

Eve glared at the back of his head as he walked in front of her, leading the way. And as she followed, Eve imagined every way you could to murder him and then murder him again.

It was only after another hour or so of their hike before Eve realized her body had loosened up and was enjoying the movement. Not only that, but she also found herself appreciating the scenery of the forest around her.

All in all, it was pretty, even though she was still sure her lungs were going to collapse sooner rather than later.

It was kind of nice.

Almost peaceful.

The conversations they shared were light, mainly because

she couldn't breathe, but Austin didn't seem to push her. Instead, he'd glance back every few minutes to make sure she was okay. He'd offer her an energy bar and kept reminding her to drink her water.

It was sweet in the, *let's hope I don't kill her because I brought her outside* kind of way.

And as Eve observed Austin, she could tell he was in his element. There was a new aura around him and even she would admit it was alluring.

You could feel how much Austin loved this.

He loved every single second of it.

And Eve got it.

Even though she was seconds from dying with every step she took, she got the beauty of being out in nature. Being with the elements and all that shit.

At least that's what she thought...

There was one problem, though. And with each minute that passed, her problem only got worse and worse.

"Wanna take a break?" Austin asked as he walked into somewhat of a clearing right off the trail. Quickly, he unhooked his pack and tossed it on the ground, turning to her. As Eve watched him, she couldn't deny how much he loved this. It was written all over his face.

She'd seen Austin many ways before, but this... this was different. This was a side of him he'd never shared with her. Not that he didn't try. Lord knows he'd asked her a million times to go out hiking with him.

There was just something about him right now as he watched her. Eve couldn't quite put her finger on it, but she liked it.

She liked the look on him.

No wonder all those dang magazines wanted to feature him. Now, if I could only find someone to look at me the way Austin looked when he was out here, I'd be set for life.

"Yeah, uh, sure."

Austin cocked his head, his brows knitting together. "You good? Not too much for you?"

Too much... Eve reached the 'too much' stage an hour ago. "I haven't seen any zombie rabbits yet, so I guess that's a plus."

Austin laughed as he pulled trail mix out of his bag, before grabbing a handful and tossing them into his mouth.

However, as they stood in the clearing, Eve realized not moving her body made her *problem* about ten times worse.

In a complete panic, Eve glanced around her, coming up empty. *Oh, no.*

"What's wrong?" The concern on Austin's face was almost too much to handle. Why did he always have to be so freaking caring when he was partially to blame for her newfound impending doom?

"Nothing," Eve bit out, squeezing her legs together with as much strength as she could muster.

Fuck me. I should've been doing a better job at practicing my Kegels.

Son of a crap on a freakin' million crackers.

Austin immediately dropped his food, and he marched over to her, concern written all over his face. "Something's wrong. Did you hurt yourself? Sprain an ankle? Why didn't you tell me?" he growled, scanning her body up and down, looking for any sign of an injury.

"I didn't hurt myself!"

"Then what's wrong if you aren't hurt? You look like you're in pain. Do I need to grab the first aid kit?"

Well, this was embarrassing. Seeing as though she had no other option than to tell him, she blurted, "Igottapee."

"Huh?" Austin's face scrunched. "What did you say?"

"Igottapee," the words flooded out of her in pure desperation.

"Eve, I have no idea what the hell you're saying. Slower, please."

"I gotta pee," she hissed, crossing her legs. "There are you happy? I'm about five seconds from peeing my pants. I know we tested a lot when I made them, but pee, I'm pretty sure, wasn't one of them."

Austin had the gall to look at her like she'd lost her mind. "Then go pee."

Eve blinked at him for a few seconds before she flung her hands through the air, frazzled. "I don't see a bathroom around here, do you?"

Austin's stupid smile was back on his face and if Eve wasn't so preoccupied with her dilemma, she would have punched it off, or at least tried to.

Bastard.

"Technically, the whole place is a bathroom, but it's rude to do it so close to the trail." Austin jerked his head, motioning behind her. "Go find a tree and pee."

"You're kidding me?" Eve's eyes rounded as she stared at him.

"Do you have to pee or not?"

"Yes, I have to pee. I've had to pee for like a freakin' hour. I was hoping we'd find a bathroom."

Austin's left brow shot up. "In the forest?"

Why did he have to look so surprised?

"I don't know. Maybe some nice people added one along the way for when you have to go pee."

"We're in the wild, Eve. This isn't a hotel."

Her eyes narrowed dangerously on him as her fists clenched. "I'm well aware, ya jerk."

"Just go behind a tree, pop a squat, and pee. It's not rocket science, Eve." He pointed toward a few trees not far from them. "Oh, and don't forget to bury your toilet paper when you're done."

"Do what now?!" Oh God, where was the zombie rabbit when you needed it? "We're gonna put aside the burying part and focus on the crucial fact you're skipping past. *Austin,* I can't just pop a squat and pee. I can barely walk. Do you really think I'm gonna be able to hold myself up?"

This was just getting better and better.

"Do you want me to hold you?" Austin winked, which caused Eve to hyperventilate.

"Over my dead body."

"We might find the rabbits then."

"Great. I'm not gonna die from heatstroke. I'm gonna get a bladder infection and die," she huffed, her body fighting against her. "Freakin' wonderful."

"Just go pee, Eve. It's not a big deal."

"To you. You have a dangly appendage that you can aim. I, on the other hand, am gonna end up peeing on myself."

As Austin shook his head, he laughed, the amusement of her torture written all over his face. The same face she was going to deck any second. "Find a tree, take your pants *off,* and lean against the tree. Problem solved. If you do it like that, you don't have to worry about holding yourself up."

"Take off my pants!" she yelled, her eyes almost popping out of her head. "That's just asking for an animal to maul me. Oh, here, let's go for the easy target. She already did half the work. Now, we don't have to ruin our claws by ripping her clothes off!"

"You have a wild imagination. Anyone ever tell you that?"

"I can see it now," Eve continued, ignoring him in her panic. "Here lies Eve Morgan. She died when she took off her pants in the forest to go pee. That's gonna go over real well on my tombstone."

"Do you want me to make sure they add in the bit about the rabbits?"

Eve gawked at him, her jaw on the ground.

That's it.

He was a dead man. As soon as she figured out how to pee, Austin was done for.

And — *oh shit.*

The peeing part really needed to come soon, because she was seconds from it running down her leg. Eve glanced around again, praying to every god and deity out there, the Universe, and for good measure, the pretty rock she saw laying on the ground next to her that she'd spot a bathroom.

Coming up empty, Eve realized she really had no choice.

This was it.

This was her moment.

I will never forget this.

Aggressively tossing her pack off her back, Eve snatched the toilet paper from Austin's outreached hand and stomped away. "If I get lost, I'm blaming you."

"You're not gonna get lost. Just go to one of those trees and pee. That way I know where you are." He pointed at the same cluster of trees he'd been gesturing to the whole time.

"So you can hear me? I think the fuck not."

"You sure are feisty when you've got to tinkle."

"As soon as my bladder is empty, I'm gonna take you."

"Sounds like fun. Don't threaten me with a good time and not follow through. Now, go."

With one last *I will kill you* glare directed at him, Eve grumbled as she stomped off to the tree he'd pointed to. She didn't know whether this was humiliating or worse. But she didn't want to think of the *or worse* part.

Once Eve got to the tree, she glanced around. Thankfully, she didn't see any animals or hear any rustling in the bushes nearby. Maybe for once the Universe would really be on her side.

But, oh man, her bladder was about to burst —

Eve eyed the tree to her right and swallowed. "Okay, it's

you and me, buddy, we're about to get real intimate." She looked down at her pants, cursing herself. "Maybe I should have designed these with a trapdoor at the crotch?"

Before she could contemplate her poor design choice a second further, her bladder gave the red alert.

Oh no.

It was time.

It was happening.

Quickly, Eve kicked off her sneaker and tore off her pants, letting them dangle from one leg as she leaned against the tree which held her weight.

"Oh, thank you, Universe. That's better than sex."

"No, it's not!"

"Go away!" Eve screamed from the top of her lungs. "Stop listening to me!"

"I had to make sure you didn't kill yourself."

As she heard Austin's voice, she realized he was close, but not too close. However, it was still a crap-ton closer than she would have liked.

Actually, Eve didn't like any of this.

As fast as she could, she finished her business, did what Austin said with the toilet paper, and walked from around the tree to glare at her best friend. "Did you really have to be involved?"

Austin tossed some trail mix into his mouth, eyeing her. "I was looking out for you."

"Yeah, yeah. I'm never going to forget this."

"Me either." Austin smirked. "And it wasn't so bad. You ready to keep going? We're not far from the campsite. And if we get there early enough, you'll be able to see the view while I build a campfire."

Eve grumbled while using some choice words under her breath as she grabbed the hand sanitizer from her bag. "The view better be amazing. While I'm at it, if you're making a campfire, you better freakin' have brought the stuff to make s'mores with you. If not, I want a refund on our friendship. There's a reason why I named my cat Marshmallow."

Austin laughed. "Have no fear, my brave wilderness girl. I have the food covered."

Eve studied him, his mischievous smile making her nervous. "Why does that worry me?"

Austin shrugged before hoisting his pack onto his back. "Have I ever steered you wrong?"

"Peeing on a tree is questionable. I never thought I'd live to see what it felt like to be a dog."

That stupid smirk was back on Austin's face, as he whistled like he was calling his canine best friend. "Come on, girl. That's a good girl. Grab your bag and let's head out. We've got ground to cover."

I'll show you ground to cover...

Chapter Thirteen

WHEN THEY ARRIVED at the campsite, Austin watched as Eve flung her bag off her back and immediately walked over to the lookout.

"Holy crap on a freaking cracker," Eve's voice was only slightly above a whisper as she stared out into the distance, admiring the view. "I kinda get why people do this now."

"Only kinda?" Austin chuckled, dropping his pack on the ground before walking over to Eve. His right arm slinked around her hip, pulling her into his side.

"It's a lot of work, but I'll admit this is pretty breathtaking."

You're breathtaking.

Austin bit his tongue to stop himself from saying the words. As Eve admired their view, he couldn't help but admire her.

Maybe it was the fresh air, maybe it was their hike, but there was something almost magical about the moment. Eve was way beyond beautiful and seeing her among one of the places he loved the most made his heart pound against his chest.

Austin pulled her tighter to his side as he closed his eyes, taking a deep breath of the fresh air. If there was a way he could, he'd sell his soul to never let the moment end. And as the sun began to set, he felt a sense of peace he didn't know he'd been longing for his whole life.

These were the moments artists strived to convey with their paintings or drawings. The writers of the world tried to replicate with their words.

These were the moments that could change the world.

As his chest tightened, Austin shifted, doing his best to get control of his emotions. There was something about this that was more than he knew.

Austin kissed the top of Eve's head, pulling her in for another hug before moving back to his bag.

It was moments like this that could change your life forever. And even though there was a part of him that desperately wanted that, he wouldn't risk it.

Instead, he'd blame the fresh mountain air.

Yeah, let's go with that. Fresh mountain air.

He'd gotten pretty good at lying to himself lately.

Austin shook his head as he knelt and unzipped his pack. The hike in had been quite entertaining and even though there were parts of it he knew Eve hated, he also saw the joy in her eyes when they'd come across a patch of wildflowers or a funny-looking mushroom they'd stumbled upon along the journey.

In a weird way, it was like experiencing hiking for the first time all over again. And being able to watch Eve explore nature made his stomach do this weird flutter thing.

It felt right.

It felt like home.

It felt like the one piece of him that had been missing was finally fulfilled as he watched Eve in wonderment as she took in their surroundings.

This really is what I've been missing. Eve— Ahh, nope wait. Back up. Let's shove that back into the box.

Austin cursed himself, pissed his mind was once again going down that path. And here he thought getting away from her apartment would help calm those feelings? Austin should've known better.

When it came to Eve, he always should've known better.

This was supposed to be just him and his best friend out in nature, enjoying something he loved to do with one of the people he loved the most.

Platonic love, he reminded himself.

Just him, Eve, trees, fresh air, and a view that would marvel any of the wonders of the world if Austin had any say in it.

Although, as his eyes migrated back to Eve, maybe *she* was what made the view spectacular. Better than anyone would ever imagine.

Maybe she —

Eve pivoted toward him, her smile spreading across her entire face with her eyes twinkling. "It really is beautiful."

"Told you." Austin's warm smile matched Eve's. "A beautiful view, for a beautiful woman. See, the outdoors aren't that bad."

"Ehh, let's not go that far. I'm pretty sure I popped a lung sometime today. I'm surprised I'm still upright." Her eyes sparkled with amusement as she walked toward him. She thumped her chest a few times with her hand to prove her point. However, in her trek over to him, she abruptly stopped and pointed at the ground. "Oh my freaking God. That mushroom looks like a dick."

Austin barked out into a deep laugh as he stood and walked to her. "Eve..."

With her eyes wide she darted her attention to him. "Holy crap, Austin, what if it's some land gnome and it's just sticking its dick out like that, hoping to impregnate some passerby!"

The hell? Austin's whole face contorted as he stared at her. "Your imagination really is wild."

"Being outside is wild." She glanced at the mushroom, crouching down in front of it. "Like its top is a mushroom head—" Eve snapped her attention to Austin. "Wait! Is *that* why they call the top of peens mushroom heads?"

Austin freaking loved this woman and the way her brain worked. "Nothing gets past you now, does it?"

Eve brushed her fingers over the top, and it took everything inside of Austin to hold back his moan.

It's just a freakin' mushroom. Control yourself, dumbass.

Eve examined her fingertips as she rubbed them together. "Now my finger is gonna get pregnant."

"Doesn't work like that."

"How would you know? This could be some weird gnome peen and the normal rules don't apply."

Austin chuckled with a quick roll of his eyes. "I'm not one hundred percent sure, but I think that's a *Gymnopilus ventricosus.* It looks very phallic doesn't it?"

"You're telling me. I'm pretty sure I could just grab it around its girth and—"

As Eve pulled on the mushroom, he lost it. "Don't disrupt the wildlife," he growled. "Leave no trace."

"I think I'm pregnant."

Fuck him, like seriously fuck him. Austin's brain betrayed him yet again as the image of Eve rounded with *his* baby popped into his mind.

In an instant, all the oxygen was sucked out of his lungs as he realized what it meant.

No, no, no. Not yet. No, not the word 'yet'. Fuck! It's the fresh air. That's it. He swallowed, knowing damn well this wasn't the fresh air.

Blowing out a strained breath, Austin moved over to his

bag. "We've got work to do." Austin's heart pounded in his chest as he willed himself to keep some sort of composure.

"What do you mean, work?" Eve stood, following behind him. "I can't work. I'm pregnant."

Austin stumbled over a rock at Eve's words, refusing to look back at her.

Fuck me.

Eve must have been still preoccupied with the mushroom since she didn't rag on him and continued on with her protest. "We worked when we hiked our butts up here. Now, we don't do anything."

Once he reached his bag, Austin had calmed himself enough to look toward her. "Getting here is only part of it. We still have to set up camp."

"Are you telling me I hiked my ass all the way here and now you expect me to make camp too? Are you kidding me, why isn't the camp already set up? You said you reserved this place. So there should be like a cabin or stuff already done. There should be *no* setting up once we get here. That's stupid."

The annoyed growl that came from Eve made Austin's brow arch while he stared at her. "It's nature, not a five-star hotel. We gotta put up the tent and start a fire to cook dinner. "

Eve flung her hand to her hip, her brows pulling together. "You're telling me some butler isn't gonna just appear out of the woods and feed me? What in the hell did you *reserve* then?"

"The campsite, babe." As she glared at him harder, he realized how adorable she was.

"You mean this lot of dirt?" Eve stared at him like he'd lost his mind.

"My smart, beautiful, Eve. You still have so much to learn." Austin's lip quirked up as he shook his head.

"Yeah, like how to hide a body," she mumbled. "I swear one second I don't mind the whole outdoor thing and then boom, you bring me back to reality and I want to jump off this overlook."

Austin rolled his eyes as he pulled out the tent. "It's a give and take thing."

"Yeah, yeah, well it sure seems like a lot of take right now. I'm exhausted. If the ground wasn't full of bugs, I'd lay down on it and take a nap, or die. Whatever works. I'd be open to both."

Eve really was a piece of work, but man, did he love it.

Chuckling, Austin pointed to a dense part of their surrounding area. "Go look for wood, so we can start a fire. I'll work on getting our shelter set up."

"Do I look like a search and find person?"

"Sticks and branches." He cocked his brow. Oh, for the love of all things. He knew it wasn't going to be easy, but damn. "That's all you have to look for, Eve. And the faster you retrieve some, the sooner we can eat."

Eve grumbled, cursing under her breath as she stomped off toward the bush. "There better be a fucking s'more in my future or I'm tossing you off the cliff, jackass."

Austin laughed, flicking his eyes to the sky. Truth be told, though, he was thankful he had a little breathing room to get his mind back in order. Quickly, he got to work on their shelter. He'd learned by now, the first thing you did was set up your tent. The sky might look beautiful and the forecast could say a zero chance of rain, but Mother Nature more often than not liked to add a little spice to things.

Although, Austin was hoping against the rain since he was positive that actually would send Eve off the cliff.

It only took Austin a few minutes to get the tent set up and ready. And by the time he heard Eve make her way back to camp, he was in the process of getting everything prepared for the fire.

When he looked toward her, Eve's arms were full to the brim of branches and sticks.

Damn, she did good. Austin was actually pretty impressed.

"That's the tent?" Eve squeaked, gawking at the shelter. "You're kidding me." She let the wood she'd gathered fall from her arms as she went to inspect where they'd be sleeping.

"Yup."

"How is *that* a two-person tent?" Eve's eyes darted to his. "It doesn't even look like a one-person tent."

"It's a two-person tent."

"Who are these two people you speak of? Are they stick figures? Is that what these manufacturers go off, stick figure people? There is no way in hell that tent will fit you, let alone *me* and you." Eve pointed between the two of them.

"It's bigger than it looks on the inside."

"That's what they all say," the words rushed out of her, making Austin laugh.

"It's a two-person tent, Eve. I promise. They're made for backpacking. Lightweight and compact."

"I'm legit the opposite of lightweight and compact."

Austin's deep laugh echoed throughout the area, as he walked over to the tent and unzipped it, showing Eve the inside. "It'll be fine. See, not so bad."

"Close the door! Close the door!" Eve jumped around on her feet, flinging her arms through the air. "You're gonna let all the bugs and gnomes in. Oh my God, did you check for gnome dicks before you put up the tent?"

"For fuck's sake, Eve Morgan, you're not gonna get pregnant by a gnome." Austin shook his head, amazed at his best friend. Holy freakin' crap. "Your brain is scary, but I promise you. You're safe from all the rogue gnome dicks."

"Don't you take that tone of voice with me, mister. It's not my fault you reserved a campsite with horny woodland gnomes running around trying to repopulate their species."

Austin blinked at her. Honestly, that's all he could do. "I don't know what to say to that, so I'm gonna ignore it. How about we get the fire started so we can eat?"

Eve enthusiastically nodded, her childlike smile appearing showing her teeth. "Oh, food sounds good. I like food. I'm starving." She thumped her stomach a few times with her hand. "Yummy, yummy, get in my tummy. Unless it's gnome dick. I don't think I'd be satisfied."

Oh, for fuck's sake. Piece of freaking work.

Eve was an absolute piece of work, but she was his piece of work.

Universe, help me.

For the next ten minutes, Austin taught Eve everything she needed to know about making a fire. And to his utter surprise, she was into it.

Austin didn't know if that was a good or bad thing. Eve and fire didn't seem like the brightest idea, but since she was into it, he'd go with good.

While Eve was on the ground preparing more sticks than they needed to keep the fire going, he damn sure wasn't going to stop her.

Plus, she was mighty cute sitting there her tongue sticking out of the corner of her mouth as she focused on bringing the blade of the knife he'd given her, carefully along the edge of her stick, feathering the bottom of it so it would catch fire more easily.

Who knew she'd end up enjoying this part? Although, as Austin thought about it, her enjoyment might have something to do with wielding a knife. But he was just going to ignore that fact. "You're a pro."

Eve tapped her temple with the stick. "Fast learner I is."

"That you are." Austin pulled out the dehydrated packs of food from his bag, watching Eve's eyes widen.

"Nope." She shook her head. "Heck no. Heck to the freakin' no. I am not some astronaut. I am a living, breathing human being here on earth. Why are you attempting to feed me space food?"

Austin chuckled, thanking everything Jake had tossed a few extra meals into their cart. Her reaction was exactly what he hoped for. "It's not that bad." He pulled out another one, watching Eve's brows nearly shoot off her forehead.

"I no longer trust you."

"Ouch, honey." Austin's hand went to his heart. "That hurts."

"Good."

Reaching over to his pack, Austin rifled through it before he pulled out a bag filled with vegetables. "You should always trust me. I have other food for us as well, the *astronaut* food is just the appetizer."

"Thank God. I thought for a second you didn't remember who I was."

Austin looked at her, his eyes warm and full of emotion. "Babe, I'd never forget who you are." He felt the tension rise as he stared at the best friend he'd ever had. And when he saw a flash of something in Eve's eyes, his stomach tightened.

Instantly the air thickened between them, and he knew she felt it too. When Eve's eyes darted to his mouth, his stomach did that weird flip again.

Wait, could this —

However, before Austin could explore his thoughts further, Eve jerked her head away, picking up one of the dehydrated meals. "Who eats this garbage as an appetizer? Or at all?"

"We do," he answered, the moment gone. Austin cracked

his neck from side to side, trying to relieve the tension, but nothing worked.

Get it to-freaking-gether man. This is just a fun, quick outdoor adventure with your best friend. Nothing more. You're getting to spend the weekend with her, and she's not half-naked asking your opinion on her designs.

However, the second Austin went there, he couldn't go back. He swallowed around the lump in his throat as the images of Eve clouded his mind.

And he'd been doing so good, too.

Austin had been so focused on Eve enjoying their hike, or well, at least not dying, he hadn't thought of her in the outfits that he was pretty sure had given him an ulcer.

Austin cleared his throat, willing his body to chill the fuck out. "I brought other stuff for us to cook up, but you needed to experience the outdoors in all its glory."

"Oh, I'm experiencing it all right. I peed on a tree."

"And you did a good job."

Eve glared at him, her lips pursing together. "You really do have a death wish, don't you?"

"I'm making stew tonight," he continued before she had a chance to hit him with the stick still in her hand. "While it cooks, we'll eat these. We're burning a lot of calories out here."

"If I burnt so many calories, I should be three sizes smaller by now."

"I don't think it works that way."

"Well, damn. First, you failed to tell me the amount of gnome peen we'd encounter and now you're telling me I didn't drop five sizes after one hike? I think I'm going back to this whole thing sucks. There is no good reason why we should be out here."

Austin dropped the bag of food before grabbing Eve's chin with his hand. He then gently turned her head to the overlook. "That's why."

"Stop being reasonable. It's annoying."

Instead of retorting her smart-ass comment with one of his own, Austin watched as the light of the fire danced on Eve's face.

The feelings he'd pushed down earlier raced through him. Maybe those feelings he'd squashed down all those years ago had been right? Eve really was the best friend he'd ever had. They'd completed each other in ways he didn't know was possible.

Where he was tough, Eve was kind.

Where he was hard, she was soft.

Where he was rough around the edges, she was warm and inviting.

Eve was his other half.

Eve made him whole.

Sure, Austin's brain kick-started after seeing Eve in her lingerie, but it was more than that.

It was more than sex.

It'd always been more than sex when it came to Eve.

And the truth was, Austin hated she was on the dating apps. He hated the mere thought she'd be wearing those pieces for anyone other than him.

It was about time he stopped fighting that.

Austin closed his eyes as a wave of adrenaline rushed through him, making his hands shake. When he opened his eyes to see Eve still happily looking out to the bright orange sky with hints of pink, he realized for the first time what his mind and body had been trying to tell him and probably for years now that he thought about it.

When was the last time he went on a date?

He couldn't even remember.

He got laid?

Oh God, even longer.

Austin would rather have been with Eve than anywhere else.

He'd rush through his week to get to her. That's all Austin ever wanted.

It was Eve.

It had always been Eve.

As the fire's light danced upon her skin, he couldn't hold back another second. "Eve, babe, look at me."

"Yeah?" Eve's head pivoted to face him, a lazy, radiant smile on her face.

"I'm going to kiss you."

Chapter Fourteen

WHAT?

There wasn't a chance for Eve to react. Before she knew it, Austin's lips were on hers.

Eve's brain couldn't keep up as her heart slammed against her chest. This wasn't supposed to happen, no.

Never.

The pure shock of the situation caused Eve to gasp, which Austin took complete advantage of to deepen their kiss.

The same kiss that sent a wave of pleasure through her body.

Austin's kiss was hungry, almost on the brink of desperation. And before she knew it, abandoning all her better judgment, Eve was kissing him back. As their mouths melded together, she didn't have time to think about the repercussions that were sure to happen once they pulled apart.

Oh my God, I'm kissing my best friend! In the woods. In the freakin' woods on the side of a damn mountain. Holy shit, I'm playing tonsil hockey with the one person I am never *supposed to play tonsil hockey with.*

Eve's head reeled as Austin's hand tangled in her hair,

pulling her closer him. And as he kissed her with such passion and so deeply, she doubted she'd ever recover from it.

No, scratch that. Eve *knew* she'd never recover from it.

Holy crap, I'm kissing my best friend.

Slowly Austin pulled his lips back, a satisfied moan coming from him as he rested his forehead against hers.

"Fuck," he growled deep in his throat as his eyes drank her in, his mouth parted ever so slightly.

And then, before Eve could process what happened, Austin's lips were on her again. This kiss was even more desperate than the one before which Eve didn't think was possible.

Holy moly, her head spun, like really spun. Absolutely all rational thought had left her brain.

Damn, who knew Austin could kiss so well?

As their mouths fought for control, all the feelings she'd hopelessly had pushed deep inside her for years came rushing back in a wave.

Every wayward desire, every stolen, hidden glance she'd lie to herself about and say something like she hadn't taken, broke through her resolve.

As Austin pulled back once more, they both struggled to catch their breath.

Holy freaking monkey balls.

They'd kissed. And not just some quick peck. No, this was the kiss you gave someone that you were starving for.

Holy freaking moly.

Earth to brain. Please wake up.

Austin's intense hazel eyes were dark as he took her in, his lips slightly swollen. The sight made Eve's breath hitch, as his gaze held such a hunger she felt like she couldn't breathe.

"Austin..."

He didn't let her ask the unspoken question as he slammed his lips onto hers again. The air thickened around them as he tasted her with such force it stole her breath away.

Eve knew it was wrong on so many levels, but for the life of her, she couldn't stop it. Instead, she let the moment consume every part of her.

And even if only for this *one* brief instance in their lives together, she'd let go. She'd let go of all the negative thoughts.

The why this shouldn't be happening.

The why this *couldn't* happen.

She'd let go of the consequences that were sure to come. Throwing caution away, she leaned into their kiss, giving Austin everything he could take and more.

As their lips danced as one, some part of Eve's brain that had a little wherewithal, noticed her arms were wet, which was an odd reaction. Then again, this was the first time she'd kissed a *best friend,* so maybe this *was* the appropriate reaction.

Did making out with the person you weren't supposed to make out with send your body into some weird hypersensitive state and it forgot how to function and now your body was randomly leaking water from different places?

For all Eve knew, they'd been transported to some alternate universe. An alternate universe where kissing your best friend was considered the appropriate thing to do.

Eve would say that could never happen, but then again, having Austin's tongue down her throat was right up there on top of the 'could never happen' list too.

"Fuck!" Austin jerked away from her panting. But as Eve studied him, his eyes held something she didn't quite understand. "We have to get inside. Right now."

"What? Wait, what?" Eve blinked a few times on the sheer verge of hyperventilating. If Eve thought her head spun before, she'd been mistaken. Because any second now, her head was liable to pop off.

Kaboom. No more Eve.

Austin snapped his head to the sky, cursed, and then looked back to her, his eyes a mix of panic and lust.

What in the freakin' hell?

Even if Eve tried, there was no way she'd get her brain to function in any way, shape, or form.

Austin grabbed her arm and yanked her to her feet. He darted his eyes to the sky and then once again to her. "Damn, Eve. What in the hell do you do to me?"

"I didn't do anything —"

Austin cut her off, pulling her into another searing kiss. This one just as desperate and deep as the ones before.

Could you end up kissing someone so intensely they'd end up pulling out a tonsil? Dear Lord she hoped not, because if you could, she was sure that's what was bound to happen any second.

As Austin cupped the back of her head with his hands, pulling her into his body, it happened.

It was as if out of nowhere the heavens opened up and bang.

Did they somehow miss the forecast for a potential hurricane? Because that's sure as hell what it seemed like.

Eve swore when she'd looked at the sky only a few moments ago, it'd been orange and pink, and all the pretty things. She hadn't seen a cloud at all. And yet, as Austin devoured her mouth with his, the rain poured down upon them, soaking them as the winds picked up.

A loud clap of thunder had Austin jerking his head back from her. "Shit!"

Holy shit, that was loud. Eve's eyes rounded as the sound echoed around them.

"Come on. We have to get in the tent."

"Tent? What tent?"

Ignoring her confusion, Austin pulled her along as the

sound of thunder rocketed throughout the area, even louder than the one they'd heard only seconds before.

That's when it hit her.

Like really hit her.

They were on the side of a mountain in a storm and a hell of a lot closer to the sky. Eve's heart slammed against her chest as panic raced through every inch of her body.

Did that mean they were a better target for lightning?

Oh God, oh God.

Eve's stomach twisted into a knot as another clap of thunder roared through the sky.

The now very dark, very angry sky.

Great. Freaking great.

Eve must've really pissed off the Universe somehow. She didn't have a chance to die of embarrassment from kissing her best friend. No, she was going to die by getting struck by freaking lightning on the side of a damn mountain.

Her eyes squinted as she glanced up. *Was this 'cause I called the mushrooms gnome peens? I don't know what you expect from me? That's exactly what they looked like.*

Not that Eve knew what a gnome peen looked like, but still.

Austin unzipped the tent in a hurry and pushed Eve inside before quickly following suit and zipping the tent shut, barricading them from the harsh storm.

"Sonofabitch."

Uhhh... Eve's eyes danced around their shelter. *Huh? I guess Austin was right. It did seem bigger on the inside. Not that much bigger, but bigger.*

Eve lifted her eyes to Austin, and for the first time in all of their friendship, she had no clue what to say.

As her gaze moved up and down his body, water dripped from him as she watched his chest rise and fall in fast succession. Austin was soaked and honestly, looking down at herself, she wasn't much better.

"You gotta take your clothes off," he grunted, wiping his hand over his face, removing some of the water.

"What?" Eve's eyes dilated as she gawked at him, her jaw nearly on the ground.

Wait a second! Now she got it. This was all some hallucination. Somewhere along their hike, Eve must have smacked her head onto some low-hanging branch. You know, payback for peeing on one of its family members and she was really unconscious in some hospital room.

Austin, seemingly unaware this was a hallucination, placed a hand behind his head and pulled his shirt off, exposing his scrumptious body.

The body she'd always admired.

The body he'd teased her with all the damn time.

Screw it. If this was a hallucination, she was damn well going to enjoy it.

Oh crap. Instantly, all those feelings Eve had thought she'd gotten rid of came flooding back again. And here she thought she'd locked them away.

Why did he have to look so damn good? It wasn't natural. People shouldn't be allowed to look the way he did.

Eve grunted as she wondered what it felt like to be the Universe's favorite.

Pushing aside her annoyance, Eve avidly watched as his hands moved to the belt buckle on his pants.

Oh yes! This hallucination is about to get a crap ton better. Take it off! Might as well live a little, right? Who the heck knows when I'm gonna wake up from this?

Just as Austin undid his belt and was ready to pop the button on the waist, he stopped.

No, keep going!

At that moment, the sound that came from deep inside

Austin sent shivers all the way to her core. "You can't look at me like that right now. Please, babe. I promise I'll fill every need you have, but let me get you safe first. I'm begging you. I'm hangin' on by a thread here."

What? What need? There was no need. Well, maybe a little. What she needed was the hospital staff to keep dumping in whatever they were into her IV to keep this going, that's what Eve needed.

Abandoning his pants, Austin crawled over to her. Once he was inches from Eve's face, his hands grabbed ahold of the hem of her top. "Off." He yanked the material with ease. "We need to get you out of these wet clothes. The storms on the mountains sometimes come out of nowhere. Usually the temperature drops pretty fast. I gotta get you warm, and I can't do that if your clothes are soaking wet."

"Naked?" Eve squeaked.

Austin growled, sending another shockwave through her. "Later. Right now, let me get you safe."

"I am safe."

Austin rested his forehead on hers, his eyes closing for the briefest of seconds before he opened them, pulling back, so Eve could look directly at him. "You're right. You will *always* be safe with me, Eve."

Her heart stopped as her stomach bottomed out. Eve didn't have much time to process his words, though, as his hands went to the waistband of her pants. Effortlessly, he hooked his thumbs in, pulling them down, forcing Eve to fall back as he removed the soaked material from her body.

Oh God.

Austin sat back on his ass, pulling his pants off, leaving them both there in somewhat damp undergarments, with her still trying to process everything that'd transpired in the last ten minutes. However, another loud crack of thunder echoed throughout the forest, causing her to jump.

"It's okay, Eve. It's okay."

Was it okay? She sure as fuck didn't think so as fear crept into her body.

As another crack of thunder bellowed through the sky, she focused on Austin. Her best friend, the person she shared everything with.

And in that moment, as the world sounded like it was crashing down around them, all while the same feelings dueled inside of her, she was scared.

She was scared for so many reasons.

She couldn't lose him.

Not as her best friend, or in any other way.

Another roar of thunder broke through the sky, causing Eve's hands to shake.

Oh God. They couldn't die out here in the middle of the woods. No one would ever find them.

As Eve's heart thumped against her chest, her eyes zeroed in on Austin even further. But if she had to die, at least she'd die with him by her side.

Austin must've seen her panic since he crawled over to her, cupping Eve's cheeks in his hands, causing her to focus on only him. "I promise you're safe, babe. It's a storm. They just sound scarier when you're out in the middle of them." His eyes darkened further, nearly matching the intensity of the storm outside. "Eve, you have to know I'd die before I let anything happen to you."

"Austin—"

That's when his lips crashed onto hers.

Chapter Fifteen

WHATEVER THREAD that had been holding Austin together snapped as he took complete possession of Eve's mouth.

He needed her and her kiss.

Austin needed every part of her. Why keep fighting when looking back, every single road had always led to Eve?

As the storm roared around them, he couldn't get enough of her. Eve's kiss was better than he ever could've imagined.

"Austin," the words rushed out of her in a desperate plea as her lips broke from his.

He nipped at her bottom lip as he pulled away. "I've got you. I've always got you." Austin didn't give her much time to reply as he reached under her sports bra, pulling it over her head, *finally* giving him the view he'd fantasized about for so long.

Austin's heated eyes scanned down Eve's body, taking in everything, as his heart pounded against his ribs.

Being able to see all of Eve was almost too much. His dick throbbed, threatening to break free.

She was perfect. Everything about her was perfect.

Eve's chest turned out to be everything Austin could have

wanted and more. Her breasts hung heavy in a teardrop shape and were far more than a handful. Thankfully, though, Austin was never one to back down from a challenge.

His eyes caught her nipples. The nipples that'd plagued him since her fashion show. And, damn, if they were better than he imagined.

The stiff rosy pink peaks beckoned him, and who was he to deny himself?

Austin's lips kissed the top of the rounded swells of her breast as his hands explored the curves he'd dreamed of.

"Austin, I —"

The moment he brought Eve's left nipple into his mouth, she moaned, throwing her head back, asking for more. No, it wasn't asking; it was demanding, and damn, that was hot. The sound would forever be burned into his brain, and he liked that. He fucking liked that a lot.

Not wanting to let her other breast feel left out, Austin's right hand pinched her nipple, causing another impatient moan to escape Eve's lips.

Yes, babe.

Her curves, oh, man her curves.

He wanted more.

No, he needed more.

The emotions in the tent ran high as his hand skimmed down her body, only stopping at the waist of her panties. Reluctantly, he tore his mouth from her nipple. "Baby, these have to come off. They're wet."

"Rain," Eve was quick to answer.

When Austin's eyes met hers, the need he saw almost unmanned him.

"It was the rain," she tried to defend herself.

Austin's hand skimmed between her legs, gently caressing her lower lips through her panties. He moaned deep within his throat. "Both."

The tent might have been small but, not that small. Austin had ripped them from her body within seconds, leaving Eve completely bare under him.

And fuck him, it was more than he could ever ask for.

Eve's curves, her skin, her fucking everything. He'd only nearly gotten a tiny look at her pussy, and it had almost sent him over the edge.

As another clap of thunder echoed around them, his eyes shot to her. The brief flash of panic he saw was not going to do. When she was with him, she never needed to be fearful.

Without another thought, his mouth found her right nipple, sucking the bead into his mouth, causing Eve to release one of the most beautiful moans he'd ever heard. Doing this, he knew Eve didn't have time to worry about the storm around them. And as she arched her back begging for more, Austin knew this was only the beginning.

Who knew his Eve was so responsive? If he'd known that years ago, he sure as hell wouldn't have taken this long to get them here.

She completed him in every damn way possible.

Austin tore his mouth from Eve's chest as he began peppering kisses down her stomach. However, the second he felt her stiffen, he jerked himself back. Seeing Eve's dark, lust-filled eyes glancing up at him had his dick throbbing and on the verge of losing it. But somehow, in her passion-filled gaze, there was also a mix of panic and worry.

No. Hell no. That would not do. Hell fucking no.

That wasn't going to fly. Whether it was from the storm or anything else. There was absolutely no fucking way he'd allow Eve to doubt what she did to him.

That shit needed to end right there and now.

Austin's left hand grabbed Eve's belly. He stared down at her, focusing on her eyes, his hunger prevalent in every move he made. "Mine."

Eve inhaled sharply as her eyes rounded, but after a split second, a devilish half-smile formed on her lips. "Prove it."

Eve was playing with fire, and Austin knew it. There was only one problem. Eve had absolutely no idea he liked to play with fire, too. "Oh, babe. It'll be my pleasure." The moment Eve's breath hitched at his response, Austin grabbed her legs, pulling them apart. "You think the storm outside is bad? You have no fucking idea what's about to happen in here."

"Austin—"

"You might know a lot about me, babe, but you don't know everything." He sat back on his heels, nestled nicely between Eve's open thighs. He laid his right palm between her breasts and slowly trailed his hand downward, caressing her curves as he kept his eyes trained on her. "I've dreamed of this—"

"You've dreamed of me?"

Austin's hand slowly drifted down her body, close to her core, as he hungrily took her in. "More than you know."

Her shocked gasp reverberated through their small space as his fingertips finally brushed against her core.

Another crack of thunder erupted around them, causing Eve to jump.

His fingers brushed lower, feeling just how wet she was for him. His whole body tightened as he stared into her eyes. "Don't worry, babe. I'm gonna distract you."

"Dear Lord, please tell me this isn't how you distract people."

Austin's middle finger parted Eve's lower lips, causing her to hiss. "Only you, babe." His eyes darkened, looking down at her. He couldn't wait another moment, even if he wanted to. Pushing himself back, he lowered himself to her core, kissing the top of her stomach as he went.

"Austin."

"Time for talking is over." His head moved to Eve's inner

thigh, biting gently, before soothing away the pain with an open-mouthed kiss. He closed his eyes, inhaling deeply, as he let his senses take all of her in.

The mix of Eve along with the aroma of the storm around them should have been illegal and if it wasn't, he was damn sure going to figure out a way to bottle it up and keep it for himself. Opening his eyes, he kissed along her thigh, finally reaching her core. Before he kissed where his mouth wanted to be the most, he looked at her and hoped his expression could convey everything this meant to him. "Beautiful."

Keeping eye contact with her, he licked along the top of her seam, causing Eve to scream out, throwing her head back in pure pleasure as her hips rocked against his lips.

Austin took that as a good sign as his tongue darted out, flicking along her nub. As she writhed beneath him, everything he'd ever wanted to do with Eve ran through his mind. And he knew no matter how long they had, he'd never be able to get through it all.

Austin needed more. He needed everything with Eve.

And it was about fucking time he got it. Wrapping his arms around her thighs, he pulled Eve's center closer to his mouth as he devoured every inch of her. Eve's pleas and moans only egged him on more as he surrendered to the feelings he'd been fighting for far too long.

Sucking her clit into his mouth, he relished in her taste. The taste of pure heaven as he worshiped her and made sure she fucking knew that's exactly what he was doing. Letting go of her thigh, Austin's hand slinked around her leg, seeking out her opening. "Fuck, how do you taste this good?" He growled against her core, humming low, making Eve buck into his face.

Yes, fuck yes. Two of Austin's fingers entered her, moving slowly at first, but as she flung her hips at his mouth, he flicked his fingers inside her center.

His whole body tightened as she took control, her hands

tangling into his hair, pushing his face between her legs. "Yesss!"

"That's it, babe. Fuck my face, Eve. Use me." And she did. She bucked against him, begging for the friction she needed. And damn if that didn't have his dick throbbing ready to explode. At this point, he didn't know how much more he'd be able to take, but he'd gladly suffer to never let this moment end.

Who in the fucking world knew Eve was a force to be reckoned with in the bedroom? Actually, as he thought about it, he should have known. This was Eve, after all.

His feisty, curvy, perfect Eve.

Passion always ran through her, from her determination to make her store a success, to her fight for everyone to feel loved and appreciated at every size. It should've been no surprise to him her passion would spill over to this.

And now that he'd seen this new side of her, he was never going back.

Austin's tongue flicked against her clit in fast succession as his fingers massaged inside her opening. Eve's legs shook around his head as she rutted against him. "More. I need more," she bit out.

She wanted more? Oh, he'd give her more.

"So close. Oh God, So—"

Austin sucked her nub into his mouth hard, before letting his teeth graze against the sensitive bud.

"Ahhhhhh," she screamed, her body thrashing around him as she came with such force, he felt her clit pulsing inside his mouth. And he fucking loved every single second of it. He rode out her wave, drinking everything she gave him.

"Holy—" She gasped, not able to get any other words out as she worked to catch her breath.

Austin propped himself onto his elbows as he watched her, licking his lips, savoring her flavor. "You were saying?"

Eve stared at him, her chest rising and falling, her eyes in a state of pure bliss. "Austin, I—"

He winked her way. "Where have you been all my life?"

The air hung heavy around them. "Right here," she answered after a beat, causing Austin's heart to slam against his chest.

She was right. Fuck, he'd been a fool. He'd been the biggest fool to ever exist. Watching Eve beneath him, her body open and ready for more, he wouldn't think of the before. All he had was right now.

And right now, with the look on Eve's face, they were far from over.

As Eve worked to gather her breathing, her eyes moved down his body, stopping at his tented boxer briefs. The moment she licked her lips, he snapped.

The fire in her eyes...

Dear Lord, any man would have lost it. His body constricted around him as his lower half ached with need. Quickly, Austin sprung to his knees, his hands going to his waist, pushing the wet material down releasing his dick.

As it bounced, Eve's eyes dilated, her mouth opening in awe. "Oh my freakin' God. Is that what you've been hiding away all this time? Holy freaking moly. No wonder you were picking apart the guys from the dating app. If they only knew."

Austin's laugh filled the tent as his hand went to his cock, stroking from bottom to top, once, twice, and then a third time. His index finger stopped at the top, pushing the pre-come around, the taste of Eve still on his tongue.

Austin hissed, the sensations shooting through him as his body filled with even more need.

Eve watched him with heavily hooded eyes, focusing on his dick. "Mushroom head. Got it."

"Oh, babe." He smirked, a small chuckle escaping him. "You will be the death of me."

"But what a way to go, right?"

He couldn't agree more. As another clap of thunder roared around him, his eyes moved to hers, ensuring she was okay.

To his surprise though, Eve was more than okay. She licked her lips again, sitting up. "Come to Momma."

Instantly, Austin jumped into action. "Not this time, my Eve," he growled. "If you so much as look at my dick, I'm gonna come. And I refuse to let the first time I come while I'm with you be in your mouth." He grabbed her outreached hand, effortlessly trapping her beneath him, all while locking her hands above her head. He brought his mouth down to hers, entangling them into another passionate kiss.

At this point, he'd never get enough of her.

Austin did a weird shimmy to get his legs out of his boxers before pushing her thighs apart, giving him the room he needed.

Damn, Eve felt good underneath him. Her softness cradled him in every way.

He loved it. He loved every fucking second of it.

Keeping their kiss deep, Austin let go of her hand and trailed his palm down her body, memorizing her curves in his mind. Once he was sure he'd committed her to memory, he reached between their bodies and positioned himself at her core.

As the tip entered Eve's center, she arched under him, forcing him further inside her. He hissed, his teeth clenching as her pussy threatened to break him.

As the storm continued around them, his heart slammed against his chest as he pushed the rest of the way inside her.

Her tightness, oh shit.

Doing everything he could to control himself, Austin

slowly pulled out, the friction sending shock waves through his every nerve ending.

With another roar of thunder, he thrust inside her, connecting them in more ways than one.

Austin's hands found her hips as he rocked inside her. As her body tightened even further around his dick, his hips sped, as he prayed to every god out there not to let this end too soon.

Not while Eve felt this perfect around him.

Austin closed his eyes, begging to keep his cool as he moved inside her, feeling every inch, and while she met him thrust for thrust... Fuck.

He opened his eyes, looking down between them. The sight of his dick thrusting in and out of her was more than he could take.

The sensation...

Oh, no. Fuck no.

He'd waited so long. There was no way he'd let this end so soon. He held onto her hips in one swift move, keeping them connected as he flipped over them, forcing Eve to straddle his waist.

Austin was ready for her protest, but instead, Eve did what she did best and shocked the absolute shit out of him.

Eve's palms went to his chest, using him for leverage as she took her pleasure into her own hands.

"Yes, yes," she moaned, her hand moving between them seeking out her core.

"Fuck no," Austin growled, slapping away her hand before it reached her clit. "Mine."

Eve fell backward, her hands going to his shins as she rocked her hips against him giving Austin what he wanted. His right hand found her center, parted her lips and found her clit swollen with need.

Feverishly, he rubbed the bud as Eve bucked against him.

Fuck, she was so beautiful above him as she rode him like an expert completely unashamed of her sexual prowess as she took what she wanted.

Fuck him, it was by far the hottest thing Austin had ever witnessed.

"I'm gonna come. Don't stop," she pleaded as she rocked back and forth against his dick. Eve's hands once again found themselves on his chest as she pushed against him, getting better leverage for traction. "Oh God, yes, please, yes. I need this."

Austin wasn't going to stop her. He'd die before he did. After all these years... Fuck, he gritted his teeth.

He needed this, too.

He needed this more than he knew.

His Eve.

Austin bent his knees, forcing Eve to fall onto his chest. He flexed his hips, thrusting inside her with more strength.

Eve's hand wrapped around the top of Austin's head, pulling him into her. He couldn't tell who was shaking more, but he didn't care.

His hands went to her hips, flipping them again so Eve was on her back. Quickly, he grabbed her leg, pushing it up as he thrust inside her, refusing to stop. His other hand moved between them, seeking out her nub.

Eve screamed out his name as she came. Her hands reached out for him, grabbing onto him like he was her lifeline.

Eve had nothing to worry about though, Austin would always be her lifeline.

This was only the beginning.

As Eve's walls clamped around him, it was too much. He couldn't hold on. Finally, after all this time, he let his body release. It started at his toes as it worked its way up, releasing everything he had deep inside her.

He'd never had a release like this before.

This one... fuck this one shook Austin to his core as his dick pulsed inside her center, milking him for everything he had and more.

And as he kept himself seated in Eve's center, he felt it.

He was home.

For the very first time in his life, he was home. And now that he'd been home, Austin knew he'd never leave it again.

As every emotion he'd ever had engulfed him, his body worked on calming itself.

Holy fucking hell. Austin gasped, trying to catch his breath.

While the storm continued to intensify around them, Austin looked down at Eve. His sweet beautiful Eve.

Fuck, she was perfect, so fucking perfect.

And now that he'd tasted heaven, he couldn't go back. Everything about her and this moment was *everything* Austin had ever wanted and more.

He just hoped Eve understood that.

And if she didn't, he wouldn't stop until she did.

Carefully, Austin pulled out of her, letting the evidence of their coupling fall from her core and fuck him if that wasn't one of the hottest things he'd ever witnessed.

Just the sight had him wanting more.

This was the moment he'd never forget, for the rest of his life. As the storm echoed around them, his eyes shifted to Eve. The lazy, satisfied smile on her face, her sleepy hooded gaze staring right back at him.

Yeah, this was only the fucking beginning.

Reaching next to him, Austin unzipped one of the sleeping bags. With heavy limbs, he quickly tucked himself inside, before gesturing to Eve. "Come."

She laughed, a lazy smile on her lips. "I just did."

Eve's breathless laugh sent something roaring through his

body as a deep growl escaped him. "And I can guarantee you'll be coming again soon enough. But right now, I gotta get you warm."

Eve cocked her brow at him, her lazy smile turning into a toothy grin. "Oh, I'm warm all right. I don't think I could be any warmer even if I were in the middle of the equator."

Austin barked out a laugh. "Eve, my Eve. Get your ass over here. The temp is dropping and we're sharing a sleeping bag."

Chapter Sixteen

WHAT IN THE world is that noise? It's loud. Like an annoying chirping.

Eve's alarm didn't sound like a bunch of wild birds out for blood.

Ouch...

And why in the hell did her body hurt? Like really hurt. Her back, her sides, her legs. Every one of Eve's muscles screamed in protest like they'd been run over and then for good measure, run over again.

As Eve worked on jumpstarting her brain, things started snapping into place. She remembered she'd gone on a hike. An overnight hike at that, and right now, she was currently sleeping on the freaking ground.

The ground!

Seriously, brain, please remind me why people enjoyed hiking?

Eve was sleeping on the ground, her whole body hurt and there was also this weird layer of moisture on everything. This was definitely going into the 'why hiking was bad and she was never doing it again category.'

And why the heck was Eve so freaking hot? What happened to that nice crisp cool air Austin always talked about? He was nothing but a freaking liar, and as soon as —

Austin!

Eve froze, her eyes shooting open.

Her stomach bottomed out as her whole body stiffened as the events of the previous night came flooding back to her.

Well, now she knew why her *every* muscle hurt.

Oh, no, oh, no, no, no... I didn't. No, we didn't. Oh no, no, no. Please tell me this is all just some weird fucked up twisted dream? Universe, if you can hear me, I'd like to wake up now. I apologize for whatever I did to piss you off. You got me back. You jokester. Haha. You really had me going there. You're so funny...

Austin's arm tightened around Eve's center, bringing her *naked* back closer to his *naked* front. If she thought she was hot before she'd been wrong because her body just broke out into a sweat.

Was she breathing? Eve didn't feel like she was breathing, as pure panic washed through her. Great, she was skipping right over the ulcer and going for a full-on heart attack. She side-eyed the top of the tent, glaring. *Fuck you, Universe.*

Eve's heart slammed against her chest with such force, she was sure she was done for. *Maybe if I don't move, it didn't happen. Breathe in one-two. Out one-two. In one-two. Out one-two.*

It was fine. Everything is fine.

Eve was really in her bed at home, sleeping soundly. Marshmallow at her feet. Yeah. That's what was going on. She was fast asleep. Not a care in the world. Her cat purring at her feet, dreaming of all the ways to take over the world.

See, fine.

Eve laid there pretending the events of the last eighteen hours hadn't happened, and she was, in fact, sleeping in her bed. However, as she lied to herself, the forest's sounds mocked her getting louder and louder as the woodland animals woke with the morning sun.

Freaking A. I guess there goes our never speaking about sex or in the pants rule. Poof, gone, right out the freaking window... or, I guess tent.

She tried to swallow, her throat completely dry. It was no use.

Eve faking none of it happened was like her saying Mildred was a quiet, reserved old librarian. Or that Marshmallow wasn't destroying things in her apartment, or secretly had a hit out on Austin.

Shit, Austin...

How could she have been so stupid? Now that those gates had opened, there was no going back. Eve knew exactly what happened between them the previous night and it was going to be burned in her mind for the rest of her life.

What in the absolute hell had she done? Lost her damn mind, that's what.

I slept with Austin... I freakin' slept with my best friend.

And to add to her misery, Eve was currently still naked with said best friend in the same sleeping bag.

Okay, at least that explained why she was so damn hot.

How in the hell are you gonna get yourself out of this one, Eve? Huh? Yeah. Good job.

Austin's hand migrated up her stomach before cupping her breast, causing Eve to stiffen while trying to stifle her moan.

Oh, no. Oh freakin' no.

Hiking, not good. Small, cramped tent, also not good. Being naked in a tent, really not good. Having your best friend grope your breast after having the best sex of your life, really freakin' not good. As everything they'd done came rushing back to her in a wave, Eve didn't know whether to vomit or cry.

Maybe both.

Both was actually a really good possibility.

Damn it! Damn it all to hell.

They'd never be able to go back to being just friends now. At least not for her. She'd kept all those feelings locked away for so long and now... *Fuck!* She and Austin would never work out. She knew that years ago. That's why she'd taken all those feelings and crushed them so far inside of her, they'd never get a chance to see the light of day.

Eve squinted, the sun beaming into their tent only taunting her. *Really, Universe, really?*

Was throwing herself off the cliff still on the table because holy shit...

Austin had been —

Eve didn't even know how to describe it. He lit her body up like no one had ever done before. Sure, she wasn't one to shy away from getting her pleasure, but dang, it was almost like *he* needed to get her off just as much as she wanted to.

The things they did...

Eve closed her eyes willing it all to go away as the memories filled her. Austin was, oh God, Austin had been perfect.

His every move set her body on fire. And she took it all and then gave it back. There was no worry, shame, or hiding.

No.

It was pure passion and since it was Austin, the person she'd shared her most intimate soul with Eve had felt free to let go and unabashedly be in the moment. She let her fantasies of them being together consume her.

There was no 'they were on different playing fields,' and people who looked like Austin weren't supposed to sleep with people that looked like Eve. Instead, they were one, and they moved together like they were always meant to be.

Damn it! Eve's heart hurt. This was never supposed to happen. There was only one person who was going to get hurt here, and she knew it wouldn't be him.

Holy shit. It felt like someone had taken an egg beater to her brain and went to town.

Okay, that settled it. Eve was going to vomit.

I slept with my best friend. My freaking best friend. And right now, his hand is getting mighty friendly with my boob.

Eve swallowed hard. The feeling of Austin's naked body next to hers made her skin tingle. Pushing down all her feelings she tried to assess the situation.

Okay well, what do we do? Run? Can we run? No, I have no idea how the hell to get out of here. Plus, I don't freakin' run. And I'm naked. I can see it now, I jump up and hightail it out of the tent and take off butt ass naked and end up getting lost and then some wolf or bear finds me and instead of eating me they feel bad and take me in. And then before I know it, I'm one of those wilderness people. My only family, the rogue animal who'd taken pity on me. I'm gonna spend the rest of my days trying to survive out here in the forest.

I'm not built for outsideness.

I don't want to sleep in a cave. And hibernating during winter... I don't want to hibernate. Although, not having to interact with people did sound appealing... Wait, no— This was not good! I'm gonna end up being someone in one of those tabloids the title reading something ridiculous like, "We Found the Missing Link."

Even in his sleep state, Austin must've realized Eve was in a panic because he tightened his hold. He gently removed his hand from her breast, going back to her stomach, pulling her into his body, almost possessively.

Eve's stomach twisted into a knot as her heart pounded forcefully against her chest.

Things couldn't get any worse at this point.

And she had no idea how to fix it. Or how to get out of the situation. She was naked in the middle of a forest.

Did she mention she was naked?

Right next to an also very naked Austin?

Eve gulped, feeling her throat constrict as her body freaked out.

Maybe that's what best friends did? They shared a sleeping bag and were naked together while one of them cupped the other's boobie in a friendly handshake.

It's what friends did on the weekends—

Duh.

Dang it. Eve couldn't even convince herself of that. And while Eve was at it, damn her body for responding to his touch. As Austin molded himself around her, tucking Eve into his side even further, lust pooled low in her belly.

Oh heck no. No, no, no, those feelings are getting locked back into that box. Stop it right the heck now.

Absolutely not.

There was no way in hell Eve was going there. Nope. Her body was just going to have to take a hike off the cliff because she was not, and she repeated, she was *not* going to get turned on right now.

Again, absolutely freaking not.

Blood rushed to her ears, defying her as she willed not only her body to stop reacting to Austin, but also to somehow turn back time.

Oh, shit. She'd slept with Austin.

She'd freaking slept with her best friend.

Eve's chest tightened as she fought the urge to cry. Everything was a mess. A complete and total mess. Tears filled her eyes as she begged the Universe to take it all away.

Maybe, just maybe, Eve could've put this past her if Austin had turned out to be crappy in bed, but no. That would make things easy.

That would mean the Universe was on her side, and it was pretty damn clear that wasn't the case.

Austin was good. No good wasn't the right word. And well, damn that tiny crush she'd had on him over the years...

Dang it, why couldn't he have sucked in bed?

Now knowing how his body complemented hers... Fuck, she wanted to scream. She'd never be able to go back to them just being friends after this. And while she was at it, she might as well throw the idea of her going on a date out of the window, too. No one would ever be able to compare to how Austin had possessed every inch of her body.

And fuck her, that was exactly what he'd done.

Eve squeezed her eyes tight as she laid there, the sounds of the forest growing even louder, taunting her again.

Hey, Universe, it's me, Eve again. Sorry about the whole cussing you out thing. I didn't mean it. Can we maybe talk this through? Give a girl a bone, you know, send in those meat-eating rabbits? Anything?

Before she got a reply, Eve's stomach growled. *No, you misunderstood, send them in to eat* me. *Why are you not listening?*

Eve's stomach growled again, this time louder. *Oh, fuck you, Universe. I must be nothing but a damn joke to you. I ask for meat eating-rabbits and you make* my *stomach growl.*

Eve's stomach clenched, begging for food as she thought back to the last time she'd eaten. In the middle of the night, somewhere along the line, Austin had grabbed the trail mix and they'd eaten a little of it before, well, he ate her again...

Ugh...

Great. Freaking wonderful. Eve couldn't even begin to wrap her mind around the events. The view, the storm, the kiss, and then—

Kill her now.

Just go ahead and send in the rabbits, please. At this point, she'd gladly take her new foster family of wild animals over this.

Maybe it'd be a wolf that took pity on her? She'd always wanted a dog. Not that wolves were dogs, and she was sure if she tried to pet one, she'd end up dead, but then again, that might be better than where she was right now.

Eve's stomach growled louder. *Crap on a freaking cracker.*

Give her a dang break.

It made sense, though, between the hike and well, fucking your best friend, it was bound to burn off some calories. Of course, her stomach was trying to eat itself.

Wonder-fucking-ful.

There was one positive about this, though. At this point, Eve wouldn't have to face Austin, since she was sure she was about to die of starvation at any moment.

Eve was adding this to the list of why hiking sucked, and she was *never* doing it again. *Yeah, fuck this shit.*

As the gravity of the situation sunk in, Eve's mind raced at a million miles an hour. How would they ever recover? Could they recover from this?

Austin was everything to her. The thought of losing him, or what they'd cultivated over the years...

Damn, that hurt.

That hurt more than she wanted to admit.

Thank everything she was lying down because she was about to pass out.

You. Don't. Sleep. With. Your. Best. Friend!

"I can hear you thinking," Austin growled, as he thrust his hips, rubbing his very hard dick along her ass.

At the friction, Eve's body instantly betrayed her as lust filled her. Damn her body, since it took everything she had not to moan as her heart pounded.

If you let go and just feel into whatever this is, you can have a different kind of pounding too... Ahhh! No. Stop! Bad body. Bad, bad body!

Austin's hand migrated back to her breast before giving it

a light squeeze. He then expertly let his fingers brush against her hard nipple, causing pleasure to shoot through her.

Eve bit her lip to stop her moan as her body stiffened in anticipation. *Damn you, body, for responding to him, you freaking hussy. Wait! Maybe, if I pretend I'm dead he'd get up and leave me here.*

"Eve."

She wasn't falling for it. Nope. Eve held her eyes closed, her mouth going dry. *Should I start snoring? I should start snoring. That would convince him.*

Austin kissed along Eve's neck, making her body heat as he worked his way across her skin. "You'd think I'd be satisfied with all that we did last night, but I'm nowhere near." His lips kissed along her shoulder before sinking his teeth in.

"No biting!" Eve snapped her head around to face Austin. Her eyes narrowed as she glared him down. "You aren't a vampire."

Austin's whole face lit as he looked at her, a pleased smirk on his lips. "I knew you weren't sleeping, babe."

"My body hurts," she huffed, as she moved her arm, trying to squeeze in between them to cover her chest.

Austin's smirk turned into a wide, toothy grin. "I'll take that as a compliment."

"Stop talking."

That settled it. Fresh air was the devil.

It made you do stupid things like freaking sleep with your best friend. And now you're both naked in a sleeping bag wondering what fresh hell this was.

Austin growled so deep it caused Eve to jump, which must've worked out in his favor since he somehow maneuvered them so he was now on top of her. His arms braced on either side of her head. "I want you, Eve."

Her heart stopped as she felt his whole body on hers. *Oh shit!*

As Austin lowered his head, Eve's flight or fight response kicked in. "I have to eat!"

Really, that's what you came up with? You can do better than that!

Austin quirked his brow, staring down at her, his half-smile back. "Babe?"

"I need to eat," she rushed out. "And we need to get ourselves home. There's so much that needs to be done. I'm positive I've forgotten stuff I had to do at the shop since you sprung this on me last minute and I need to check on Marshmallow." Eve knew it was word vomit, but she couldn't stop herself.

Self-preservation and all that shit.

Austin must have sensed something was wrong, since he unzipped them and sat back on his heels.

"Ahh!" Eve flung her hands over her eyes. "You're naked." *Oh, fuck!* "Wait, I'm naked!" Eve grabbed the forgotten sleeping bag next to them and tossed it over her body.

When I said could the morning get any worse, that was not *a challenge.*

Austin cocked his head, a slight smirk on his face as he watched her. "Nothing gets past you, does it?" He laughed, but as he did, Eve peeked through her fingers, her eyes honing in on the dangly appendage between his legs.

Eve jerked her head away. "It's staring at me!"

"It likes you, what can I say?" Austin's deep laugh echoed throughout the tent.

Eve snapped her head to him at his smart remark, her eyes narrowing, daring him to go further. "Don't."

Austin wiggled his brows, his eyes lighting with pure amusement.

Well, at least someone was enjoying her downfall.

"And here I always thought you were a morning person, babe?"

That's it. She was going to kill him. How in the hell could he be so calm? Eve was seconds from losing every thread of anything she had inside of her, and yet, Austin was ready to have a morning coffee and take a freaking walk in the woods.

Was there a point you had to worry if your heart was beating too fast? Because if so, she was positive she was there.

Eve flung her hands around, knocking the sleeping bag off her. *This is it. I'm having a heart attack. The hike didn't do it, but this sure as hell was.*

No more Eve.

Austin grabbed her arms, pushing Eve backward, effectively pinning her under him. His legs resting on either side of her very naked hips. "You're adorable when you're all flustered."

Adorable? A-freaking-dorable.

Eve was going to kill him. However, her brain turned to mush the moment Austin lowered his head, kissing along her exposed neck.

She couldn't fight her body as it responded to him. Moving her head out of the way, she gave Austin more room.

"What in the hell do you do to me?" he rumbled, before biting the base of her neck, lightly nibbling on the skin. "I think you're right, my Eve. We do need to eat." He pulled back, his eyes devouring every inch of her. "And, babe, just so you know, I'm starving."

How could anyone think clearly when someone looked at them the way Austin was looking at her?

It wasn't possible.

Austin kissed down her neck, peppering kisses between her breasts.

She fought her body, but it was no use. He felt good, and he made her feel good.

Eve's eyes moved to his, and that's when she realized the

sun was no longer coming up, it was full-on there, and beaming right through their tent.

A wave of adrenaline washed through her, causing her stomach to bottom out.

Last night had been dark. The only light they had came from the small lantern Austin had set up. But now, well, crap, now *everything* was on display.

Eve gasped for air, her skin flushing. *He's gonna see it all. Everything. All of it. Boom, right in the light of the freaking day.*

Austin, completely oblivious of the war raging inside of Eve, continued his kiss down her lush stomach, his eyes catching hers and the moment they did, her breath hitched.

The passion that looked back at her... *Oh, God.*

Austin's hand squeezed her stomach, just as he did last night. "Mine." He said it with such force, she forgot how to breathe.

Trying to jumpstart her brain, Eve opened her mouth to protest, but no words came out as Austin reached her center.

She shouldn't let this happen, not again. Where it stood right now, Eve might be able to mend her heart back together, but if they continued...

And yet, her body had other plans. "I'm not supposed to be on the menu." Eve's words were strained even to her own ears.

Austin parted her legs, fitting himself perfectly between them. "That's for me to decide." He lowered himself, kissing the top of her lush mound. "Best meal I'll ever have."

Eve's back instantly arched as Austin began to devour her, his tongue flicking over her clit, causing her whole body to quiver as he took his fill of everything she had.

The only thing Eve could do was wrap her legs around Austin's shoulders, pulling him closer to her center, encouraging him.

The sensations caused her body to ignite all over again. Just as it did the previous night, as Austin's fingers found her center immediately finding the spot that had her entire body tingling.

He pulled her clit into his mouth; the pressure too much for her to handle as her body exploded around his mouth, forcing her to shake and convulse as euphoria blanketed her.

"Oh, God!"

Eve's chest heaved as she fought to breathe, the explosion still racing through her.

"I'll repeat, best meal I'll ever have." Austin sat back on his heels in between Eve's parted legs.

Eve's stomach clenched as her eyes shifted to him, seeing her juices coating his chin had her breath catching in her throat.

Holy freaking moly.

Eve's eyes flicked to his, and the fire she saw staring back at her was her undoing.

In for a penny, in for a pound. She'd deal with the fallout later. But right now. Fuck, right now, she needed him.

Austin was her everything, and right now she was willing to throw aside everything telling her no and go for it.

Eve was on her knees, grabbing Austin's shoulders and flipping him onto his back. She tossed her left leg over his hip, positioning herself directly above him.

"Yes, take me, Eve. I'm yours."

Eve hovered over him, using her hand to align his dick with her center. Feeling his thickness in her palm sent another wave of lust through her. Glancing into Austin's eyes as she stroked him, the head of his cock brushed against her sensitive clit as she flicked it back and forth.

"Fuck me, Eve. Please," Austin pleaded, his eyes dark full of primal need.

Grabbing the base of his dick, keeping him steady, Eve

lowered herself. And the moment the tip entered Eve's core, her body rejoiced begging for more.

Instantly, Austin hissed as his hand shot to Eve's hip, forcing her down onto his member. "Fuck!"

She couldn't agree more.

Eve circled her hips, feeling how full Austin made her.

His hands gripped her hips with such a force, Eve knew there'd be bruises, but she didn't care.

Eve flung her head back exposing her neck as she rode him.

She guessed Austin must have seen that as an opportunity since his hand went between her breasts before trailing upward to her neck.

"Yesss," she hissed out at Austin's hand going around her throat.

Fuck, that was hot.

Hotter than she ever thought. Austin didn't squeeze hard, it was just enough pressure to heighten the sensation flooding through her. Austin's other hand stayed on her hip, encouraging Eve to rock back and forth.

It was too much.

It was all too much.

The feeling... Oh, God.

Eve's movements became erratic, and Austin must have sensed her need. He flipped them with zero effort, causing Eve to land on her back without breaking them apart. Immediately Austin began to push inside her with such force that Eve thought she would break in two.

"Austin," she begged, her hips meeting him thrust for thrust. "Please, I need—"

"I know what you need," he grunted, his hand moving to her pussy. And the second Austin flicked her clit, she exploded harder than she ever had before. Eve clenched around him, pulling him in as Austin growled out his own release.

"Damn, Eve. What do you do to me? I think I just lost a year off my life."

As she laid there desperately trying to get herself under control, Austin pulled out of her sitting back on his ankles. "But I'm okay with that." He lowered his head to her knee, kissing it gently as he panted, his chest rising and falling.

After giving her knee another gentle kiss, Austin's eyes shifted to hers. The smirk on his face was almost too much for Eve to handle.

Oh, God.

Austin eyes lit as he winked. "I think it's about time I feed *you*. Don't you agree?" With that, he grabbed his pants and unzipped the tent, leaving Eve there with her mouth hanging open.

Chapter Seventeen

AUSTIN HAD to admit breakfast at the campsite had been interesting. Actually, the entire morning after they'd left the tent had been on the side of weird and he wasn't a fan.

Austin had tried to get closer to Eve and she'd either push him away or brush him off.

Again, weird.

That wasn't their relationship. It'd never been like that. Sure, they'd play around and joke with each other and stuff, but this was... whatever the hell it was Austin didn't like it.

Tearing down the camp was strange, too. They'd pretty much worked in silence as they got everything packed up. Once they were done, Austin watched as Eve walked over to the cliff admiring the view one last time, before turning to him with a forced smile on her face, asking the way to head out.

Austin didn't like it.

Not at all.

Truthfully, he fucking hated it.

Austin had no idea what to do to fix it. Every time he'd try to talk about anything, she'd inadvertently brush him off again.

Everything had seemed so perfect when he left the tent, and then it wasn't.

And that shit just wouldn't fly. Not another second. This wasn't him and Eve. Whatever the issue was, they'd fix it.

It was Austin and Eve against the world always, and this was no different, even if he needed to remind her of that.

Especially now.

Eve was the other part of Austin's soul, and he'd be damned if he lost her. Clearing his throat, he spoke. "Eve, babe?"

She'd been walking slightly in front of him, but at his words, Eve turned to face him, that forced smile on her face again.

Oh, fuck no. Absolutely not. See, he knew something was wrong.

"Yeah?" Her voice was low, almost pained.

Panic washed through Austin as he thought the worst. Was she hurt? Was that the reason why she'd been acting strangely? Fuck him, he was an idiot. She'd probably been hurt or sore this whole time and he'd been off in fucking la la land not paying attention. "Are you okay?" he asked, his eyes scanning her up and down for any sign of an injury as he walked toward her.

Eve snapped her hands up, stopping Austin from moving closer. "Yeah. I'm okay. Why wouldn't I be okay? I'm like *super* okay. So okay, I should get a crown that says Queen of Okay."

Austin quirked his brow. "Eve—"

"That's my name. Fun name isn't it? You'd think it would be short for something, but nope, it's just Eve. Eve, Eve, Eve. Three letters. That's it, nothing more, nothing less." Her eyes shifted from left to right before focusing back on Austin, that same pained expression on her face.

Okay, yep, something was definitely up. "Eve?"

"See!" Eve threw her hands in the air. "So simple. Even you

can say it with ease. There isn't much more to it. You can draw it out if you want, but you don't have to. Plus, it sounds silly. Eeeeevvvvvveeee."

"Babe—"

"But when you do that, it kinda sounds like the hum from some appliance. Eeeeevvvveeee, hot damn, look at me I sound like a dishwasher. Did you hear that? I bet I can do it again, maybe sound like a deep freezer this time. Eeevvv—"

"Enough, babe, I get it." Austin chuckled. "You can morph into an everyday household appliance."

"That's talent."

"Sure thing, babe." He nodded. "I've got to ask though, other than the last few seconds demonstrating your immaculate dishwasher impersonation. What's up? You've barely said a word on the trail. You're starting to freak me out. I'd thought you'd be spouting off about dying by now."

Eve crossed her arms over her chest, jutting her chin out toward him. "I'm focused. I'm *trying* to concentrate on not *dying*."

"And that makes you quiet? You're never quiet."

Eve gasped, her jaw hitting the ground. "Rude. I can be quiet."

"When?" Austin cocked his brow.

"I'm offended." Eve's hand flew over her chest. "Here I was thinking I was doing us both a favor focusing on the path... " She eyed him. "You know trying not to die and all that shit, and here you are saying I can't stop talking. Again, rude."

Austin held up his hands, a slight smirk on his face as he watched her being completely flustered. Damn, she was adorable. "My apologies. I only wanted to make sure everything was okay." His eyes focused on hers. "*We're* good. You know that, right?"

Eve's hands swung around through the air between them. "Of course, I know that. Why wouldn't we be good?"

Austin watched Eve for a few beats, analyzing her answer. Maybe fresh mountain air was too much for her?

"Stop looking at me like that. I'm hot and gross. My body hurts. Plus, I'm trying not to trip on a rock and die. All I really want is to go home and shower. I'd give my left boob to take a shower right now."

"Not the left one, that's my favorite."

Eve's mouth fell open, her hand snapping to her right. "No one gets to play favorites with my tatas. They are equally prestigious. They'd get their own scholarship to an Ivy League school if they could figure out how to apply."

Austin growled low in his throat, his eyes focusing on Eve's plentiful chest. "I couldn't agree more."

As his hand reached out, Eve slapped it away. "Nope. No way. Abso-freaking-lutely not. We are headed out through this death trap of a forest and getting into the car. There'll be hell to pay if I don't get home soon to check on Marshmallow. She's probably thrown a party already and the whole damn apartment is trashed."

"You're probably right." Austin nodded as a wicked smile formed on his face.

"I know I'm right. That cat lives for moments like this."

Austin burst into a deep laugh, some of the tension leaving his body. Maybe he was overreacting and thinking way too much into everything that'd happened. After all, this was Eve's first time hiking.

Eve must have decided their conversation was over and stomped past him, causing Austin to shake his head. Had he mentioned she was a piece of work?

At least she was *his* piece of work.

"Babe," he called out, the corner of his mouth tugging upward.

"I can't hear you," she hollered, continuing on her path. "I'm an expert backpacker, hiker, dude, person, now and I'm getting in all the steps. Might as well sign me up to climb Mount Everest. That mountain ain't got shit on me—"

"Eve," he cut her off, holding in his laugh.

She spun toward him. "What are you a slowpoke now? Let's get a move on. My phone is in your SUV, probably dead."

Austin's smirk turned into a full-blown grin as his eyes lit. "Those are some mighty ballsy statements from someone who is going the wrong way."

SHIT! DOUBLE AND TRIPLE FREAKIN' shit. Could this be going any worse? Probably not.

Eve flicked her eyes to the bright sky. *Please, don't take that as a challenge.*

She closed her eyes tight before opening them, struggling to take a deep breath. *Crap on a million crackers.*

If there was an award for the most idiotic person, she'd win it hands down. The only thing Eve wanted to do right now was to find her way out of the damn forest and back to her apartment where she could figure out what in the ever-loving hell she was going to do next.

It wouldn't have been so bad if she hadn't had a serious talk with herself before she left the tent that morning. You know, one of those "go get 'em" talks. It's about time. All the signs lead back to Austin... blah blah blah. Why not take a chance?

She'd decided to open all those boxes inside her and was ready to see where it went.

Eve figured why the hell not, right? Who said it couldn't be their time?

Sure, she'd slept with Austin, and it was good. Damn good, but there was also their connection. The connection they'd shared their whole friendship, and it only heightened after spending the night together. And who cared if they didn't seem like they belonged together?

They'd gotten that a million times. Besides, Eve fully admitted their friendship was weird, but that's what made it perfect. It was perfectly weird, and that was fine by them.

So, in that tent, after another brief panic attack, Eve decided she wanted to try.

It wasn't just sleeping with Austin, though. Yeah, like she said that'd been fantastic. She felt free, and it felt right no matter how much she tried to deny it.

It was more.

Way more.

She'd decided in the tent, she'd pull up her big girl panties and see where it went. Of all the years she'd known Austin, granted she didn't really know about his sex life, because, Lordy because if she had... Whoo-boy.

Anyway, Austin never seemed like one of those guys to sleep with someone and move on. Even with all the women throwing themselves at him.

Austin was a long-haul guy.

He might love the outdoors and being out in nature, but Austin also loved hanging out at home or in her apartment, watching movies, and staying away from the crowds just as much.

So why not give it a try, right? Why not throw caution to the wind? Why not open up that tent and see what happened?

Why not push aside the safe option for the first time in her life and go for it?

Why couldn't Eve be the main character for once?

And look how that line of thinking turned out for you, dumb-dumb...

Eve's chest squeezed as she cursed herself, trying to make sense of where she'd gone wrong. Or, if she'd magically be able to find a time machine in this crap forest and go back to that morning.

Eve groaned, her body fighting as hard as it could to stay in one piece.

When Eve pulled herself out of their tent, ready for something new, ready to try, Austin was there acting like it was any other day.

To him, Eve was still just Eve, his best friend. The best friend he just so happened to have a lapse of judgment and sleep with.

It turned out her whole revelation and pep talk was a complete waste of time, and now that she'd gone there...

Like she said, it hurt.

Her heart actually hurt.

It hurt like hell.

Some reaction, even a negative one would've been better than what she got...

Closing her eyes, Eve thought back to her sitting in the tent, nearly hyperventilating as she convinced herself to let down her guard. You know, finally let those walls around her heart fall where it came to Austin.

Because this was it. This was their moment. This was going to be what changed them forever, and Eve was ready.

Austin wouldn't sleep with her, especially with that much passion just to throw all of what they had away.

Eve saw it clear as day.

She was going to get dressed, unzip the tent, and magically Austin was going to be there stoking the fire. He'd turn to Eve and confess his undying love.

The same love she had for him that she only *now* was willing to let out.

Her adrenaline coursed through her, but she'd been

excited. This was going to be it. Sure, Eve might've fought it initially, but why keep fighting what was meant to happen?

Eve's voice inside of her should've been a hype person because as she sat there in the tent, she *knew* they were meant to be. That little voice was cheering her on, screaming to go get Austin.

It was about damn time.

Mildred would've been proud.

Hell, she'd been proud of herself.

Eve was going to pop out of the tent and their lives would be changed forever.

That was what was supposed to happen, right? That's what happened in the movies, so why in the hell could it not happen to her the same way?

In a weird way, it did happen, just not the way she'd hoped.

Eve had swallowed her fear and popped out of the tent, only to be met with a paper plate full of scrambled eggs and a conversation about how they needed to break down the tent and get a move onto the trail.

Eve stood there stunned, holding her plate of eggs like someone had knocked the wind out of her, and that someone was Austin. Not a word was spoken about their night together. Instead he glanced at her, a half-smile on his face, before he carried on with what he was doing.

Like nothing happened.

Eve couldn't keep her heart together even if she'd tried. The walls that once surrounded her crashed down, but along with them went her heart.

And as it shattered into a million pieces, Eve forced a smile on her face, willing her legs to work.

When Austin turned back to the fire without a care in the world, Eve realized the mistake in her pep talk.

This wasn't a movie.

It wasn't a romance novel.

This was life.

Austin wasn't about to sweep her off her feet.

Nope. Instead, Austin handed her a plate full of eggs and acted like they did every Friday night.

And, damn, did that hurt.

Eve had fought her feelings for so long, but when she'd finally let herself believe, to feel, to pretend to be the main character in a movie, she was wrong.

She'd been dead wrong.

All while her heart broke the impossible inch more, Eve quickly finished her eggs. For being outside, it sure as hell felt like she'd run out of air. And on wobbly legs, Eve pulled herself together enough to walk over to the overlook as Austin worked on packing up.

Eve stood there doing her best to memorize the view. Because she knew once they left, she'd never be the same.

She'd be leaving a piece of her heart at the campsite.

And no matter how badly Eve wanted to place the blame on Austin. How she wanted to hate him for making her feel anything in the first place, she couldn't.

Eve couldn't blame Austin in the least.

And she wouldn't.

Austin was a stand-up guy. He'd always had been, and he always would be. That's why he was her best friend.

The tensions had been high; the storm was loud, and even if she didn't want to admit it, Eve knew she'd gotten a rise out of Austin with her designs.

Any man would've broken at some point.

And if she were being honest with herself, maybe that was subconsciously her plan all along. Now that she'd opened up that box, she could see how she liked getting him all hot and bothered.

Her.

Eve Morgan, the plus-sized, very opinionated, somewhat of a walking disaster with a cat who was out for blood, was able to turn on a guy like Austin.

She was able to turn *him* on with all her lumps, bumps, rolls, cellulite, stretch marks, and all.

And that felt good.

It'd felt damn good to know she could do that.

But to think he'd magically be in love with her now was foolish, and that was putting it lightly.

Her and Austin sleeping together, no matter how much passion was involved, had been done in the heat of the moment.

That's it.

Eve's stomach knotted as she willed herself to keep her composure. Because she knew, at least for her, she'd never be the same.

She'd never be able to fully go back to the way things were.

And that hurt.

That hurt a hell of a freaking lot.

It was her worst fear come to life.

All the things she'd debated about in the tent, the good, the bad, the what-if's... A fresh wave of bile rose in Eve's throat.

Austin carried on like nothing happened, and they were still good ole best pals, Austin and Eve.

Austin might be able to put aside their torrid affair out here in the wilderness, but there would be no way Eve would be that lucky.

Her hand went to her heart trying with all her might to ease the pain she was fighting with. How was she supposed to just walk away? Like she finally hadn't given a part of herself to Austin. The one-piece she'd so desperately tried to keep from him for years.

Oh God, it hurt.

It hurt worse than she could've ever imagined.

Fuck nature and all its nature-filled things.

It was safe to say she'd never go hiking again. This one outing not only cost Eve her heart, but it was also going to cost Eve her best friend.

It felt like time was slowing down, as the whole situation solidified the fact Eve would never be one of the elite. She'd never get the guy at the end of the movie. She was just Eve, and that's how she was going to stay for the rest of her life.

Eve's heart broke into another million pieces as the realization thickened around her. She was good enough to sleep with if everything aligned the right way, but Eve wasn't good enough to get her happily ever after.

She was just Eve.

She'd always been just Eve in the world, and apparently, that's how she was destined to stay.

A tiny snort escaped her while she shook her head.

The whole thing had been a colossal misstep, but in a way, Eve was glad they slept together.

Because now she knew.

That little part of Eve that'd always pretended, even if she didn't want to admit it, there could be more between her and Austin, now knew for a fact that would never be the case.

A sharp pain ran through Eve's stomach as she mourned what was never supposed to be.

And although it was going to hurt like hell, and it was going to take everything inside of her, she'd eventually be okay with being just Eve.

Let's get home. Once I'm home, I can figure it out from there. All I need to do is get home. Home is safe.

Pushing down everything inside of her, Eve's eyes scanned Austin. The worry matched with amusement on his face sent another pang through her heart.

She might end up being just Eve to him. The person he

slept with on a hiking trip while Mother Nature raged a war around them, their emotions raw, but to her, Austin would still be the best friend she'd ever had.

And would ever have.

His concern for her right now was enough to prove that.

Taking a deep breath, Eve swallowed hard around the lump in her throat desperately trying to ease her grief.

You can't help who you fall in love with in your lifetime, just like you can't make the person you've fallen in love with love you back.

And that realization sucked.

But none of that mattered. This was her problem and she'd deal with it. It was going to hurt for a while, but this was Austin.

It wouldn't ever be the same but having Austin as a friend was better than not having him at all.

Eve knew that.

And even though her heart shattered with every breath she took, she'd do everything she could to build her walls back around her heart, and yet still be there for him.

It was Austin.

And he deserved the world. Even if that world didn't involve her any more than her being *just* Eve.

She might need a few days to get herself back in order, but she would.

She'd come out of this stronger.

What was that stupid saying? It's better to try and fail than not try at all...

Eve might still somewhat wish she could be the main character... But hey, in a world full of so much uncertainty, she guessed being the side character wouldn't be that bad.

At least she'd still get to be there.

Even if she'd be there as just Eve for the rest of her life.

How many cats do you need before you become the stereotype?

Eve shook her head, clearing her throat as she walked back, staring at Austin as she worked on building the barriers back around her heart.

She could do this.

She had to do this.

Eve only needed a few days to get herself back together. "You could've told me that before I went this way."

Austin's entire face brightened as a toothy grin appeared. "I just did, babe."

Babe...

Eve swallowed hard as she walked past him, doing her best to remind herself she was just Eve. This wasn't her happily ever after and it never would be.

As soon as she realized that, she'd be able to move on with her life.

When I get home, I can have a total mental breakdown. I'm sure Marshmallow will be right there, judging the shit out of me. And then, once I've gotten it all out of my system, I'll do what I do best. I'll put myself back together and move on.

It's what I've always done and will do now.

All I need is a break from Austin to push everything back into its rightful box, never to see the light of day again.

Now, all Eve needed to do was get out of this forsaken forest and learn to start her life as just Eve.

Chapter Eighteen

AUSTIN WAS PISSED, annoyed, concerned. You name it, he was it.

What a shit way to start his week.

It was now Tuesday and he hadn't seen Eve since he'd dropped her off at her apartment early Sunday afternoon. Which even that turned out to be a fucking disaster. Austin had every intention of going up to Eve's apartment with her, showering together—

Might as well get dirty while you're getting clean, right?

And then spend the rest of the weekend together. That's how it was supposed to be and was honestly how Austin thought it would've gone.

The whole way to Eve's place Austin contemplated about where'd they get takeout from, what movies he'd convince her to watch. Hell, he was ready to bribe the cat to leave him alone just once so he could enjoy their time together without the fear of an attack.

All he wanted was Eve.

Oh, and he couldn't forget getting her to model for him again.

Damn, his knuckles had turned white as he gripped his steering wheel, imagining being able to *finally* untie that little bow. He'd take his time, and ever so slowly let the ribbon fall open, revealing to him his beautiful Eve.

Austin lost track of the number of times on the ride, he'd reached down and adjusted himself to give his dick more room.

Austin planned on making up for a lot of lost time and getting back to Eve's apartment was only the beginning.

Austin would never be able to get enough of her, and he knew it.

Now that they'd finally reached this place, he was all in.

Truth be told, he'd be lying if he said he also couldn't wait to get Eve into her bed, on the couch, the floor, the kitchen counter. Oh, and he couldn't forget his own bed. As soon as she'd make some excuse for him to leave so they could get ready for work the following day, and how he needed to get back home to unpack, he'd march right up to Eve toss her over his shoulder. He'd tip his chin to Marshmallow with the promise she'd be back and then bring her to his house to do it all over again.

Granted, his home wasn't as homey as Eve's. It's why they'd spend all their time in her apartment versus his house.

But he could see it now, his house wasn't homey because Eve wasn't there. *She's* what made a house a home and he knew it.

And Austin was damn well looking forward to building their home together... or so he thought.

However, Austin was thrown for a loop the second Eve jumped out of his SUV holding up her phone babbling about how she'd forgotten a client was picking up a custom piece and Mikayla needed help. The expansion had taken up most of her time over the last few weeks. She was also behind on custom orders and just a whole bunch of things she'd forgotten.

Austin didn't even have a chance to argue with her. Before he knew it, Eve pretty much pushed him back into the SUV rambling about everything and anything, and then she was gone, off to her apartment and he was left there in shock. Austin was about to head upstairs to figure out what the hell had happened when he got a text from Eve saying they'd talk soon, and how she'd had a good time and thanked him.

Everything inside of Austin felt off. This was not how they were supposed to start their new chapter.

Not in the least.

As Austin made his way toward her apartment, he got another text from Eve, this time with a heart emoji.

That caused him to stop. There was still something that felt off, but this was his best friend. They'd been through everything together. And when there was a problem they always talked it out.

He had to give Eve the benefit of the doubt since she hadn't mentioned anything was wrong between them. In her defense, they'd never avoided each other when there was a problem.

Against his better judgment, Austin sent back a text saying he'd see her later, and they'd get dinner along with a heart emoji.

And that was it...

When he thought about it, though, Austin had sprung the hiking trip on her and this *was* Eve. She'd never disappoint a client. If she'd promised them something by a certain date, she'd deliver.

She'd always deliver.

It's not like he wouldn't see her later anyway, he still needed to pick up the inventory for the week. But as he drove away, he couldn't help the feeling he was leaving a piece of himself with her.

And he'd been right.

Hell, he didn't even get a goodbye kiss.

And it sucked.

Own Your Curves was Eve's life. And her mission was to help everyone feel beautiful just as they were and if she had a client waiting, he wasn't going to mess with that. So even if it frustrated him he wasn't with her and his plans had been derailed, he understood.

Austin didn't like it, but he got it.

It wasn't like this was goodbye; it was only the beginning for them. He knew it.

He'd quickly gotten home, unpacked their stuff, showered, then headed to Own Your Curves to pick up the inventory for Anytime Adventure, and to see if he could help Eve.

Even if it was just moral support.

And once her client was satisfied, Austin vowed to do the same with Eve. He hadn't thought of christening her shop yet, but now he was looking forward to it.

See, he really couldn't get enough of her and he doubted he ever would.

It was all bound to work out...

Until it didn't.

Austin walked into Own Your Curves ready to sweep Eve off her feet only to find Mikayla in her place handing him his inventory, saying she had no idea what he was talking about.

And that's when everything spiraled out of control.

When Austin called Eve to ask what happened, she'd said she went home early not feeling well.

Instantly, Austin jumped into action.

As Eve continued on about her almost getting sick, he was out of her shop headed to their local soup restaurant, ready to take care of her. She'd complained that nature couldn't kill her out on the trail, so now it was trying to do it with a cold. Even when Austin tried reassuring her it was just her body probably reacting to the hike, and he should really come over to take care of her, Eve wouldn't have it.

Austin's concern only solidified when he turned up at her apartment with the soup, only to find her deadbolt in place so he couldn't get in.

What originally had been the best weekend of his life, quickly turned into a panic-filled mess. After hollering through the door begging Eve to let him take care of her and her refusing, saying she'd get him sick, spouting off about him being in tiptop shape for work, he had no choice but to leave the soup at her door and head back to his SUV.

He waited in his car, a war raging inside of him, trying to figure out what to do next. When she messaged him a picture of the soup in a bowl and Marshmallow eyeing it down with a thank you, Austin chuckled, grateful she'd at least taken the soup.

Not long after he'd gotten the picture, she'd sent another of a thermometer showing a fever, a high one at that. Which made Austin feel even worse. Apparently, taking her out on a hike almost did kill her.

And what was he to do? She wouldn't let him in. Austin had no choice but to leave and head back home to his house ultimately feeling like everything was a disaster.

Which left him where he was now on Tuesday morning, completely fucking lost, ready to snap his desk in half.

How had things gotten so fucked up so fast?

It was like the past two days had all mushed into one. It wasn't not being able to see or speak with Eve, no it was more. It was like a piece of him was missing.

Eve hadn't really replied to any of his text messages, and it hurt.

He couldn't sleep, eat, or anything, really. And he had no fucking idea how to fix it.

"Yo, dude, what in the hell has gotten into you? You're worse off than you were yesterday." Jake walked into his office, his face scrunching as he gave Austin the once-over.

"Fuck off."

Jake's brow cocked. "Someone's in a bad mood."

Great, to add to his misery, he was now going to have to deal with Jake. Austin massaged his temples while glaring at his friend. "I don't have the time right now. What do you need?"

Jake plopped himself onto the couch, looking at him like he'd grown an extra head. "A million dollars, a month-long vacation, and to get laid. Honestly, I need a lot."

"Really?"

"You asked." Jake winked as he shrugged. "But for real, man, what's going on? I barely got a word out of you yesterday. Every time I tried to talk, you'd growl and then stomp off. At first, you seemed pretty panicked and concerned, but you became more and more of an asshole as the day went on. Here I was ready with popcorn for you to tell me all about the hiking trip and instead you were just a fuckface. I think you almost made Lindsey cry when you snapped at her."

At Jake's words, Austin's eyes widened, his mouth opening.

Fuck.

He hadn't realized he'd been taking out his frustration on others. But now, thinking back, Austin could see it.

Shit.

"I'll go down and apologize to Lindsey. I shouldn't have snapped at her."

"You do that." Jake nodded, still eyeing him. "But you still haven't answered why you're being a Grade-A asshole. Do I need to play twenty questions to figure it out?"

"Fuck off."

"Twenty questions it is." Both of Jake's brows shot to the ceiling. "Did everything go okay on the hike?"

Fuck him, Austin didn't want to talk about the trip, and he definitely didn't want to be sitting behind his desk right now. All he wanted was to get ahold of Eve and figure out if she was okay or not.

There was more to all of this than her being sick. He could feel it in his gut.

Austin pulled his phone out of his pocket, swiping through to his text messages.

When he saw nothing new, his stomach knotted as the now-familiar wave of unease surged through him. His hand tightened around his phone as he debated tossing it against the wall.

If he could just talk to Eve for even a few seconds, he'd be able to put his mind at ease.

Austin didn't get it.

He didn't get it at all.

This was supposed to be their start, the beginning of whatever they were going to be.

"Was the trip bad? I heard about the storm that came out of nowhere from some of the guys on the floor. Did you get caught up in that? Is she not talking to you because you almost killed her?"

Austin looked up at his friend, not even knowing where to start. "The hike was better than I ever would've imagined. The storm..." He would never experience storms the same again. "The storm was fine. We handled it the best we could. Eve was a champ."

"So if the hike was fine, then what the hell is the problem?"

Austin avoided Jake's eyes as his stomach tightened. He fucking wished he knew the answer to that. "Nothing."

"Okaaay. How was Eve, did she enjoy it? I'm begging for crumbs here, Austin. I thought you'd have tons of stories to spill."

Oh, he had stuff he spilled alright... *for fuck's sake.*

Sitting back in his office chair, Austin let out a breath he didn't realize he'd been holding. "Eve had her issues, but it wasn't anything too bad. Overall, I think she enjoyed it. She seemed to be obsessed with rabbits killing her and woodland gnomes trying to get her pregnant." Austin laughed, thinking back. They might be in this weird place right now, but he enjoyed every second with Eve on the trail.

Austin wouldn't change any of it for the entire world. Well, he'd change what came after... Austin sure as shit wouldn't have driven away from her apartment the first time. But he wouldn't change a thing that happened on their outing.

"Really, gnomes?"

Austin shrugged. "She's special." She really was. Eve was more than special, though. Eve was his other half, and that's why everything right now was killing him.

Jake sat back on the couch, stretching his arms out in front of him before putting them behind his head, kicking his feet out. "That she is. Can't argue with you there. But I have this feeling you're neglecting to tell me something. What else happened?"

Austin studied Jake for a moment before answering. "Nothing."

"Bullshit."

"She peed on a tree."

Jake cocked his brow, sitting up. "Was that a monumental event for both of you?"

"Nope. That would've been us sleeping together," Austin said it so matter-of-fact it even surprised himself.

Jake's eyes nearly popped out of his head, his jaw dropping. "Excuse me? Can you repeat that? I don't think I heard you correctly."

Good freaking going, why in the hell did you just blurt that out?

Damn, not having Eve around really did screw up his brain. "Forget it. Go watch the floor."

"Oh, fuck no. You don't drop something like that and then brush it aside. Back the train right up there, bud."

When Austin's only reply was an annoyed grunt, Jake slapped his knee, his smile growing from ear to ear. "About fucking time."

Austin's eyes widened, his heart thumping against his chest. "What?"

"You heard me. It was about fucking time. You've been in love with Eve since the moment you walked into her shop." Jake bounced his head up and down, his toothy grin growing even wider. "Half the employees here have a bet on when you two would finally get together. I'd have to check the white-board in my office to see who won—"

"Is that what that is?"

"Yup." Jake shrugged with a smirk. "What did you think it was? We've all got good money on this. Whoever won, I think can take a cruise. Fuck, I hope it's me. Maybe I can convince Mikayla to—"

"Jake!"

"What? You can have Eve, but I can't have Mikayla? I thought we've talked about this already? Besides, what's the issue here? You finally got what you've wanted all along. Why isn't your head in the sky, walking around like you're on cloud nine and all that shit? Have you started planning the wedding? Is Eve gonna make her own dress?" Jake's eyes narrowed on Austin for a split second. "I better be the best man. Consider this my acceptance right now." He clapped his hands together. "Fuck yeah, you're gonna have the best bachelor party." He pulled out his phone. "I'm gonna start planning it now."

Austin sat there, his mouth open as the blood rushed to his ears... *wedding dress, love, bachelor party?* His throat tightened as he tried to swallow around the lump that'd formed.

"Dude, what in the hell is going on with you? Why do you look like that? You definitely don't look like someone who just got laid by the woman he's in love with."

"Fuck off, Jake."

"Do you want me to call Eve to see if she can come down here and settle you? I can lock you guys in here, 'cause you're kinda freakin' me out. Your face is going all red, I can see the vein in your neck—"

"Jake, I mean it. If you want to keep your job, shut your fucking face." Austin couldn't breathe, his stomach knotted while he forced his brain to work. If Jake would just shut up for a minute, he could think—

"Wait..." Jake cut off Austin's thought. "Something's not right. Are you guys okay?"

Austin couldn't answer.

"You're kidding me." Jake's brow quirked. "I got it. I should've known. What did you do to fuck it up?"

Austin snapped his attention to him, his eyes hard. "What do you mean, what did I do? I didn't do anything."

Jake watched him, his head cocked to the side. "Not buying it. You did something. Lay it on me. Let's get this fixed so I can start planning my cruise and your bachelor party."

"I'm gonna punch you in the eye. That's what I'm gonna do."

"Violence nice. Eve's really got you twisted into a knot." The corner of Jake's mouth turned up. "I love her. The fact she can rile you up makes my little heart happy."

"Shut up, Jake."

"Fine, be that way." Jake stood from the couch, taking a

step toward the door. "Maybe I'll go talk to her myself. I'm taking my lunch."

"Sit down."

"Nah, I think I'll take my chances with Eve. Maybe I'll take her to lunch with me."

Something snapped inside of Austin as a wave of possessiveness raced through him. "Don't you fucking go near her. And if you say you love her one more time, I'll—"

"You'll what?" Jake cut him off, plopping back down on the couch.

"I'll kill you."

Jake's grin spread across his entire face, his eyes brightening. "I'd like to see you try."

"Don't test me, Jake. I'm not in the mood."

"Maybe you suck in bed." Jake tapped his chin. "That would make sense."

The man had a death wish. "Jake," Austin warned.

"If you aren't gonna tell me how you fucked up, I'm gonna have to come to my own conclusions."

"I didn't fuck up. No one fucked up. It's just—"

"Just what?"

"I don't fucking know, man. I thought things were fine. Sure, she seemed a little off, but we did go out hiking and there was a big storm. I thought we'd go back to her apartment, play with Marshmallow a little, shower, and just spend the rest of the weekend together—"

"And none of that happened?"

"No. We got back home and it went downhill from there and now she's sick. She's blaming it on the storm, but I can't shake the feeling it's more. We slept together. This was supposed to be the start of, I don't know... us. But instead, I'm at a fucking loss. She's barely even speaking to me."

Jake nodded.

"That's it. That's all you got for me, a nod? I tell you what's going on and you just nod?" *Fucking great.*

"What else happened?" Jake eyed him.

"That's it. Didn't you just hear me?" Austin was about two seconds from saying fuck this shit and leaving. Clearly, talking to Jake wasn't getting him anywhere.

"I'm not talking about when you got home. I'm talking about when you were out on the trail. What else happened?"

"I don't know what you're asking. I took Eve to one of the most beautiful places around here, and it happened. There was the storm and honestly, I was tired of fighting it. Like you said, it was about damn time."

He wanted Eve. He knew that with every ounce inside of him. Eve was the endgame for Austin, and even if they hadn't gone on the trip or if she hadn't started her expansion at the shop, it still would've always been Eve.

Eve Morgan was it for him.

He was supposed to be this tough, hard guy, who climbed mountains and took risks, but he'd never been willing to take the biggest risk of his life in fear of losing Eve.

And that's what it felt like right now.

It felt like he lost her.

Austin felt like a part of his soul was missing.

He wasn't whole anymore.

And fuck him, that hurt.

Austin didn't want to fight it anymore. He wanted to be with her, but now not having her at all...

It hurt.

And he knew, he freaking knew she was hurting too, either because she was sick, or something else and not being able to take care of her was killing him.

He'd always take care of her. He'd tuck her in with a warm blanket and keep her comfortable. Fuck, he'd even hold her hair back if she got sick.

Austin didn't care what he needed to do, he just wanted to be with Eve.

"So you bow-chika-wow-wowed and then came home. That's it?"

Austin looked at Jake, his face holding the duh expression. "I just told you that."

Jake sat up, pushing himself to the edge of the couch. "Let me get this straight. You get Eve out into nature with you. You have a grand ole time. She pees on a tree. There is some weird conversation about gnomes and there is a storm. You let the passion take over and you finally confess your feelings for her and—"

Austin froze, his heart sinking as he slumped into his chair, Jake's words hitting him hard.

Oh, shit.

"For fuck's sake." Jake's brows shot off his face as he stared at him. "Austin, please tell me you told her. Please fucking tell me you told Eve you're in love with her?" Jake asked. "And I hope to God you did it *before* you slept with her. You're a smart man, Austin. You built Anytime Adventure from the ground up. And you're sure as fuck smart enough to tell the woman you love that you are in love with her before you sleep with her."

Austin's mouth went dry, his heart beating against his chest. "I—"

"You're an idiot," Jake cut him off, snapping to his feet.

Austin's mouth opened and closed as everything fell into place, the world collapsing around him as he realized his fuck up.

"Maybe you aren't so smart after all." Jake shook his head, the disappointment written all over his face, before he turned to leave, not once looking back at Austin.

Chapter Nineteen

EVE LEANED against the counter of Own Your Curves cursing herself for what seemed like the hundredth time since Austin had dropped her off on Sunday.

That time machine was looking pretty good if you asked her.

Hiking: bad — okay, it had its good points. But she'd take those to her grave.

Peeing on a tree: bad.

Getting caught in a storm: bad, and also scary.

Sleeping with your best friend: very bad.

Have the best sex of your life: okay, that one was good.

Finally admitting to yourself you're in love with said best friend: really bad.

Not having that love reciprocated: painfully bad.

Pretending you had a client you needed to help to get out of being with said best friend: also bad.

Faking being sick and going as far as sticking a thermometer in soup to make it seem like you were running a fever only to see it was too freaking high so you needed to pop it in the freezer so your best friend wouldn't be suspicious: the worst.

Eve let out a frustrated groan. The headache she'd had since Sunday was in full force, pounding behind her eye.

Freaking A —

If the ground would just go ahead and swallow her, she'd be mighty grateful. Eve's eyes flicked to the ceiling for a split second, hoping the Universe would finally be on her side.

Nothing. Damn it.

Idiot.

What made everything worse was Austin, once again, being the absolute best friend she'd ever had, and had been willing to jump in to take care of her.

I guess this is why you don't lie. When you do, shit gets out of hand. Way worse.

Universe, please help her and her poor naïve mush of a brain.

All Eve needed was a day or two away from Austin to get her mind settled. That's it. In her defense, it'd been a lot. And, she just needed a few days, just a few to get herself back together so she could put on the happy front and pretend nothing ever happened.

That wasn't too much to ask for, was it?

There was only one problem. Who knew being away from Austin and actively avoiding him somehow made her heart hurt more?

Eve grumbled, her headache getting worse by the second.

Life wasn't supposed to end up like this.

And now here she was, fully aware of her feelings, and she hated it.

Eve hated it all.

She hated that she loved him.

She hated she'd lied to him.

She hated it was by far the best sex of her life.

She hated he'd ruined her for all men.

And she hated the thought of having to see Austin and not being able to run into his arms and tell him she loved him.

That she had always loved him.

Eve didn't know where it happened in their friendship, but it did. Eve was in love with Austin, the generous, kind, caring, annoyingly handsome Austin.

Eve wanted to scream, cry, throw up, all of the above.

Closing her eyes, the familiar ache in her chest came back as Eve thought about their ride to her apartment. As each mile passed, her anxiety heightened as she willed her heart to keep it together.

Austin seemed tense on the drive back to her apartment.

And they didn't joke about Eve being a master of jumping to conclusions for nothing.

Eve had no idea what to expect when they got back to her place. Would he want to go upstairs with her and start a what? Friends with benefits, or would he slump on her couch, order takeout, and it end up being like a regular Friday night for them?

Neither one of those options sat well with her.

Jumping to conclusions wasn't the only thing Eve did best, that would also be panicking. And boy, had she panicked.

Eve rolled her eyes at herself, thinking of her lies.

He freaking brought you soup, dumb-dumb. Gahh, why did he have to do things that just make my heart ache for him all the more?

Stupid heart.

Eve glared down at herself. *And stupid body. Did you really have to go all in? You do know we'll never be satisfied like that again now don't you?*

Stupid body.

Stupid everything.

Eve would punch herself, but it would do no good. It wouldn't change the outcome or where she was right now. Austin was back to being totally fine with everything that happened and they were still just best friends, and Eve was... just Eve.

For fuck's sake, this is why you don't fall for your best friend.

Eve banged her head on the counter. "I'm an idiot." She was destined to die alone with a hoard of cats.

I hope Marshmallow wants tons of brothers and sisters. Eve lifted her head to glare at the ceiling. *Why did you have to make him still be, well... him? He brought me soup! Freakin' good soup too. Better yet, why in the hell did you have me sleep with Austin and accept I was in love with him and him being all my good ole buddy ole pal. What episode of this sitcom are we on now?*

How in the hell am I supposed to just go back to how things were? How? Please, tell me. I'm all ears, how do I get back to B.F.M.B.F - before fucking my best friend, and all those pesky feelings coming to light? How am I supposed to pretend we're all good when I know just how fantastic it feels to be with him?

She growled deep in her throat, her fist clenching at her side. *I'd like a refund, please.*

Eve's eyes moved to the front window of her shop, seeing the beautiful day outside. Birds chirping, the sun bright, the flowers blooming.

"I guess I know where the Universe stands in all of this." Give her a break. "Bleahh. No."

That's it! No more. We're better than this.

Eve straightened, shaking her shoulders. She stuck her hand in her top lifting her boobs putting them in their perfect place. *Come get me now world. I am not going to let this tear me down. No more pity party. They had sex. It's done and we're moving on.*

Besides, it was bound to happen Eve's feelings would eventually go away. That's how adulting worked, right?

If you ignore it hard enough... poof, gone.

Magic.

Ugh. Who was she kidding? Even she didn't believe herself.

Alright, Eve. No more. We're getting ourselves back together. This is getting ridiculous. You said yourself you'd rather have him as a friend than nothing at all, so buck up. Let's do this. Harden your heart, and keep those memories of his kiss, his touch, his everything deep inside.

You've made it through every tough day you've had in your life so far, you can get through this too.

Eve's eyes glanced at her phone sitting on the counter instantly making her stomach flip. She'd been avoiding his texts, and that wasn't very best friend like of her.

Neither is sleeping together. Ahhh! Stop it.

Eve grabbed her phone, quickly unlocking it. When she spotted a few of the dating apps, a new wave of disgust hit her.

Yeah, like anyone would ever compare to Austin...

Damn. Being an adult was hard. What an absolute fucking disaster.

Eve grunted, pushing aside her phone annoyed. "And I never got my damn s'more. I mean, come on, I named my freaking cat Marshmallow. I could have at least gotten a s'more out of all this."

You got your best friend's dick, though. Eve blanched, her head jerking back. *Oh, for the love of all things.*

Eve had been doomed from the start.

And now she was left here, trying to get her life back in order so she could be the best friend again.

Even if that involved always being just Eve.

Maybe she should look back at those dating apps...

"Okay, that's enough." Mikayla walked out of the back-room, plopping folded shirts on the counter. "You and I are having ourselves a little chat. I let it go yesterday, since you seemed like you weren't in the mood. Which is understand-able, because I thought you were recovering from the hike, but this is more. I can tell. Plus, I knew something was up when Austin picked up the inventory and was surprised you weren't here making a custom piece for some mysterious client. I handle your schedule and we haven't had anyone on the books for a few weeks while you figure out the expansion." Mikayla leaned her arm onto the pile of shirts. "You haven't even told me about the trip. Was it really that bad? I'm starting to worry."

"Nothing to worry about."

"You're a horrible liar." Mikayla moved her hand to Eve's arm. "Sweetie, talk to me. What's going on?"

Eve shook her head, mustering up everything she could to keep herself together. How do you even begin to explain the shit show of the hike or the fact that she was in love with Austin? Oh, and how they'd slept together only for him to want to go back to how things were before.

How she couldn't ever look him in the eyes again knowing how his body felt against hers? How he ignited everything inside of her? How now that she'd gotten even the smallest taste of him, she'd never dream of being with another man? "It's nothing."

"Bullshit."

It *was* bullshit. Eve knew it, but what else could she say?

"Just the people I wanted to see!" Mildred came hustling into Own Your Curves like a bat out of hell on a mission. And when it came to Mildred, that was usually the case.

Freaking crap on a million crackers. Not now. Please, not now.

"My chickadees, how are you doing this fine beautiful

Tuesday?" Mildred propped her hip to rest against the counter, eyeing both of them. "Holly's birthday is coming up and since she's at the library, I wanted to run down here to see if I could order one of your new sexy, make the world fall at your feet and drool, lingerie pieces for her. I'm sure Benny Boy will be more than thrilled. I've also ordered her a new vibrato—"

"Mildred!" Mikayla snapped. "Not the time."

Mildred cocked her brow, her hand darting to her hip. "It's always the time for —" She stopped in mid-sentence, her eyes honing in on Eve. "Oh no, deary, what happened here?"

"She said nothing," Mikayla answered, sending Eve a pointed glare. "But she's lying."

"That is not the face of *nothing*," Mildred tsked, shaking her head. "Do you want me to guess, or are you gonna inform the gallery?"

The headache Eve had migrated to behind both her eyes as she stared down the old woman, while begging her brain to come up with a believable lie... although, lying had screwed her over with Austin, so maybe lying wasn't a good idea.

Eve glanced at the ceiling.

I really do want a refund at this point, please.

Eve took a deep breath, looking back at them, hoping to change the subject. Forcing a smile on her face she focused on Mildred. "I don't have any designs finalized so I can't help you on your quest to have Ben lose his mind. Sorry."

"That's not true," Mikayla corrected. "The bodysuit drove Austin wild. And we just got the fabric I ordered for it in this morning."

Hearing Austin's name made Eve's stomach bottom out.

"Ahh, now I see what's going on." Mildred nodded, giving Eve a sympathetic look. "Although, I will say I'm a little hurt you were using him for opinions rather than me." She scoffed.

"Seeing as you're in distress, I'm gonna let it slide just this once." Mildred stretched out her hands in front of her, cracking her knuckles. "Stop me if I'm wrong, and I'm rarely wrong. You don't get to my age without using your noggin." She tapped her head with her index finger. "You had your hunky outdoor lumberjack fine piece of ass of a best friend of yours help you with the new expansion. Did you try on designs for him?"

"She sure did."

"Mikayla," Eve growled.

"What? You did."

"I see, and he liked them?" Mildred gave Eve the once-over. "A little too much, I'm guessing?"

"That's not what happened," Eve grumbled, annoyed at the whole damn world, for real was she ever going to get a freaking break?

"He liked them all right," Mikayla answered for Eve. "And to get his payback for Eve torturing him, he made her go hiking this past weekend."

"It wasn't payback," Eve protested. Although it kind of was. It didn't matter now though, did it, since they both lost.

"Bleahh." Mildred shook her head. "Nothing good about the outdoors unless it involves sex—"

The groan that came from Eve was involuntary. She wouldn't have been able to stop it, even if she wanted.

Instantly, the room fell deathly silent as both sets of eyes turned on her.

Oh, crap.

As Mildred watched Eve, a devilish smile spread across her face as she punched the air. "Hot damn."

"Did you have sex with Austin?" Mikayla rushed out. "Oh my God, you did! You had sex with Austin."

"Could you both just shut up?"

"Nope," they answered in unison.

Eve glared at them, her lips thinning. Oh, for the love of all things. "Nothing happened. Can we just drop this and move on? Mildred, the only thing I have would be the bodysuit. If I agree to make you one for Holly, will you get the hell out of my shop?"

Mildred strolled around the counter like she owned the place, pulling up a chair and plopping down into it. "Not on your life, missy. All I'm missing is some popcorn."

"Fuck me."

"Sounds like Austin already did," Mikayla retorted.

"Mikayla, knock it off." The smile on her face told Eve this was only the start. Again, fuck her.

"She's right, it sounds like you took a ride on that big ole sexy lumberjack."

"Austin isn't a lumberjack. He's an outdoor man. There's a difference."

Mildred's face brightened as the corner of her mouth tugged upwards. She then reached into the pocket of her skirt, taking out a pad of paper and a pencil. "Care to tell me the difference? I hope it's in the body parts."

"Holy shit. You two are a piece of work."

"I'm waiting." Mildred tapped her pad with her pencil. "I'll take any details you've got. Please throw this old lady a bone. Holly refuses to indulge me."

"I wonder why." Eve glared at her.

"I wonder that myself." Mildred's hand went to her heart. "I'm just a wee old woman trying—"

"Mildred," Eve warned.

"Fine. It's my turn for the gossip in my knitting group. Spill and leave nothing out." She leaned forward ready to take notes.

"That's it I'm leaving."

"No, you're not." Mildred jabbed the pencil in Eve's direction. "You're gonna stand there and tell us what's got you all worked up. Was he bad in bed? I never pegged him to be one who didn't know what to do with his man meat or not knowing how to satisfy the ladies, but I will admit, although it doesn't happen often, I have been wrong."

"Seriously, please stop talking."

"I wonder how big his dick is. By any chance, do you have a picture?"

"Fuck me, you're kidding, right? Please tell me you are kidding?"

"I would never kid about such a thing." Mildred held her hand over her heart again in shock. "You should know this. Now, would you mind informing the rest of the class what's going on in that head of yours. You're a lot like Holly and I can almost guarantee it's not good whatever you're cooking up in there. Shouldn't you be jumping for joy? You finally got into that hunk's pants."

"I'm not cooking up anything other than the truth, Mildred."

"And yet something is off." The old woman cocked her brow. "Give it to me straight, my heart can take it. Is Austin lousy in the sack? Do you want me to have a talk with him on how to pleasure a —"

"For the love of all things, I am begging you to please stop talking."

"No can do. Not until you fill us in on the whole story."

"I see why Holly avoids you."

"Holly loves me."

Eve rolled her eyes. At this point, she knew there was no way of getting out of this and the sooner she told them, the sooner she could put it all behind her and move on. "There isn't much to talk about. We slept together, and it was a huge freaking mistake. Does that make you happy?"

"I doubt that," and "doubt it," was said in unison.

"Trust me on this."

Mildred crossed one of her legs over the other sitting back in her chair. "I think you're wrong, but please inform us why it was a mistake?"

"Yeah, we all knew this was bound to happen," Mikayla remarked, nodding her head.

Eve quirked her brow, staring at her employee like she'd lost her mind. "You knew what was going to happen?"

"You'd sleep together. As soon as you said he was helping you, we all knew it was gonna end up here. Only a best friend, my ass."

What! Hold up.

"She's right. Although, I didn't know he was who you chose to help with your designs." Mildred narrowed her eyes at Eve. "But, since he was, I'm not at all surprised."

Well, Eve was.

"I don't get what the problem is?" Mikayla asked. "It was always bound to end up like this, so why are you sulking over here? What are you neglecting to tell us?"

Eve closed her eyes, her heart hurting all while wishing this conversation was over. "You know what, fine. We are gonna have this talk but once it's over, we are never gonna bring it up again." She looked at both of them, glaring. "Deal?"

Neither Mildred nor Mikayla spoke.

"Deal?" Eve asked again.

"How about I agree to not tell my knitting group?"

Eve's shoulder stiffened as she groaned, wishing she was anywhere but there. "Why do I feel like that's the best I'll ever get out of you?"

"'Cause, it is. Now, missy, I'm not getting any younger. What's got your panties in a twist?"

I'm damned if I do and I'm damned if I don't, so why not just let it all out? Maybe then I can get past this disaster.

Taking a steady breath, Eve stood straighter. "I am

completely and utterly in love with Austin. My best friend. The one person I was never supposed to fall for, I fell for. I tried to deny it for years and look where that got me?"

"Laid," Mildred answered.

Eve growled in her direction but kept going. "I don't know what happened. One moment we were looking at one of the most beautiful views I'd ever seen and the next we were in a storm. Tensions were high, and it happened. It happened more than once. And it was good." She side-eyed Mildred. "Too good. I'll never be the same."

"I knew I wasn't wrong."

"Anyway, I panicked—"

"As you do," Mikayla chimed in.

Eve's eyes darted to her with a grunt. "Yeah, well, I did. At first, I freaked out. I thought we'd ruined everything, but it's hard to explain. When we were together, it was like... I don't know. It'd never been like that." Eve swallowed the pain of their passion creeping back up into her. "I never knew it could be like that. So the next morning I decided to say screw it and go for it. Let's see what could happen. Why can't a guy like Austin fall for a girl like me? Why couldn't I get my happily ever after?" Tears pricked behind her eyes as that morning replayed through her mind. "And then I walked out of the tent and he handed me a plate of scrambled eggs."

"And?"

"And what? That was it. Austin was back to being friends. Nothing more." Damn, it still hurt. She'd been such a fool to think it was finally her time.

Idiot. Party of one.

"Eggs mean friendship in your mind?" Mildred cocked her head slightly to the side, observing Eve.

"No, it was just..." she trailed off.

"Just what? I'm trying to understand where the only friends come into play."

"It's hard to explain, Mildred." Everything was hard to explain, but she would try her best. "Did I think he was going to confess his undying love for me, it would've been nice, but no," she lied, trying her best to rebuild the walls around her heart. "But I thought we'd, I don't know, talk about it. See what it meant. But there was nothing. Trust me, no matter how bad I want it, he doesn't feel the same way. And then the hike out and ride home..." She groaned. "It was so freaking awkward. I panicked again and lied about a client needing a custom piece and then I lied again and told him I was sick."

Mikayla's eyes widened. "Is that what he was talking about?"

Eve shrugged, refusing to look at her. "I've made a mess of everything."

"I think you might be wrong. I've known Austin just as long as you and I don't think—"

Mildred held up her hand stopping Mikayla from continuing. "And you think his silence on the matter was him, what? Pretending it didn't happen?"

"Wouldn't you?" Damn, this sucked. Really sucked. Eve sadly looked at the old woman, her heart breaking all over again. "But, it's fine. It's nothing I can't get over. And I am."

Mildred gave her the once-over, her brow slightly cocking. "I'm sure you are."

"Hold on, something isn't right here," Mikayla spoke up. "That's not Austin. I know this. I see the way he looks at you. I've always known this."

Eve placed her hand on top of Mikayla's shoulder. "It's friendship. I'm his best friend. I'm *just* Eve."

Mikayla gasped, her brows shooting off her forehead. "No, you're not."

"I am."

Mikayla shook her head, her eyes still wide. "You've got this all wrong. I know you do. This is coming from me. All men are pigs. I hate them and the world would be better without them but trust me. You've got it wrong with Austin. I wouldn't say that if I didn't think it. I am very much in the hate all men club, but Austin doesn't belong there."

Eve watched her, the sadness filling her all over again. "It's funny how the world changes, isn't it? Usually, you'd be on the side of fuck all men, but here you are on the opposite."

"That's because I know I'm right. Men are assholes, but Austin isn't."

Eve smiled, but it didn't reach her eyes. "You're right. Austin isn't an asshole. He's far from it. He's probably one of the best men I've ever met in my life. But that doesn't mean he has to be in love with me or even like me. What happened between us was a fling. That's it. And even though it hurts to not have your love reciprocated, it's okay. Because Austin is the best guy out there. He deserves the world and I'm lucky enough to be a part of it any way he'll let me."

Even though Eve still had that pang rush through her heart, the more she said it, the less it stung. There wasn't much more she could do about it anyway. One of these days she'll get over him or she won't.

They had a perfectly good friendship before they slept together and she admitted to herself she loved him. Thank God she hadn't admitted it out loud. There would be no coming back from that. And truth be told, it is what it is. It might hurt like hell, but what was Eve to do? You can't make someone love you. And having him as a friend was better than nothing.

Eve shuddered, while she thought about it though, friendship is where it would stop. She sure as hell would never be a booty call. Definitely not with Austin. She'd rather have her vajayjay dry up, adopt fifteen more cats than ever go down that road.

And Eve meant that.

This was only a bump in her road, a major bump, but a bump nonetheless. In a few years they'd be able to laugh about it.

Life was fine.

Life was beautiful.

"You know what you need?" Mildred interrupted her thoughts. "You need to go home, relax, and have some self-care."

That didn't sound so bad to Eve.

"Take a hot shower, put on a face mask," Mildred continued. "Masturbate—"

"Mildred!"

The old woman's eyebrows wiggled. "I can send you some links to a few movies if you'd like? It'll help take the edge off."

"Please don't." When Eve glanced back to Mildred, only to see the wicked smile on her face, Eve laughed for the first time in days.

Leave it to Mildred to somehow flip the script. "Never change."

"If I haven't changed yet, I doubt I will." Mildred pocketed the pad and pencil before standing. She walked over to Eve, pushing her shoulder toward the door. "Go on and get out of here. The least you could do for yourself is take a day. Missy over here and I will watch the shop."

Eve didn't know if she liked the idea of Mildred in her shop, she was positive she'd come back to a section of Own Your Curves dedicated to selling vibrators but taking the day for herself sounded like a good plan.

She worked hard and she owed it to herself.

Plus, Eve trusted Mikayla, so Mildred wouldn't get into too much trouble.

But this is Mildred we're talking about...

Screw it. Why not take the day for herself? Maybe she'd

246

journal out her feelings or meditate. Hey, why not get all fancy and go to the local bar for a drink?

Just because no man would ever compare to Austin didn't mean she couldn't look. And if she was feeling extra ballsy, maybe she'd open up those dating apps and see what she'd been missing.

If she was going to have to start her life over as just Eve, she was at least going to get a move on.

"I don't know what you're thinking, but I like it." Mildred nodded.

Eve laughed, grabbing her bag tossing it over her shoulder. "I just decided I am not gonna sit in my pity party. It's done and over with. I'm gonna take today and I don't know, maybe I'll head to the bar or check out the dating apps again."

"Eve—" Mikayla tried cut her off with worry in her voice.

"What's that saying? The best way to get over someone is to get under someone else?"

"That is not—"

Eve held up her hand, stopping her. "I'm joking. But I am gonna take the rest of the day. I already have Holly's measurements, and I've got some of the black material at home. I'll start planning it out."

Mildred nodded, her eyes soft. "You do that, honey. We'll take care of the shop."

Eve pointed at her, her lips thinning. "No sex toys."

Mildred waved her hands in the air. "We'll see."

"I mean it."

"Yeah, yeah," Mildred replied, pushing Eve out the door. And the moment the sun hit her face, Eve took a deep breath.

In the grand scheme of things, life wasn't so bad. This was her story, and she might not be the main character, but she sure as hell was going to live her life the best she could.

Being just Eve wouldn't be all that bad. Over time, she'd learn that being just Eve is pretty damn okay. She'd bring a lot to the world, even if it wasn't the way she thought she originally would.

And that was the thing.

No matter what the future held for her, she was going to be the best *just* Eve there ever was.

Chapter Twenty

Austin raced into Own Your Curves, barely avoiding a collision with one of the front displays. "Eve! Where are you? Eve!"

As Austin stormed through the shop headed to the office, Mikayla and Mildred walked out of the backroom. If he wasn't in a full-blown panic, he'd question why Mildred was there, but he didn't have the time, nor did he care.

"She's not here." Mikayla crossed her arms over her chest, sending him the death glare.

"Fuck!"

"I'd say so. Actually, I'd go as far as to say you really fucked this one up." Mikayla shook her head, her eyes flicking to the ceiling. "I was rooting for you. I really was."

"Down, killer," Mildred interjected, placing her hand on Mikayla's shoulder. "We don't know the whole story. We only know what Eve said." Mildred's head pivoted toward Austin. "Care to enlighten us on how you stuck your foot in it?"

Son of a bitch… damn it.

Adrenaline raced through every part of his body. His hands shook, his muscles clenched, and his brain clocked in at a million miles an hour. Austin needed to get to Eve, and that was the only thing he cared about. He could deal with them later. "I don't have time for this." Austin turned on his heel to head out the door but stopped when he heard Mildred's voice.

"Young man, you turn your ass around and march yourself over here. If you think even for a second gallivanting off the way you are will get Eve to listen to you, you're sadly mistaken. For being her so-called best friend, I wonder if you even know her at all?" Mildred mimicked Mikayla's stance, crossing her arms over her chest.

Fuck him, and fuck everything that was running through his body. He really didn't have time for this. What he needed was to get to the woman he loved and explain what she meant to him. And apologize for not saying it sooner.

He needed Eve, and he needed her right now.

Austin's eyes moved to the door once more.

"You can try, but I'm telling you right now you won't get anywhere." Mildred walked out from behind the counter, staring him down the whole time in a way that made the hair stick up on the back of his neck.

Mildred might be an old woman, but she was one not to cross. "Fuck," he growled, his fist clenching at his side.

"From what I've heard, it sounds like you already have," Mikayla blurted, her eyes scanning him up and down with disgust as she moved to stand next to Mildred. "I don't know what you did, but you really fucked up. How could you let her walk away thinking she was *just* Eve? You better tell us right now. I have enough pent-up anger from my ex, I could level you to the ground. Was she just a quick roll in the hay for you? Playing with her emotions, is that a game? I thought you were different, but I guess not. In the end, all men are nothing but trouble and you're no different."

"You've got it all wrong," Austin's words ground out of his mouth, the shock stunning him. "You've known me for years. How could you think that low of me? You know for a fact, I'd never hurt Eve—"

"And yet you did."

Mildred placed her hand on Mikayla's shoulder. "Now, missy, I know you have your own misgivings about the male species, but we need to give him a chance. You yourself said Austin would never hurt Eve when she told us what happened. Let's see what he has to say." Mildred gave him the once-over before jutting her chin out. "Get to talking, mister."

Austin didn't know what to do. It felt like everything was falling apart around him as his eyes flicked to the door once more, his adrenaline pulsing through him.

He had to get to Eve.

If I could—

"Don't even think about it."

Austin's jaw clenched as he snapped his attention back to the women. "There is nothing to talk about other than I'm an idiot."

"Agreed," they both said.

"I am in love with Eve, and I have been for a long time. And I foolishly thought after we slept together she'd know that," he grunted, realizing for the hundredth time how stupid it sounded. He really was an idiot.

Austin could punch himself in the head.

"That wasn't very smart of you."

Austin's heart slammed against his ribs. "I'm getting that now. That's why I have to talk to her. I have to tell her," he rushed out. "I need to make sure she's okay. She's sick and—"

"She's not sick."

"Yes, she is. I brought her—"

Mikayla flicked her eyes up. "You really are a dumb man."

Austin growled deep in his throat, the tension in his body rising. "If you're not gonna help, then why the hell am I still here talking to you?"

"Who said we aren't gonna help?" Mildred replied. "Groveling is only gonna get you so far. I hope you're an expert with your tongue. If not, I suggest practicing licking the brownie batter off the mixing tools. Get that tongue of yours a proper workout before you go back to Eve begging on your knees."

Austin's eyes rounded as he gawked at the old woman, his jaw nearly hitting the floor. But then again, this was *Mildred.* Clearing his throat, he stood straighter. "Rest assured, I don't need any help in that department."

Mildred's eyes gave him the once-over again. "Hmmmm."

Fuck this. This conversation wasn't getting him anywhere. "I really don't have time for this. I need to see Eve. I need to—"

"Do you love her?"

"I'd give my soul for her," Austin answered, without missing a beat. "I fully admit I am the idiot here for assuming she understood how I felt. Which does make me an idiot. I've known her long enough that I shouldn't assume anything when it comes to Eve. She's my other half, and the past two days not having my other half has nearly killed me. Now, if you don't mind, I'd really like to get back the other piece of my heart."

"Damn," Mikayla spoke, her eyes rounding. "I'd start with that. The woman you love thinks she's *just Eve* to you."

"She'd never be just Eve."

"Then go get her. Convince her she's not *just* Eve." Mildred narrowed on him for a second. "I still think you might need to practice on egg beaters though, but who am I to stop you? She's at her apartment." Mildred waved him off before turning around and headed toward the sewing room. "How many vibrators do you think we need to fill the back right corner? I bet she wouldn't even know if we added the display. Maybe we can spice it up with a few other toys. Some lube..." Mildred's voice trailed off as she walked out of the room, continuing on her quest, Mikayla following behind.

Austin stood there for a split second trying to process what he'd heard.

Screw it.

He'd let Eve deal with it, or they'd deal with it together later.

Right now, Austin had one thing he had to do: get to the love of his life.

Quickly, Austin ran out of the front door and jumped into his SUV and raced toward Eve's apartment. Nothing mattered other than getting to Eve.

Once Austin parked at her building, he took the stairs two at a time, screeching to a halt in front of Eve's door. Hastily, he grabbed his key and unlocked it, thanking every God out there Eve didn't have the deadbolt in place again.

He flung open the door, stepping through. "Eve!"

As Austin made his way inside, Marshmallow sat at the entrance, staring him down, only blinking once and then focusing back on him. Austin would be lying if he said the 'you're my next meal' look on the cat's face didn't make him shudder. "I'm sure your mom told you all about it. I get it, I'm the enemy. I promise you can take me out as soon as I fix it with your mom."

"Her mom says there is nothing that needs to be fixed."

Eve walked into the room wearing black leggings that molded perfectly to her legs and a formfitting green top that plunged low, showcasing her ample chest.

Fuck, she was beautiful. Was it possible for her to become more beautiful in the few days he hadn't seen her?

Austin's eyes scanned Eve up and down, taking in every last inch of her.

Holy shit.

"Austin, what are you doing here? Shouldn't you be at

work?" He took a step closer to her, making Eve hold up her hand. "Cough, cough. I'm sick. Don't come any closer."

"Bullshit."

Eve's eyes widened as he took another step toward her. "You aren't sick. You never were sick."

"I – I..."

Austin grabbed Eve's arm, pulling her into his embrace. He held her tightly to him, his head resting on top of hers.

And for the first time in two days, his body relaxed. To have her in his arms again... "I'm so sorry."

Eve placed the palms of her hands on his chest before pushing Austin away. "Why are you sorry? You have nothing to be sorry about."

It was at that exact moment he watched as Eve stood a little straighter, and he could see her building the walls around herself. He shook his head, his stomach bottoming out at the thought of her closing herself off to him. "No. No, don't do that."

"I'm not doing anything other than trying to figure out why you're here instead of at work."

Austin shook his head. His brave, stupid Eve.

However, as he looked at her, Austin's stomach bottomed out. Seeing the anguish on Eve's face was enough to do him in. And knowing he was the one who caused it made him feel even worse.

For fuck's sake, he'd been an idiot.

He should punch himself.

"How could I be at work when the only thing I want in this world is to be with you—"

"Don't." Eve's hands shot up as she took a step back.

Hell no.

Absolutely not.

The fact Eve backed away from him was like a knife going

straight through his heart. "Babe, I'm so fucking sorry I didn't say it sooner and I made you question anything—"

"Austin," she cut him off.

The tears he saw in Eve's eyes broke him.

"I'm in love with you." The moment the words were out of Austin's mouth, Marshmallow leaped through the air, his ankle the cat's only target.

Chapter Twenty-One

THERE WASN'T any time for Eve to process Austin's words since her cat decided at that exact moment to unleash her master plan. Although a part of her wanted to thank Marshmallow for momentarily getting her out of whatever disaster was about to happen, Eve jumped into action.

"Marshmallow, no!" Eve lunged toward her cat. The same cat going to town on Austin's leg. However, instead of jumping away, her cat doubled down, wrapping her arms around Austin's calf, only to start kangaroo kicking while biting him.

"Ouch. Fuck. Okay, I deserved that, but damn." Austin reached down and unhooked Marshmallow from his leg. He lifted his pants to check for bleeding while glaring at the cat. "Really? I know you hate me, but did you have to do that right now? Couldn't you have waited a few minutes? I'm trying to pour my heart out here and convince your mother I'm in love with her."

"Hey, don't yell at her. She's protecting me," Eve rushed out, picking her cat up into her arms, doing her best to ignore the part where Austin said he was in love with her. However, the second Eve got ahold of her cat, Marshmallow hissed batting at Eve's face before jumping down and running toward the bedroom. "That was rude." Eve narrowed her eyes in the direction her cat took off in.

And to think I was just about to thank you.

"Why does your cat always have it out for me?" Austin grumbled, checking out the damage to his leg.

"She's a good girl." Eve scoffed as she took a few steps over to Austin to inspect his leg, but stopped as his words ran through her mind.

Deciding she didn't want to deal with it, she twisted away and headed toward her bathroom. "I'll get something to clean it up."

You've got this. Just laugh everything off and move on with your life, Eve.

She'd only made it a step before Austin grabbed her arm, pulling her back to him. "Babe."

"I need to get you cleaned up," Eve squeaked, willing everything inside of her to take a chill pill since it felt like she was seconds from breaking in half. Why did he have to show up here? Why did he have to say those words?

They weren't true. No matter how bad Eve wanted them to be, she knew they weren't.

She wanted to scream. How could you work on getting over the person you loved, when they kept showing up solidifying reasons why she'd fallen in love with him in the first place?

Eve searched his eyes trying to figure out what to do next. Austin somehow, someway knew she'd been upset, and Austin being Austin needed to fix it. That's what he did and always did.

He always fixed it.

But sometimes you can't fix everything.

See, he really was an amazing friend. He'd lie about loving

her just to make her feel better. Although Eve wasn't a big fan of that.

Once this all blew over, she'd have to talk to him about it.

As Eve did her best to keep herself in control, her mind raced. *You should've known he'd show up here. This is Austin. He's your best friend for a reason, dumb dumb.*

Come to think of it, Eve had to give it to Austin, he'd waited almost forty-eight hours to rush to her side. Even if she was sick for real, she knew he'd only stay away for so long. Austin really was the most stand-up guy in the world, and Eve loved that about him, even if it did complicate her trying to keep her distance.

Who am I kidding? You really are an idiot.

Eve's eyes shot to her deadbolt on the door. It'd kept him away Sunday night, maybe if she'd—

No, no more of that line of thinking. Buck up, Eve, we're doing this. Harden your heart because this was bound to happen sooner rather than later.

"Eve, stop."

Austin reached for her hand, but she yanked it away. Eve knew they had to have this conversation to move past it, but that didn't mean she was ready for touching.

"Don't walk away from me." Austin's eyes were filled with so much emotion, it made Eve nearly choke. "Not now, babe."

"I'm not walking away. I'm helping you."

Austin cocked his head to the side, examining her, and as he did, it made her skin prickle. Damn, this was harder than she thought it would be.

"Eve, babe, I know I should've said it before and I'm sorry I made you think anything else. But you gotta know. I'm *in* love with you." He grabbed her hand, pulling it to his chest placing it right on top so she could feel his heartbeat. "You own my heart, Eve. Every beat is for you. I am madly in love with you. You're mine. You've always been mine, even when I was too stupid to claim you—"

"No." Eve jerked her hand back, her own heart racing as it slammed against her rib cage, the blood rushing to her ears. "No. No. That's... no. You don't love me, Aust—"

"Yeah, I do," he cut her off. "You don't get to tell me I'm not in love with you."

"I do when it's not true." Eve's chest squeezed, her body temperature rivaling a volcano as she shook her head, refusing to listen.

Universe, I'd really appreciate some help here. I know we've had our off days, but come on. I'm begging. I'd either take the time machine, or you know, death. Either is fine. I'm not picky right now. Just let me survive this, even if my heart is only somewhat intact.

If I promise to never call you a mean name again, will you —

"It *is* true. I'm in love with you, Eve Morgan."

Screw you, Universe.

That's it.

This had to stop.

This had to stop before Eve started to believe it. "No, you're not. You only *think* you're in love with me because I turned you on wearing the designs I made. You're mistaking love with lust, and I get it. I might be bigger, but I'm sexy as hell. We let the tensions get the better of us and we had sex." She cleared her throat, straightening her shoulders. She could do this and once it was over, they'd both be better. "It happened. We can either pretend it didn't or accept it did and move on. But please don't pacify me by saying you're in love with me. That doesn't help anyone. Just because I foolishly fell for yo—" Eve stopped herself as she did her best to stay strong as she spoke her next words. "I'm okay with being *just* Eve. I've been just Eve my whole life. This isn't anything new."

Austin stared at her wide-eyed with his mouth open. "I don't even know where to start with that."

"How about not at all? Let's just move on. We can pretend none of this happened. I can put on a movie and make some popcorn—"

"Move on?" Austin blinked at her, all the color draining from his face. "No. Fuck no. I know what you're doing here. You're putting on a brave front but you aren't listening to me. I am in love with you. Full stop." His face contorted, his brows pulling together as he stared her down. "And please explain to me why you being bigger has any bearing on whether I'm in love with you or not?"

"People like you don't fall for people like me," Eve shouted, her resolve tipping over to anger.

Anger at Austin.

Anger at the Universe.

And anger at herself for wanting to believe his words.

Austin took a step back as if she'd burned him, the hurt etched all over his face. "What do you mean, people like me?"

Why was he making this so damn difficult, couldn't he just leave this all alone?

Fuck, she wanted to scream. Taking a strained breath, she waved her hands between them. "Overly attractive hot guys are not supposed to fall in love with whatever the fuck I am," she snapped out, angry that once again Eve had to be reminded how she would only ever be *just* Eve.

"Since when have you ever given a shit about what is *supposed* to happen? You preach that from the top of your lungs, all day, every day."

Eve's eyes rounded, Austin's words hitting her hard, causing her stomach to bottom out.

"Fuck, Eve. I'm *in* love with you. I've been in love with you longer than I even know. I don't give a flying fuck what society thinks and you shouldn't either. That's not the Eve I know and love. And here's the thing, babe. I know I'm mostly to blame for this. I'll admit I should've said it a lot sooner, but I'm a dumb man. Not that me being a dumb man is an excuse, but it's true. Fuck, man. How in the hell could you think of yourself as *just* Eve when it comes to me?" She felt like Austin's eyes were piercing directly into her soul. "You could never be *just* Eve. It's you. It's always been you. You'll never be *just* Eve. Because you're *my* Eve. My other half. And yeah, you fucking drove me wild wearing your test pieces. It was simultaneously the best and the worst moment of my life."

When Eve opened her mouth to speak, he stopped her with a sharp look. "I only say worst because I couldn't act on what I was feeling. It took everything inside of me not to untie that fucking bow and finally have you. Do you know I nearly rubbed myself raw fantasizing about us? About you. I think you're by far one of the sexiest people on this planet but newsflash, babe, I thought that before you ever walked out of your bedroom wearing the lingerie. But you turning me on doesn't even scratch the surface of the hold you have on my heart. I think somewhere deep down I've always known it would be you, but I was too fucking scared of losing the best thing that'd ever happened to me in my life, so I ignored it. I pushed it aside. But you can only fight your feelings for so long. And when you started talking about the dating apps, and then—" Austin's fists clenched. "Fuck, you'd be wearing your designs for *them* and *not* me."

"That's —"

"Sure, I laughed that first night when you told me about the date who spun you around and ripped your favorite dress," Austin growled, his nostrils flaring. "That fucker. You still need to give me his name so I can take care of that."

Eve watched as he took control of himself, taking in a deep breath before looking at her again.

"I was an idiot, Eve. I didn't realize you talking about

another guy would cause a wave of possessiveness within me. And that's on my dumb ass. I lied to myself saying it didn't bother me that you went out with some guy instead of hanging out with me because I was too much of a pussy to see what was right in front of my face this whole time. Instead I sat on your couch, irritated you chose to hang out with someone other than me." He grunted, his jaw tight. "I could have lost you to some faceless asshole. What if that date had been perfect? I almost lost my chance with you because I was a fucking idiot."

"Austin..." It was hard to speak, hell it was hard to breathe. His words rattled around her brain as Eve tried to make sense of them.

The way he looked at her right now... it was... Oh God. Eve swallowed, her stomach tightening.

"I was so frustrated. I was pissed you were on those dating sites. I was also pissed guys were sending you pictures of their junk. The only dick you should be looking at is *mine*."

Eve's eyes involuntarily flicked to his crotch causing her cheeks to heat.

"And I was fucking pissed you weren't mine. I was fighting myself every step of the way because I'm a moron. Do you know I'd fly through the week just to get to you on Friday night? I spend every free moment I have with *you*. Because I am fucking in love with you." He threw his hands in the air. "Fuck! If you think about it, we've been dating this whole time. The only thing we were missing was the sex. And me, being the stupid man that I am thought once we added that in over the hike, it was a done deal. We'd do everything we always did, but now I got to call you mine. Because that's what you are, Eve Morgan. You're mine. So no, you don't get to tell me I'm not in love with you. 'Cause looking back, it's safe to say I've been in love with you from the moment I walked into

Own Your Curves. And I am so fucking sorry for ever making you think otherwise."

Eve stared at him, her heart pounding against her chest as his words echoed through every part of her. "You aren't supposed to fall for your best friend."

"Tough shit." Austin grabbed her pulling her in, bringing his lips down on hers in a searing kiss. A kiss that rivaled every single one they'd had before. This was the kind of kiss someone that was starving gave to their only salvation. She melted into him, their mouths becoming one.

Austin jerked his head back, his movements sharp as he looked directly into her eyes. "Do you love me? Tell me that you love me, too."

The tension around them was thick, but Eve couldn't deny it. And hearing what Austin just said, she couldn't think. She couldn't process.

She'd fought falling in love with him because you weren't supposed to fall in love with your best friend. And when you add in how annoyingly perfect and handsome Austin was, it just added fuel to the fire. Men like him didn't fall for women like her.

But that's the thing.

Men like Austin... There was no one in the world like him. Austin Flynn was more than a best friend. He didn't care about her size, he didn't care her cat enjoyed messing with him. He cared about her. He cared if she was safe and happy.

He supported her like no other ever had.

And he was right. When had she ever given a shit about what society thought or what was supposed to happen? Eve built her whole career around going against that notion.

Oh God, she'd been an idiot too.

"I can see it in your eyes." He cupped her face in his hands, kissing her once more.

"Austin," Eve whispered.

Instead of letting her continue, he brought his lips to hers again, sealing them into another passion-filled kiss. "You forgot something, babe. I'm your best friend. I know you better than you know yourself. We were both stupid for us to take this long to get here, but we're finally here. We can start now. This is our time."

Eve's eyes filled with tears as she looked into the eyes of the man she loved. "I didn't want to love you. I didn't want to fall in love with you and watch you fall in love with someone else. I kept my feelings locked away because I never thought I'd be good enough for someone like you. I didn't want to be the big girl that pined after her attractive male best friend. But somewhere along the line, even though I tried to deny it, that's what I became. I don't know when my heart became yours, but it did."

Her pain from the past came rushing forward as Eve spoke her next words, her tears finally falling over the rims of her eyelids. "I've been the side piece before, Austin. It hurt. But at the time, I didn't love myself enough to stand up for me." Eve jabbed her finger into her chest. "When we slept together and the next morning it just seemed like everything went back to normal. I just couldn't do that again. I didn't want—"

"Eve," he cut her off, grabbing her hand pulling her into his arms. "I'm so sorry. I should've told you that morning I loved you. You would never be a sidepiece to me. You're my *whole* piece. Everything went back to normal because we are meant to be, babe. Things with you *are* normal. They *are* easy. That morning after we'd slept together, I felt whole for the first time in my life. You completed me and I was an idiot not to say the words. I cannot stress that enough. I should've said it right then and there. I will regret that for as long as I live."

As a tear fell down Eve's cheek Austin wiped it away with the pad of his thumb. "For being your best friend, I did a shitty job forgetting you jump to conclusions, and sometimes you need the actual words."

"Don't put all the blame on you," Eve stated, resting her head on his chest, feeling like a fool herself. "I could've asked."

Austin held her close for a second before pulling back, looking her softly in the eyes. "Babe, you and I both know that wouldn't have been the case. I can guess the second you popped out of the tent and I handed you breakfast you assumed we were just... I don't know screwing around in the heat of the moment. Something along those lines."

"Am I that obvious?" The corner of her mouth rose as she chuckled.

Austin kissed her before resting his forehead against hers. "Just to your best friend."

They stood there in each other's arms for a few moments before Eve spoke. "What do we do now?"

"We be in love. It's you and me against the world." Austin kissed her again. "I'm in love with everything about you. From your insistent need to talk during every movie, to your cat who wants to kill me, to the fact that your whole life's mission has been to make others feel beautiful when society does a shit job and tears them down. I am madly in love with you, and if you can forgive me, I want to continue loving you for the rest of my life."

"I didn't get my s'more," she blurted, her smile growing from ear to ear as she wiped away the last bit of her tears.

Austin barked out a laugh, kissing the top of her head. "I'll make it up to you."

"I doubt it." Eve snorted, a half-smile on her lips. "I should rethink being in love with you. If you can't deliver on the s'mores, what good are you gonna be?"

"You little shit." Austin grabbed her waist, picking her up and tossing her over his shoulder just as he'd done the night she said he couldn't pick her up.

"Put me down you, Neanderthal."

"Hell no. I'm never putting you down. In fact, I plan on making up for lost time and do what I wanted to do when we got back from hiking." Austin marched straight toward Eve's bedroom, his hand on her ass, keeping her still.

Eve was about to yell at him, but before she could, Eve found herself flying through the air. "Austin!" She landed on her bed with a bounce. "That was rude!"

"Nah, that was the start of foreplay."

"I need to get you a dictionary."

Instead of laughing, Austin sobered, his face serious as he stared at her. "If there is ever a problem between us again, don't shut me out. The past two days nearly killed me, Eve. It hurt not having you near me. It felt like a piece of my soul was missing."

The air in the room around them thickened as she nodded. "I felt that too. Even though my heart hurt, being away from you hurt just as much."

"Don't ever lie to me again."

"I'm sorry. I didn't know what to do. My heart hurt."

Austin closed his eyes, and she could see him battling with himself. "I'm sorry I ever made your heart hurt."

"I think we can agree we're both sorry. I'll never shut you out again," she promised, her heart filling with all the love she had for him.

"Good."

Eve's eyes scanned up and down his body, her skin heating. "We have a lot to make up for and what a better time than to start right now..."

There was no point in wasting another moment. Not when Eve Morgan had the love of her life standing above her, reminding her love was meant for everyone, *including* her.

Austin's eyes heated a promise-filled smile on his face. "Babe, my plan was to bring you back here, shower *together*, and then show you how much I love you," he stated matter-of-fact.

There was no denying it as she saw the love Austin had for her in his eyes.

Eve quickly pushed herself onto her elbows, her brow cocked. "What's stopping you from showing me now?"

Austin growled deep in his throat as he reached behind his neck, pulling his shirt over his head giving Eve a view she would never grow tired of.

"I plan on it."

Chapter Twenty-Two

AUSTIN POSITIONED his knee on the edge of the bed, his hands going to his belt as he kept his eyes glued to Eve as he undid it. "My Eve."

"Prove it."

"Oh, babe, you have no idea what you unleash inside of me." His right hand braced himself on the mattress as he began to crawl toward her.

However, before he made any progress, Eve sat up. "Wait."

Austin's brow cocked as he watched her. "What do you mean wait?"

Instead of answering him, Eve jumped off the bed and ran to her sewing bag in the corner. She looked over her shoulder at him, a devilish smile on her face. "I'll be right back." With that, she ran out of the bedroom leaving Austin still crouching on the bed a little confused. After a few seconds, he flipped over to sit, his brows furrowing together.

Huh.

That just so happened to also be the moment Marshmallow appeared from under the bed. She stretched her body before turning to face Austin. The cat sat perfectly still, staring him down as she licked his lips.

"Are you here to attack me?"

Marshmallow blinked once, keeping her eyes on Austin.

"Great, can you make it quick? I got a lot of time to make up for with your mom. I'm trying to make her a happy woman. I'd appreciate it if you'd give me a break for once."

Austin watched Marshmallow look him up and down before standing and strutting off to the living room, her tail flicking in the air.

"Okay then. I'm going to consider this a truce, possibly even a win."

"I'd hope so." Eve walked into the bedroom wearing one of her designs that had nearly given him a heart attack.

"Oh, fuck." Damn, she looked good. She had on the robe she'd made, the one that had the little tie between her breasts. The same one he'd been fantasizing about. Fuck him, his dick throbbed as his body heated.

Eve's mischievous smile spread from ear to ear. "I hope that's what we're about to do."

Austin shot off the bed, a primal growl coming from deep within his chest. He took two steps to stand in front of her. "This..." His voice was deep and demanding. "This has given me an ulcer. I can't even tell you the number of times I've imagined reaching my hand out and untying this." Austin's hand moved to the bow, gently pulling on the ribbon. "I'd be slow. Meticulous. I'd let the bow undo itself."

The ribbon untied, opening to reveal Eve hadn't put on the bodysuit underneath. His heart pounded against his chest as he gave her the once-over, her breasts on full display. The only thing she had on was a thin pair of black panties that matched the robe.

Austin groaned, his eyes closing as he took a deep breath.

"This is by far the best present I've ever gotten in my life."

His hands moved to her shoulders gently opening the robe the rest of the way before slowly pushing the material off her shoulders, letting the robe fall to the floor. "I must have been a very good boy to deserve you."

"Maybe." Eve smirked as she winked his way.

Austin sucked in his breath through his teeth. "Babe, you love to play with fire, don't you?"

His eyes meet hers and the moment they did, Eve's breath hitched, her eyes widening. "Now, I think you get it."

He cupped her face in his hands bringing his lips to hers. Moving her slightly to the side Austin intensified their kiss, pouring everything he had into it.

He'd been such a fucking fool. "I'm never letting you go." He pulled away, looking into her eyes.

Austin's hands caressed down her body stopping at her waist, before picking her up and tossing her onto the bed. "Mine," he growled, glancing down at her in nothing but her panties.

Fuck, she was beautiful. Every part of her.

"Yours."

Hearing the word made his chest tighten. He could have lost this. He could've lost it all. The thought alone made his stomach knot and his heart ache. It might've taken them a while to get here, but it was Eve. It had always been Eve. "Always."

Austin crawled up the bed. When he reached her lips, he kissed her, hoping to convey everything he was feeling.

Eve moaned, letting him deepen their kiss, allowing it to consume both of them.

This was Eve, *his* Eve.

And this was only the beginning.

Austin pulled back and glanced down at her, his hand going to between her breasts, resting there. As he felt her heart beating against his palm he looked Eve in the eyes. "You're so fucking beautiful."

The air surrounding them thickened even more, the tension high as he marveled at her heartbeat against his hand. "And you're mine."

Eve let out a tiny gasp, her eyes focusing on his, and he knew she understood what he was saying.

His hand trailed down her stomach, letting his fingers caress her soft skin.

He'd never get tired of this.

Once he reached the top of her panties, he smirked, admiring the design. "I like the new addition you've made." His eyes flicked to hers, his smirk turning into a full-blown toothy grin. "I'm sorry to inform you, though. You're gonna have to make more." With that, Austin fisted the material, twisting his hand, ripping it with ease.

"That was the prototype!"

"Oops." Austin's eyes brightened as he failed to hold back his promise-filled smirk.

Eve pushed herself onto her elbows, glaring at him. "You have zero remorse. Ya jerk."

"It was in my way." Austin shrugged, his eyes scanning down her body. As she laid there completely naked in front of him, he swore he'd never seen a more beautiful sight in his life.

This was *his* Eve and he was going to enjoy every last second of it.

However, as he went to position himself between her legs Eve stopped him.

"If we're gonna play like that, then your pants are in *my* way." Eve sat up, shooting to her knees. She quickly grabbed Austin's shoulders and pushed him so he fell onto his back.

"If I'd known you were this demanding in bed, I wouldn't have waited this long. Fuck, Eve. Damn." His skin heated as his dick throbbed, begging to be inside of her. "My little wild-cat. Now I know where Marshie gets it from."

Eve laughed, her hands going to the waist of his pants. "She is feisty." She winked at him. "And so am I." Eve quickly undid his pants, hooking her fingers in the top of his boxer briefs before pulling them down his legs, his dick instantly springing free.

"Babe," he hissed, his body tingly at the sensation of the air hitting him.

"Mine." Eve looked into his eyes just as he'd done to her.

The moment she licked her lips anticipation coursed through him, sending every nerve ending he had on fire.

Fuck.

Eve positioned herself between his legs, her hand going to the base of his shaft. "Don't you think it's about time I returned the favor?"

The feelings racing through him were too much. "You don't have to." He gritted his teeth, peering down at her between his legs, his heart pounding in his chest.

Eve licked her lips. "Time for talking is over."

He tossed his head back, closing his eyes as he begged the Universe to give him some control.

However, the moment she kissed the tip, his eyes shot open, his muscles tightening as he looked down. "Eve."

"That's my name," she whispered, blowing lightly over the head making Austin's entire body shudder in response.

Oh, fuck.

He couldn't breathe as she kissed the underside before finally encasing her lips around him, swallowing him down. Austin's eyes rolled to the back of his head, as his hand reached out fisting her hair as Eve worked him with her mouth.

"Fuck, babe," he panted.

The sensations. The feelings. Oh God, it was too much. The moment she wrapped her hand around him, he snapped.

Her mouth felt too good. The number of times he'd pictured exactly this didn't even hold a candle to the real thing.

Fuck.

Clenching his teeth, he sat up, pushing at Eve's shoulder. "Stop."

Eve gawked at him, his dick still in her mouth, and fuck him it was too much. He scooted back, causing Eve to release him with a pop.

"Why?"

"'Cause I don't want to come in your mouth after I finally tell you I love you," he growled, watching her cheeks heat.

Eve sat back, her breasts bouncing as she did. She then used the pad of her thumb to wipe her swollen bottom lip before putting it in her mouth. "Fair enough." The corner of her lip quirked up. "Although, I don't think I've actually said the words."

That little shit.

Austin's growl echoed throughout the room as he grabbed hold of her, flipping them so she was on her back, her arms pinned above her head. "Why must you insist on messing with me?"

Austin looked down at her, his eyes heated as his body hummed. She was going to kill him. He knew it.

Eve's smile grew wide spreading across her face. "It's fun."

"I'll show you fun." Austin's lips were on hers in an instant, making her laugh.

"You're going to be the death of me."

"Sounds like a plan, but can you wait another forty-plus years? We finally got here. I don't want it to be over too soon."

"I'm gonna tie you to this bed for the next *sixty* years," he roared, making Eve's eyes widen as she bit her bottom lip.

Fuck him, she liked the idea. And damn if he didn't like it too.

He leaned down kissing along the nape of Eve's neck as he spoke. "Don't forget, babe, I'm a master of tying knots. It comes with the territory."

"Damn, I feel like I'm missing out. I wish I had some rope here."

Austin moved back, winking at her. "Don't worry, babe. We've got tons of time and I have lots of rope." He lowered his head again, kissing along her neck before biting her collarbone.

Eve gasped, moving so he would have more room.

"What you do to me..." Austin let his words trail off as he licked where he'd just bitten.

"You talk an awful lot of game for someone who isn't delivering."

Eve's comment made Austin jump back his eyes rounding as he shook his head. "So brave, and yet so fucking stupid."

"Hey—"

She had no time to argue as Austin grabbed her hips, flipping her onto her knees. He used the palm of his hand to push the upper part of her back, forcing Eve onto the mattress. He quickly moved behind her, using his knees to kick her legs open giving him the most perfect view of her ass high in the air.

"Austin."

"I believe you were the one who said the time for talking was over." His fingers trailed down the middle of Eve's back, brushing over her plump ass before seeking out her core. "So wet."

She pushed back against his fingers, causing a hiss to escape from her.

Austin's hand went to his dick as he worked himself before lowering his lips to her core, flicking his tongue over her clit.

"Austin, please," she begged, pushing into him.

"I just need a little taste, that's all," he murmured low in his throat knowing the hum of his voice would send an intense wave of sensation through her clit.

"Austin!"

Ignoring Eve's plea, he sucked her nub into his mouth while working his dick up and down. He'd never get enough of this.

"I... oh God."

He flicked his tongue around her clit. "My Eve." As he felt her legs quiver, he knew she was close.

"I need—"

Austin instantly stopped, pulling his head back.

"No!" Eve snapped her head around, glaring at him from over her shoulder.

He tsked, his head shaking. "Sorry, babe, that's what you get for lying to me." His fingers brushed against her swollen lips, making her gasp.

"I'll kill you."

"No, you won't." When she lifted herself up to flip over, Austin stopped her, his hand shooting to the middle of her back pinning her down once again. He grabbed the base of his dick, dancing it along Eve's seam, before bouncing it onto her sensitive clit.

His fist tightened around his dick as he lined himself up. He had every intention of slowly entering her, but Eve had other ideas. The moment he was at her core, she pushed her ass back, forcing him in. "Fuck." Austin grabbed her hips, her walls clenching around him.

"I'm trying. Dear Lord, I'm trying."

As Austin thrust inside her, he kept one hand on her hip. The other he moved to the middle of her back, keeping her steady.

"Please, oh God."

"Mine." Austin's hand trailed up her back to the base of her neck, letting his fingers spread into her hair before closing his fist, pulling her head back making her gasp out as he rode her.

"Yes!" Eve screamed as she met him thrust for thrust. "Yes, please yes. Harder."

His movements were fast and precise as he took her. "*My* Eve." He let go of her head, his hands going to her waist, helping guide her.

"*My* Austin." At her words, Eve's walls clenched around him. "Yesss!"

Eve was close, he knew it. And fuck him, he wanted to feel her come all over his dick. No, he needed to feel her come. Just like he'd done in the tent, Austin grabbed Eve, flipping them so she was facing him.

Eve didn't miss a beat as her hands went to his chest as she used him for leverage.

"Yes, please yes." Her legs vibrated around Austin's hips.

"Give it to me," he growled, pushing inside her, his muscles clenching.

"I can't, I need..."

He knew what she needed.

Austin took hold of her shoulders pushing Eve back so she'd fall the opposite way, her hands going to his legs. Looking up, he nearly choked at the view of his beautiful Eve open to him on full display as he watched his dick move in and out of her.

The muscles in his neck strained as he reached his hand to her core, finding her clit. He rubbed hard and fast, as his own body began to betray him.

She felt too good.

He flung his head back, closing his eyes as he willed his body to not lose control. But how could he not?

This was the woman he loved and would love for the rest of his life. "Eve!"

She sat up, looking him in his eyes, and that was the

moment he lost it. Austin's hands went to her hips, guiding her up and down. "I can't—"

He didn't have to worry, though, since she was right there with him. Her legs tightened around his, as he slammed her hips down into him, keeping her still as they both came with such force it almost knocked the wind out of him.

Holy hell.

If it was going to be like this with Eve each time, he was going to need to get his heart checked out... holy shit.

He panted, sweat dripping from his body as pulled her into his arms making Eve collapse onto him.

As he held her close, he moved them so Eve was laying right next to him, his leg resting over the top of hers. "What you do to me..." He shook his head.

She smirked. "Right back atcha."

As Austin looked into her eyes, he saw the love there making his heart clench.

He was whole.

Eve made him whole.

Eve made him a better person. She always had. He'd been an idiot for waiting as long as he did, but Austin knew no matter how many mistakes he'd made when it came to Eve, she was his world. And he'd stop at nothing to prove that to her, time and time again.

Gently, Austin brushed the hair out of her face tucking it behind her ear. "I love you."

Eve's smirked turned into a warm smile, her eyes shining bright. "I love you too." She kissed the tip of his nose. "Took us long enough to get here."

Austin chuckled, making his chest bounce. "But we're here." He held her face in his hand. "It's you and me against the world, babe."

"Always."

A half-smile formed on Austin's lips. "Speaking of

which..." He looked at her, his eyes lazy as he took her in. "Mildred is putting up a sex corner in at the shop. When I left she was trying to figure out how many vibrators to buy."

"Oh, fuck me!" Eve tossed her head back, falling onto the pillow as her arms flung through the air.

Austin took that as an opportunity to pin her under him. "It'll be my pleasure."

Epilogue

SIX MONTHS LATER

"I HATE YOU."

"You love me." Austin laughed as he spun to Eve with a massive smile on his face while the snow fell around them.

"Not right now, I don't," Eve grumbled. "Can you please tell me why we are hiking in the freakin' snow?"

Austin shrugged, his smile growing even wider. "'Cause you didn't like the hiking we did in the heat last time."

Eve was going to kill him if he didn't wipe that smug look off his face. Better yet, if her hands weren't frozen, she'd do it herself. "And you thought the snow would be better? I'm gonna freeze my tits off."

Austin scanned her body up and down, his eyes holding far too much enjoyment in the situation. "But, are you hot?"

He was a dead man. "No, but I can't feel my toes and I'm pretty sure I'm gonna die of frostbite."

Austin walked toward her, pulling Eve into his arms, the snow crunching under his feet. "Good thing I get to warm you up in our sleeping bag, then."

Eve jerked out of his embrace, sending him a death glare. "Oh no, mister, if you think I'm getting naked in this weather you are dead wrong. I'd rather get eaten alive than strut around here in my birthday suit."

"Babe," Austin growled, his eyes filling with heat. "I can promise you'll be getting eaten all right."

Eve waved her hands in the air. "No touchy!"

"You didn't say that last night."

"Austin!" Eve crossed her arms over her chest, her eyes narrowing on him. "You know, you've gotten very cocky since I let you get into my pants."

At her words, Austin threw his head back, barking out a deep laugh that echoed around them. "I've always been this way and you know it. I just get the added bonus of knowing how good it feels to slide between your legs now."

Eve's eyes nearly popped out of her head as her mouth hung open. "Dear Lord, you're as bad as Mildred."

"Hey, you could have told her to remove the display. It's not my fault you didn't." Austin laughed again, grabbing Eve's arms encouraging her to continue on the trail.

"Yeah right. You ever try to tell Mildred she had to do something?"

"Good point."

As they walked through the snowy forest, Eve grunted, her face frozen and her body cold.

What a freaking whirlwind.

It'd taken Mildred less than two days to have, as she liked to put it, *the sex corner* in her shop up and running. It'd gone up right next to the expansion with the lingerie pieces Eve kept in stock.

And as much as Eve wanted to deny it, the woman might be a horny old bat, but she'd been right. Own Your Curves turned a bigger profit in the last quarter than it ever had before. Eve could barely keep the *sex corner* stocked. She'd ended up acquiring a crap ton more clients with most of them wanting custom pieces as well.

Almost to the point of Eve needing to hire someone to help her and Mikayla. But all in all, Eve didn't mind. The idea she now had a hand in making everyone truly feel beautiful in their own skin meant the world to her.

It's why she started Own Your Curves to begin with.

The expansion, and subsequently the sex corner, had been the best thing she'd ever done in her life for her boutique.

Plus, she'd be lying if she said it wasn't an added bonus she got to model all her new designs for Austin. Although, Eve quickly realized she needed to make two prototypes of each new design she came up with.

The man had zero remorse for taking her pieces and ripping them to shreds without a care in the world he'd ruined them.

The jerk.

She loved him, but he was also a piece of freaking work. Then again, she guessed he always had been. It had just gotten a little worse now.

Eve huffed as she made her way down the snowy path. "And while we're having this heart-to-heart while you try to kill me out here, can you *please* stop sending me dick pics? For the love of all things, I almost opened one of them while Mikayla was looking over my shoulder the other day. Thank God I know better not to click when I see *Austin sent you an image* pop up on my phone."

"Not on your life." Austin pivoted toward her, his toothy grin on full display. "Only dick you'll ever see now is mine. I gotta keep reminding you of that."

"Mildred thinks otherwise."

Austin growled low in his throat, his brows pulling together. "Is she still sending you links to porn sites?"

"She never stopped."

Austin's lips thinned. "I'll have a talk with her," he grunted.

"Please don't. It's best to just leave her be. Lord knows what her and Mikayla get up to when they're in the shop alone."

Austin side-eyed Eve. "I don't think Jake would be thrilled to know Mikayla's looking at porn sites."

"Well, Jake doesn't get much say about what she does or doesn't do, does he?" Eve's brows shot up. "Until he makes a move, he gets to keep his mouth shut."

Austin's smirk reappeared as his eyes lit. "I'll be sure to inform him on Monday."

"You do that."

"I still don't want you looking at any other dick than mine," he reiterated, making Eve roll her eyes.

"Yeah, I know. You promptly deleted all my dating apps after we said we were in love with each other. You didn't even let me check my messages first."

"Damn right I did. You're mine, Eve. End of story."

Here we go again. Secretly though, Eve loved it when he got all growly and possessive, but that didn't mean she couldn't egg him on.

"You can put the Neanderthal shit away there, bud. I don't belong to anyone," Eve grumbled, failing to hide her smile. Although, it wasn't like she could smile all that well, anyway. She was pretty much out of breath. She was cold and her face hurt. At this point, she didn't know if she was going to die from the hike or the elements.

Probably both.

"It seemed like you belonged to me the other night when I had you tied to the bed."

Eve gasped, glaring him down. "I thought we weren't going to bring that up?"

"Of course we are." Austin licked his lips. "Who knew my girl like being restrained?"

"Shut up."

Eve huffed, focusing back on the path. She crossed her arms over her body, holding herself close, trying to keep warm. Why in the hell she agreed to go hiking again was beyond her, but Austin had insisted on it, to the point Eve had no choice but to give in. At least they were going to the same place they went before, so Eve was somewhat familiar with the area. However, in the snow, everything looked different.

Eve's eyes scanned the ground, coming up empty. "I guess no gnome peens this time?"

Austin burst out into a laugh, shaking his head. "I love you."

"I'm beginning to doubt that. The man who loved me wouldn't have taken me out to the pits of hell to die in the snow."

"We can't be in the pits of hell if we're in the snow, babe." Austin rolled his eyes pulling Eve into his side. "Besides, I already told you I'm more than happy to warm you up. All you gotta do is ask."

"You're a piece of damn work, Austin. Now stop blabbering and tell me how much longer this death journey is gonna take. I can't feel my toes. And I think my eyes are freezing shut."

"I'm your piece of work, just like you're mine." He pointed to the area right in front of them. "The clearing is right there."

Eve surveyed the area as she took everything in while they walked the last few feet to the campsite. "Wow. Everything looks so different."

Eve watched as Austin unhooked his pack, placing it on a fallen tree.

"It's like hiking for the first time again, isn't it?"

"Ehh, I wouldn't go that far. But it is kinda cool to be back here. It's got this familiar feeling to it, and yet, also mysterious." She glanced at the overlook, remembering what it looked like last time.

Before, it was stunning, but right now with the snow-covered ground it was downright breathtaking. It honestly looked like a painting.

Austin walked over to her, grabbing the top of her pack, helping Eve unhook it before placing it next to his.

"Ahhh! Great, now my back is cold."

Quickly Austin returned, putting his arms around her shoulders molding her back to his front. "That better?" He kissed the side of her icy cheek.

"I guess."

"I'll always keep you warm." Austin barked out a laugh as he pulled away from her. "Go check out the overlook while I get the tent set up. You know the first rule in backpacking is setting up your shelter." His eyes heated as he grinned at her. "You already know the weather can change at any moment and we need to be safe."

"Don't remind me." Eve shuddered. "At least there won't be thunder this time."

Austin winked at her. "Oh, there will be thunder all right."

Rolling her eyes, Eve ignored him trudging over to the overlook that had changed her life all those months ago.

It was weird but in a good way.

As her eyes took in the snowy mountainside, she couldn't help realizing the last time she'd seen this view, she thought she was leaving a part of her heart here, but instead she found it.

In this spot, her heart became whole for the first time in her life.

Who would've thought the man who stormed into her shop years ago asking a million questions about plus-size clothing would end up not only being her best friend but also the love of her life?

Where he'd been an expert at all things outdoors, she'd been an expert in all things plus-size attire.

Eve chuckled to herself, shaking her head. *Tents & Tights. That's what I'm gonna call us from now on. I'm sure the girls would love it. Plus, it'll probably annoy Austin.*

Double win.

Eve's face broke into an amused smile as she turned to tell him about their new nicknames.

However, the second Eve spun around expecting to see Austin setting up their tent, he instead was behind her down on one knee holding up a ring.

Eve's breath caught in her throat as her heart raced in her chest. "Austin?"

"I know it's cold, and I know this isn't your idea of a good time. But I couldn't think of a better place to do this," he started. "There is one thing I know for certain in this world, babe. I am so in love with you, it hurts. When you aren't with me, I feel like a part of me is missing. I don't want to spend another moment without you in my life. Yeah, you moved into my house, and you've made it a home but it's not enough. I want more. I need more. I need you, Eve, always." He chuckled, his eyes crinkling with enjoyment. "I need for us to bring home brothers and sisters for Marshmallow, maybe then she'll stop trying to kill me." Austin held the ring toward her, the emerald glistening against the snow. "I need to have you by my side for the rest of my life. Eve Morgan, would you do me the honor of becoming my wife, my partner, my everything?"

It might have been cold outside, but Eve's whole body heated as she watched the man she loved more than anything in the world. Tears pricked behind her eyes as she jumped into his arms, causing them to topple back into the snow. "Yes. A million times, yes!" She cupped Austin's face, bringing her lips down to his.

Austin's hands went to her hips, keeping her steady as they kissed. "Good. Best decision you ever made."

When he winked at her with that stupid smirk on his face, Eve cocked her brow. "I'm not disagreeing, but I have to know, did you really have to bring me out here in the dang snow to do this?"

Austin's chuckle filled the air as he flipped her onto her back. "I had to make it a memory we'd never forget."

Eve barked out a laugh, her head falling back in the snow. Thank everything she'd made quality plus size outdoor jackets with insulated hoods. "Trust me, I'll never forget this. I think I just got snow down my pants."

"Then let's hurry up and build the shelter so we can take them off." His eyes heated, drinking her in.

"Austin!" Eve pushed at his shoulder. "Hey, wait a minute. I thought you said the number one thing you have to do when you get to camp is put up your tent?"

"I thought this was a little more important."

She couldn't argue with him there. Eve's heart warmed as she looked at him, the love of her life. "Okay, I'll let it slide this time. I'm just following through with your rules."

"That's mighty kind of you." Austin laughed as he grabbed her hand, taking off her glove before gently placing the ring on her finger. "My Eve." He kissed the emerald, locking his eyes with hers.

"My Austin." Eve took a deep breath, their love coursing through her as she held up her hand to look at the ring on her finger.

Life was perfect.

Well... kind of.

Eve darted her eyes back to Austin. "Now give me back my glove. It's cold out here. You don't want me getting frostbite, do you? Then we'll end up having to chop off my fingers. No more ring."

Austin handed her the glove with a laugh. "You always jump to the extreme. But I wouldn't have you any other way." He leaned down kissing her, the snow continuing to fall around them.

"Yeah, I'll show you extreme. If I don't get a s'more this time, we're done-zo." She glared at him, but try as she might, she couldn't keep the smile off her face.

How could she not? She was going to marry her best friend.

"Sure thing, babe." Austin sat back on his heels. "Good thing I've got everything we need for s'mores in my pack then, huh?"

"You said that last time."

Austin burst out into a deep laugh as he shook his head. "I love you."

"Then where's my s'more?" Although her face felt like it was seconds from breaking in half from the cold, the corners of her lips turned up meeting her eyes. And before Austin could answer, Eve pushed him back, climbing on top of him.

Once she was there, she glanced down her heart filling with so much love.

Who would have thought happily ever after was in the cards for Eve all along? If you'd asked her before she would've laughed it off and say happy endings weren't meant for people like her.

At least that's what she thought.

Eve's eyes flicked to the grey sky. *Thanks for letting me be wrong, Universe. I guess I should trust you more often. While I'm at it, also thanks for not sending in the meat-eating rabbits. I'd be pissed if I missed out on this.*

She looked down at Austin knowing her goofy smile matched his. "I love you too, more than I ever thought possible."

As long as Eve had her best friend by her side, she knew

without a doubt she'd be able to take on anything in the world.

And apparently, that included hiking.

Eve blanched.

Figures.

The Universe might finally be on her side, but it still needed to jab at her every once in a while.

As she looked down at her best friend, the love of her life, and now her fiancé, she couldn't help the joy that radiated through her. They might've been complete opposites in every way, but in the end that's what made them special.

Austin and Eve.

Best friends to lovers and so much more.

And Eve couldn't wait to see what adventures were in store for them next. As long as it wasn't hiking... she gulped. *Oh no, what if it's other outdoor things—*

Eve narrowed her eyes to glare at him. "Just so we're clear, I'm never going rock climbing."

Austin burst into a round of heavy laughter. "I'm not that stupid. I finally got you and I wanna keep you alive."

"Thank God."

Austin's hand moved to her cheek as he pushed a piece of her hair that'd fallen out of her hood away from her face. "My Eve."

Her heart fluttered as her smile warmed her body. "Always. Now, let's put up the tent, I'm freezing." Eve reached beside her, grabbing a handful of snow before tossing it in Austin's face.

"Hey!"

Eve jumped up quickly, but didn't get far.

"You little shit." Austin pulled her to the ground, their laughs echoing around them as the snow continued to fall, giving them both a memory that would last a lifetime. "What in the hell am I gonna do with you?"

Eve's heart tightened as she looked at her best friend. "Love me."

"Oh, babe. I plan on it." Austin cupped her head in the palm of his hand before bringing his lips down to hers. "Forever."

Thank you so much for reading Tents & Tights! I absolutely adore this story and I hope you did as well.

Are you curious about the widely inappropriate librarian Mildred? Or how about the walking lovable disaster that is Holly? If so, check out Stumbling Into Him, there is a sneak peek on the next page.

Stumbling Into Him Sneak Peek

CHAPTER ONE

"WATCH OUT!"

Holly Flanagan heard a commotion coming from the other side of the park.

Ignoring the shouting, she bent over focusing on picking up her Corgi, Waffles', most recent deposit. With Holly's track record, though, she should have known anyone yelling "watch out," "take cover," or "that's about to fall" was directed at her. Even after years of being the spokesperson for unlucky, klutzy, and clumsy she still disregarded the shouting as she carried on with her dog parent duties.

Before she could register what happened, she was knocked onto her back with a pain radiating from her mouth and nose.

"At least the sky is pretty today," Holly mumbled as she tried to get her bearings. She reached for her mouth as she felt the pain start to spread.

"Ma'am, are you okay?"

Holly closed her eyes as she thought about it.

Was she okay? She'd just been hit with something. She was pretty sure some part of her face, she didn't know which part, but she was sure something was bleeding. Waffles barked uncontrollably, and her head hurt.

So, was she okay?

Holly let out a heavy sigh.

Yeah, she was fine. This was just another day in her life for her. And so far, if being hit by an unknown projectile to the face was the worst thing that happened to her, she'd considered it a good day.

Deciding to face the music she opened her eyes.

Holy shit!

Above her, only a mere few inches from her face was by far the most handsome man she had ever laid eyes on.

He had dark brown hair and deep blue eyes that were richer than the ocean. His jaw was chiseled, with a light dusting of scruff, in the alpha male, I'm in charge here kind of way.

Wonderful. Okay, let's add embarrassing yourself in front of a Greek God to your list of attributes for the day. Hey, it can only get better from here, right?

When she realized she'd been staring at him for what could have been considered too long, she quickly jerked her head forward trying to right herself. Unfortunately for her, though, she slammed her head right into the Greek God's forehead.

Freaking wonderful.

Not only was her mouth hurting, her head now pounded.

Absolutely freaking wonderful!

"Shit," she heard the Greek God say as the wave of pain coursed through her body.

Taking the chance, she opened her eyes again only to see her Adonis holding his head. *Great.* And to make matters worse, Waffles started barking directly at her before looking at his recent deposit still on the ground then back at her.

"For the love of all things, dog. I was trying to pick it up," she growled, before taking her hand away from her mouth to deal with his majesty, *Lord* Waffles. However, the second her hand came into view she saw the blood and screamed.

"Oh shit. Lady, you're bleeding," the Adonis said, putting his hand under her chin moving it from side to side as he examined her face.

"What happened?" Panic ran through her. *Did I break my nose? Am I unconscious? Am I dying?*

The Adonis tilted her chin back to get a better look. "I was tossing the Frisbee with Ripley, and somehow it veered off course. I tried to warn you with the 'watch out.'"

Typical. Holly groaned. *Hot guy throws Frisbee. Said Frisbee hits me in the face. Hot guy then insinuates it's my fault for not getting out of the way fast enough. I mean, I know I'm generally invisible to men like him, but, damn. You'd think these extra wide hips would make me more visible.* She glared at the Frisbee sitting next to her.

Ignoring the object, she moved her eyes back to the Adonis.

"I can't tell if it's a busted lip or worse." He tilted her head further back like she was a child.

Holly ripped her face from his hand. She'd be able to tell if it was just a busted lip. She'd had too many to count in her life, from falling down, objects to the face, and even falling up the stairs. She reached into her pocket and pulled out the napkin she had stuffed in there from her soft pretzel. She blew off some stray salt and started feverishly wiping at her mouth.

"Let me see," he demanded, before taking one of the napkins from her hand. He then started dabbing at her lips.

She froze.

Well, Holly. This is the most action you've had in months. And, if some hot guy is all over you, you might as well enjoy it while it lasts.

Waffles crawled onto her lap demanding attention and started kissing the underside of her jaw.

Thanks, Waffles, for bringing the attention of my double chin to the Adonis. She rolled her eyes.

"Thanks for trying to help me clean up your mom," the Adonis remarked before quickly abandoning his job of cleaning the blood off her mouth to pat Waffles on the head.

"He's not trying to help you," Holly scoffed. "He's *trying* to remind me I still need to pick up his poop and then give him a treat."

"Shouldn't your mom be the one getting the treat if *she's* the one picking up your shit?" He cocked his head at her dog.

Waffles, ever the one to argue, looked at the man that now had a mischievous grin on his face, with the most judgmental side-eye he could muster.

No one came between him and his treats.

Ignoring Waffles' attempt at a threat, the Adonis once again pat the dog on the head before moving back to Holly's mouth dismissing him. "I think it's just a busted lip, but your front tooth..." He coughed as he sheepishly looked away.

"My front tooth?" Holly quickly ran her tongue along her front teeth. Shit, she felt a jagged piece. "Oh, crap." She quickly pulled her phone from her pocket and launched the front-facing camera.

As soon as she saw her face, she jerked back. Her hair was all over the place, her face red, there was still blood on her...

You've had better days, Holly. She took a deep breath before he hastily opened her mouth to see the damage.

"Oh no."

Staring back at her was a chipped front tooth along with a busted lip. *Wonderful. Thank you so much, Universe. Thank you, so very much.* She didn't know whether she wanted to laugh or cry. *Clumsy Holly, strikes again. Do you ever take a break?*

As her eyes flooded with tears a sudden cold nose hit her arm distracting her. Realizing it wasn't Waffles she looked to

293

her left and saw one of the most beautifully colored gray and black Australian Shepherds she'd ever seen.

"Aren't you a cutie?" she softly said. Thankfully, her love of animals overrode everything she was feeling.

"That's Ripley." The Greek God chuckled. "I'd thought you'd be more concerned about your mouth than a dog."

Ignoring him, she reached out to scratch Ripley's chin. "You're so pretty." Ripley must have agreed because she barked before kissing Holly's hand.

"Uhh, ma'am, I'm not a human doctor but I think we should pay more attention to your injuries instead of the dogs."

"Human doctor?" Her brows shot up. "As opposed to what, an alien doctor?"

"I haven't worked on any aliens that I know of, but I did neuter a cat named Alien once. Does that count?"

Her eyes widened at the realization. "Oh great, you've got a body of a Greek God, and now you're also a vet. Which of course means you love animals. *Freakin'* wonderful. You're like the most perfect guy, and here I am on the sidewalk with blood pouring out of me with a chipped tooth." She pushed Waffles off her lap and stood. "Please excuse me while I find a place to die of embarrassment."

A corner of the sexy man's mouth lifted. "You're funny."

"And you're hot. So, we've now successfully established which groups we belong to." Annoyed at herself more than anything she angrily started to stomp away from the Greek God.

"Hey, wait up!"

She spun around to glare at him. When Holly saw Waffles sitting at the foot of the Adonis looking up at him, her left eye started to twitch.

Of course, her dog would betray her. She wouldn't expect anything less. "Waffles, come." She pulled on the leash slightly, but the dog wouldn't move. "Lord Waffles, get your butt over here."

The man cocked his brow. "Lord Waffles?"

"Yeah," she answered. "He thinks he's a freakin' king. Hence the "lord" and I love waffles. Do you got a problem with that, buster?"

The Adonis burst into laughter as he scratched Waffles on the back. To make matters worse, that betraying Corgi rolled over onto his back asking for belly rubs.

The Audacity! *That's it. No more treats for you!* She glared at her dog.

"Who's a good boy?" the Adonis cooed. "You've got a weird name, but you're the best boy aren't cha?"

Holly's eye started to twitch harder.

She stomped back toward her bastard of a dog and the Greek God when out of nowhere her foot hit an invisible rock causing her to trip. Within a split second, she ended up falling right into the arms of the bane of her existence at the moment.

"Whoa, are you okay?"

"I'm fine," she grumbled as she righted herself. *Go ahead and add this to the, "it can only happen to me" list.*

"I feel like you need to walk around with a warning sign or at least a crash helmet," he joked.

"Not the first time I've heard that." Quickly she bent down and retrieved Waffles. "If you'll excuse me. Not only do I really need to find a secluded place to die of embarrassment, I also need to call my dentist, or go to the walk-in. Maybe both." She turned on her heel and started power walking down the sidewalk.

As she passed the spot she'd tripped at, she examined the cement. Figures, there'd be absolutely nothing there. If there were a sporting category on tripping over invisible objects she'd win gold twice over.

"Hey!"

She kept walking, doing her best to hide her humiliation and ignore the Greek God.

Unfortunately, that was short-lived. "Hey, I want to make sure you really are okay," he said, as he caught up to her in two point three seconds.

Stupid short legs! "I'm fine."

"Your lip's still bleeding."

She glared at him. "Wonderful."

"Hey..." He reached for her arm stopping her escape.

"What?"

"Let me help you. My practice is only a block from here. I've got all the supplies to clean up your lip. I can also get a better look at your tooth."

"You're a vet." Her eyes started to twitch again. *Could today get any worse?*

"I am pretty sure if I can surgically remove nuts from an animal I can look at your busted lip." He shrugged before smirking at her.

A laugh escaped her lips. He did have a point after-all. "Thank you for the offer...." she trailed off.

"Ben. The name's Ben Richman." He held out his hand to her.

"Thanks for the offer Dr. Richman, but there is a walk-in clinic not far from where I live."

"Call me Ben. And please let me do this. It'll help me sleep at night knowing the woman I maimed with a Frisbee is somewhat okay." She watched as his eyes pleaded with her. Even Waffles, the jerk, who was still in her arms looked up at her and whined. "Oh, for the love of... fine. Lead the way, Ben."

"Perfect." Ben's mouth curved into a smile. "Follow me."

When he whistled Ripley sat instantly by his side. He quickly bent down and fastened her leash before walking toward the street.

Holly looked at Waffles who was clearly enjoying being carried. "Guess you get an extra trip to the vet."

She couldn't help but burst out laughing when Waffles closed his mouth and glared at her.

CONTINUE BEN and Holly's story in Stumbling Into Him...

Also By Molly O'Hare

Stumbling Through Life Series

Stumbling Into Him

Stumbling Into Forever

Stumbling Into the Holidays

John & Emma's story – *Coming soon*

Teased by Love Series

Teased by Fire

Teased by Tinsel

Lucas & Miranda's story – Coming soon

Hollywood Hopeful Series

Hollywood Dreams

Risking It All (Danny and Lexi's Story) – *Coming soon*

Standalone Novels

Nothing But a Dare

Learning Curves

Tents & Tights

Stay Connected

Sign up for my newsletter or check out my website.

If you just want to hang out, come join my reader group: Molly's Badass Babes.

About the Author

Molly O'Hare is a USA Today Bestselling author of plus size romance books.

She grew up with severe dyslexia and neurodivergence, trust her, spelling is not her strong suit. Over the years, she's become a huge advocate of "just because you learn something a little differently than others does not make you less in any way." She also advocates for body positivity in all shapes and sizes. And, to say Molly is obsessed with all things animals is probably an understatement.

When she was younger, she had a wicked case of insomnia most nights, and to help herself fall asleep, she would create stories in her head, always picking up where she left off the night before. Then, one morning she figured if she got endless enjoyment out of her imagination, others might as well. And thus started her career as an author. And as she always likes to say, never forget how absolutely unique and beautiful you are. The world is better because you are here.

Stay Connected